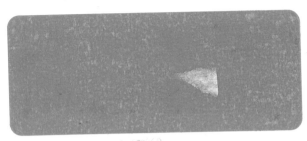

2/09

WRACK

WRACK

A NOVEL

JAMES BRADLEY

Henry Holt and Company | New York

Fiction
Bre

Henry Holt and Company, Inc.
Publishers since 1866
115 West 18th Street
New York, New York 10011

Henry Holt® is a registered trademark of
Henry Holt and Company, Inc.

First published in the United States in 1999 by
Henry Holt and Company, Inc.

Originally published in Australia in 1997 by
Random House Australia

Library of Congress Cataloging-in-Publication Data
Bradley, James, 1967–
Wrack : a novel / James Bradley.—1st U.S. ed.
p.   cm.
ISBN 0-8050-6108-8 (hb : alk. paper)
I. Title.
PR9619.3.B655W73   1999
823—dc21   98-41603

Henry Holt books are available for special promotions and
premiums. For details contact: Director, Special Markets.

First United States Edition 1999

Designed by Kelly Soong Too

Printed in the United States of America
All first editions are printed on acid-free paper. ∞

1   3   5   7   9   10   8   6   4   2

This book is dedicated to the memory of my grandfather,
Richard Francis Haren (1907–1994)

wrack: *1. To suffer or undergo shipwreck; 2. To wreck; to ruin; to cast ashore by shipwreck; 3. Remnants of or goods from a wrecked vessel, esp. as driven or cast ashore; wreckage; 4. To cause the ruin, downfall, or subversion of (a person, etc.); to ruin or overthrow; 5. Retributive punishment; vengeance, revenge; 6. A thing or person in an impaired, wrecked, or shattered state; 7. Marine vegetation or seaweed cast ashore by the waves or growing on the tidal seashore.*

CONTENTS

WRACK

Prologue

"Oh but it is true . . . Things need not have happened to be true. Tales and dreams are the shadow-truths that will endure when mere facts are dust and ashes, and forgot."

NEIL GAIMAN,
"A Midsummer Night's Dream"

From the personal journal of William Townshend, Surgeon, aboard His Majesty's Vessel *Berkeley*.

It comes as more than some little surprise to me that I am able to write these words: if I had been asked only twelve hours ago whether I believed I would survive to see the dawn my answer would have been a simple negative. Yet here I am, alive and, in good part at least, intact. The night just passed was truly the most terrifying I have ever known, and more than once I offered up prayers to the Almighty in the sure belief my hours on this earth were at an end.

The ship has been cast upon a shore unknown to the crew or the captain, yet we are some hundred leagues or more to the south of Port Jackson. I hope this place is not an indication of this land's true temper, for it is a miserable place; cold and windswept in the extreme, with little to offer in the way of comfort or succor after our long journey.

LATER

I am writing this several hours later, wishing to record a most worrying and curious sight I and several others have witnessed. The seas having subsided somewhat, the Captain and a group of a dozen or so men, including the repulsive Colvey, who seems to grow more repugnant with each passing day, put ashore in the longboat. I accompanied them at the invitation of the Captain, who continues to treat me as a gentleman, although I detected in his offer to "let me see the temper of my new home" a note of mischief. The seas, although smaller, were far from calm, and the landing of the boat was only achieved with some difficulty; all of us were soaked fairly to the skin by the time we landed, and the wind, which seemed to blow straight from the icebound lands of the Antarctic, cut through to our very marrow.

Once there, however, my thoughts were not on my physical discomfort. No, for it was a quite singular pleasure to step onto dry land again after all these months of rolling swell, and the mere fact of my being on land was more than enough to distract me from the wind and the dampness of my situation. Once again I underwent that same phenomenon I experienced in Cape Town, where the solid land took on the feel of the ocean, seeming to swell and move underfoot.

But I digress. Once upon the land all of us ran and sported like children, so delightful was the sensation of being on dry land once more. Even the dour Captain Bell could not resist a smile and a few quick steps. The country itself is bare and miserable in the extreme, the sand of the beach rising into low ridges, covered in a dismal growth of grass and low bush, but before long the men's games took them up the face of the first rise, and when they reached the apex, their hoots and cries of glee stopped all of a sudden.

This sudden silence drew my and Captain Bell's attention and, looking up, we saw the men gathered unspeaking on the peak of the hill, gazing in silence at what lay beyond it. For a long moment nothing more happened, the Captain and I standing, watching the men watching whatever it was they had seen. Then one of them, the repulsive Colvey or maybe young Berridge, called and motioned to us to join them. We hurried, a spirit of urgency having descended upon the pro-

ceedings, and upon reaching the top of the hill were greeted by the sight that compels me to make this record: a ship, much damaged by the elements and the passage of time, but a ship nonetheless, and even to an eye as untrained in these matters as my own, one of some antiquity.

Upon descending to it there was much discussion between the Captain and the more intelligent of the men, and I understood they believed it to be a ship of Portuguese or Spanish origin, its reddish mahogany construction confirming its Iberian ancestry, but, and this is the source of my amazement, of a design not seen for over two hundred years.

The discovery of the ship was a source of much excitement among the men, who clambered through the wreckage with the clear intent of discovering for themselves some item of value. Many small keepsakes were to be easily found scattered in the sand and among the remnants of the ship, but so too were grimmer discoveries. In the stern of the vessel we came upon the bones of several men. I say they were the bones of men, although I doubt an eye less expert than my own would have known this for certain, since they were of a great age, and had been set upon by beasts or savages and spread throughout those gloomy chambers. In the bow there was charring and evidence of an unsuccessful attempt to burn the ship.

The discovery of the remains coupled with the evidence of attempts to destroy the ship caused the mood of the men to change, and concern grew over the possibility of a confrontation with the natives. Captain Bell posted Berridge on watch with a rifle and allowed the men to continue searching for another half-hour or so. By then numerous small relics, bottles, coins, and an exquisitely carved bone knife handle, apparently of Tamil origin, had been found, together with the remains of navigational instruments, much corroded, and a slim wooden box containing many papers, much water damaged, but still legible in parts. On these papers we found a name, de Cueva, and a date, which even now, I still find hard to credit, namely 1519.

At the expiry of this half an hour the Captain sought my counsel, which I took to be a sign of his increasing trust and respect for my personage and rank. He confided in me his opinion that the ship was Iberian, and of more than two hundred years in age, an opinion that I found hard to resist. But it was not this that he sought my counsel upon. Rather he was concerned, being a man of strategic wiles, by the implications of this ship's presence in New South Wales. For if sailors of Portugal were in this land over two hundred years before Mr. Cook, then our King's claim to this land may be in dispute.

Upon reflection I took to sharing this concern of the Captain's, and after some discussion we cautioned the men not to breathe a word of what they have seen. In order to forestall their indubitable protests, the Captain granted them the small treasures that they had found, on the proviso that each and every one of them undertook to dissemble should they be interrogated as to its place of origin. The Captain took into his possession the papers, and granted to me the bell and several coins. And, as we left, I took upon myself the liberty of levering forth a sliver of the ship's red timber with my knife, secreting it upon my person as we made our way back to the longboat.

Upon our return to the ship the men were duly silent, and I am as sure as one can be of such types that they understand the importance of their silence. This discovery of ours must remain a secret, locked close as this journal.

I

The various discoveries which had been made upon the coasts of Terra Australis antecedently to the present voyage are of dates as widely distant as are the degrees of confidence to which they are respectively entitled . . . In tracing a historical sketch of the previous discoveries, I shall not dwell upon such as depend upon conjecture and probability, but come speedily to those for which there are authentic documents.

Within these few years however, two curious manuscripts have been brought to light which have favored an opinion that Terra Australis had really been visited by Europeans nearly a century before any authentic accounts speak of its discovery. One of these charts is in French, without date; and from its almost similitude is probably either the original or a copy of the other, which is in English; and bears a dedication to the King of England. In it an extensive country is marked to the southward of the Moluccas under the name Great Java; which agrees nearer with the position and extent of Terra Australis than with any other land; and the direction given to some parts of the coast approaches too near to the truth for the whole to have been marked from conjecture alone. But combining this with the exaggerated extent of Great Java in a southern direction, and the animals and houses painted upon the shores, such as have not been anywhere seen in Terra Australis, it should appear to have been partly formed from vague information, collected probably by the early Portuguese navigators from the eastern nations; and that conjecture has done the rest. It may, at the same time, be admitted that a part of the west and northwest coasts where the coincidence of form is most striking might have been seen by the Portuguese themselves before the year 1540, in their voyages to and from India.

MATTHEW FLINDERS,
Voyage to Terra Australis, 1814

*H*ow to tell this story, where to begin? Perhaps it begins in a storm, the wind-whipped sand cutting deep into a child's skin, bullying him, driving him, pushing him deeper into the darkness, this unkindness of wind a purification, slicing flesh, bleaching bone, pushing all that obscures before it as it rolls back the sand to expose what is hidden beneath. For surely this story should be like the wind, cutting away at what does not matter, at what is extraneous, until there is nothing left but what is essential; this purity of form a distillate of the truth. Or maybe the truth is not what lies beneath the sand but the sand itself, always shifting, never certain, so that once we cut away that which we cannot be sure of we are left with nothing but space. And echoes.

Yet maybe there are patterns we can detect in the motion of the sand, eddies and flows within its ceaseless flux and ebb. Not skeletons or truth, but feelings, encoded bumps and ridges that might make letters, then a word, then a sentence or maybe more, a secret Braille of touch and faith. A quiet urgency of form. Or they might be no more than they seem.

Here, were you to try and decipher them, these symbols might trace out a story about love and death. About loving and dying. And surely that is all they could be. For in the end that is all there is, all there can be. The transformation of heavy flesh into light and sensation. Emotions moving like tides, like rivers deep within the sand. Feeling stealing across years like the shifting hills, slowly, inexorably, burying all that lies before them; leaving what lay hidden exposed to the harsh sun, the freezing air of winter, a movement of form, a disturbance in the shape of the world flowing from the past into the future. Like the bones of the dead. Like words scrawled on paper in haste.

avid shimmers, adrift in the white sea of the sand. Around him heat rises from its baking surface, light glaring from every angle. Not far away the sea rolls in against the beach, out of sight, the steady breath of the surf streaming thin moisture through the boiling air. A seabird wheels overhead, its voice creaking as it rides the waves of heat upward. The air smells of salt.

For a long time David stands like this, aware of the sun's rays against his unprotected skin, unmoving, unwatching, unlistening, just being, drinking up this place. The sun bounces up and out from a million angles, shattering over the rolling mirror of sand. Then from behind him there is the blast of a car horn, then again, and David starts, turning toward the sound. Behind him he sees the shapes of several four-wheel drives bumping across the sand toward him. The heat haze shivering around them, making their outlines jump and flow. The horn sounds once again, and David lifts his arm to wave, the fact of its motion suddenly marvelous to him. A grind of brakes and the cars slide to a stop beside him, their thick wheels sledding through the hot sand, ploughing it up into furrows. Music blares from the cars as the doors open, spilling refrigerated air outward, turning his sweat suddenly cold against his skin. Figures pile onto the sand, feet slipping beneath them, surrounding him, a riot of colorful shorts and baseball caps and mirrored glasses. David steps back, trying to take it all in, the tide of voices, movement, music washing against him.

A woman's voice beside him asks him something, and he feels his mind reengage, falling back into its webs of analysis. He turns to her, his hands describing arcs of exploration, assigning tasks, delineating borders. Equipment is unloaded, deployed. David watches his students move outward, the flat feet of metal detectors sweeping across the ground. Stakes are driven into the sand and nylon rope strung between them, marking out a perimeter on the face of the hill, a ridge of tussocked marram grass containing the downward spill at its center. The handheld detectors beep and whistle, drawn together at the clump of grass.

Anna, one of the other archaeologists on the dig, pauses beside him.

Last chance? she asks. David is unsure whether she is serious or joking, and turns to look at her. Her face screwed up against the sun reveals little.

This time at least.

She snorts. Ever the optimist, mate. Unless we can find something conclusive in the next few days there isn't going to be a next time. You know that as well as I do.

We know from the aerial scans that something's down there. His voice dogged, unflinching.

She looks at him intently for a moment before replying. The anomaly's too small. We both know that.

David pauses. It's all we've got, he says at last, then turns and steps away.

As she watches him walk the ten meters toward the nearest group of students, Anna feels her irritation with the determination of his belief fade, become annoyance at the hesitancy of her own, and as it does she wishes he would turn so she could smile, wave, reassure him that she too believes. But he doesn't turn. Instead, after a moment's unheard conversation, he takes a shovel from one of the students, shifts its weight experimentally in his hands, then in one swift movement plunges it downward, the blade slicing deep into the spilling sand, a foot on its back driving it deeper again before he pulls upward, grunting with the effort, casts the brimming flat of the shovel's blade behind him in a shower of pale powder. Moving closer she hears him address the students, his voice low, unwavering. OK, he is saying, let's start digging.

As HE DIGS, David listens to himself, careful, scholarly, cautioning his students against allowing their hopes to be raised. All the while the blade of his shovel hacking away at the roots of the grass that web the loose sand, cutting, slicing, tearing at the ribbed strands straining outward and downward in search of water. He does not need Anna to tell him that the anomalous signal the aerial magnetometer has detected is too weak to be anything significant. He too has scanned the pages of the computer printouts; their whorls and eddies describing the lines of force that lie unseen beneath these hills; the ghostly shadows of water and ferrous metal written within the swirling patterns. He more than anyone knows that none reveal what he has spent years hoping lies somewhere just beneath their feet. It cannot be the ship, he knows that, but it is hard not to succumb, to believe. He knows the students can hear his excitement, the catch in his voice, and he almost hopes that his desire infects them as well. Perhaps it does, for as the digging proceeds, although it is he who digs the fastest, ignoring the burning of his hands chafed by the handle of the shovel, the sweat on his face, he is dimly aware that the students are digging faster, too. Lured into the past.

Overhead the sun arcs inland, shadows creep down from the crests of the hills, playing in long winding furrows through the shifting sand. A snake moves through the search area, liquid quick, provoking shrieks and wary fascination from the students, who follow it across the sand at a careful distance until it eventually disappears into a knot of tussocks. David and the others take it in shifts, digging for half an hour, then swapping over, carting sand and sifting for half an hour. The heat on the sand making the shadows dance and twist.

Just before dark David feels the hair on his neck rise, as if he is being watched. Turning, he half sees a figure on a dune behind the cars. He blinks, wiping the sweat from his brow, but the figure is gone. For several seconds he stands, not quite convinced it was just a mirage, but then he shakes his head, trying to clear it. As he does he hears a cry from behind him and looks around to see one of the students kneeling down, everyone else converging on what she has uncovered. He feels his chest tighten in expectation, his breath coming faster, and he steps forward, almost forgetting his unease of a moment before. Halfway there he pauses, glancing back in the direction of the figure, but seeing nothing continues on, his step lengthening to a run.

In the middle of the ring a scrap of cloth pokes out of the sand. No one speaks, their faces turned to David and Anna. He glances at Anna, who nods, and David steps forward, moving through the line of the circle, kneeling beside the tiny flap of cloth. His instincts tell him it is nothing, but his voice trembles as he turns, issuing instructions for more precise tools, tiny spades, brushes and sieves. His breath coming in ragged gasps, he scrapes the sand away, his tools carving a form out of the sand. A long khaki line slowly becomes a mound. David pauses, peering at the mound in the failing light. Anna appears with a torch, and its light picks out the frayed fabric of a blanket, then black letters on the peeling fibers, a crest, a rearing sunrise of bayonets, a serial number. David slumps back, his hands falling to his sides, hears sighs from behind him. He turns, shrugging, says something about that being how things go, then settles to the task of pulling the mound free.

His arms encircle the mound, and nodding to one of the students they pull, loosening their find from its grave. Exposed now it is a rolled blanket, army issue, containing something about six feet long. A student asks him what he thinks it might be and David shrugs, noncommittal. Anna's glance telling him she too knows what it is, but he shrugs nonetheless.

Let's see, he says, stepping forward and carefully opening the bundle. The material of the blanket begins to give way in his hands, but he perseveres, drawing it open like a curtain. Slowly something appears, shreds of hair, dried skin, the blind socket of an eye. A heaviness filling his chest, David steps back and a ripple of surprise runs through the group. The students unable to look away.

Finally one asks, What now?

David rubs a hand across his mouth.

I guess we call the police.

$\mathcal{I}$t takes three phone calls to find the local police. On the phone they are friendly but unimpressed. Twice David is asked whether he is sure the body isn't that of an Aborigine, and he explains again the blanket, the scraps of uniform. Finally they agree to come, and David clicks the mobile off, watching the glowing green window for several seconds before it dims and fades. The phone in his hand, he returns to the waiting students clustered around the pit. They turn to him, anxious to hear what he has to say. He smiles as he speaks, trying to reassure them.

The police said they'd be here as soon as they could, he says. But if any of you want to head back now, do. It's getting cold now the sun's down.

Several of the students nod, talking among themselves, then drift off, bidding farewells as they go. David and two or three others remain. They talk, voices low in the darkness. Finally Anna asks the question everyone else is skirting around.

Who do you think it is?

God knows, David says, then pauses before continuing. But

I'd give you good money somebody put him there and that that somebody didn't want him to be found.

Murder? asks one of the students.

That seems the obvious conclusion, but I think we should wait until the police arrive before we start making any assumptions. Whoever he is he's certainly been there a while.

Do you think the police will investigate? After all, whoever it is has been there for years.

That depends, David begins, but the sound of a police car heading over the sand toward them interrupts, the white shear of the halogen dazzling them so they turn away, covering their eyes.

THE POLICE DO little but cordon off the area and take down names. They are local police and, as one confides to David, can do little until more senior officers arrive from Sydney. David stands by, watching the two men in uniform taking down the names of his students in the glare of the police car's spotlight. Finally the policeman who had taken David into his confidence announces that they should leave now; nothing more was going to happen until dawn, when the detectives were supposed to be arriving. Once the announcement has been made, Anna and the students begin to move back to the cars. David doesn't follow them, looking instead at the policemen in their dark uniforms by the excavation, a sense of panic, collapse, rising within him. Suddenly Anna is at his side, her hand on his arm, leading him to the car. He complies, looking back at the two policemen. One turns and waves, the gesture friendly and slow, in the manner of those who live outside cities.

At the door to the four-wheel drive David pauses again, gazing out into the darkness. Then he climbs in and pulls the door shut behind him. The radio blares, the vehicle skidding away through the sand.

ALONE IN HIS tent, David cannot sleep. This piece of land, the ghosts of which he has been acquainted with for years, has changed. There are new ghosts now, shades of violence and death.

That there are ghosts here does not surprise David. Although he calls himself an archaeologist, and believes in the coded and ordered knowledge of science, the structured discourse of academic debate, he feels the pull of other places, other times. Whether they are real or mere echoes of other times, David has learned to believe in ghosts. Of the dark-skinned tribes who gathered shells and hunted here for tens of thousands of years. Of de Cueva and his men, irrevocably and hopelessly lost in this alien place. Of the others who came later, and through neglect and greed remade this place in their own image.

The shadowy dunes suddenly full of hidden secrets, knives in the darkness.

CITY DETECTIVES ARRIVE at dawn, men in suits, somber, commanding. David arrives soon after. Yellow tape is twisted between stakes, encircling the sandy depression. The sun is hot, the air cool. David watches them lift the body from the ground, onto a tray like a stretcher. Men in uniforms do the lifting, while other men in uniforms stand about chatting. As the body is carried from its shallow grave David moves closer.

A detective holds the yellow tape to the ground with one foot to allow the body to pass.

What happens now? asks David. Where are you taking it?

The detective speaks without looking at him. Away.

The body moves toward a police van, David following.

Away where?

The detective looks round. To the police labs in Sydney, but I'm sorry, that's all I can tell you. This is police business now.

David looks the detective in the eye, taking his measure.

Listen, mate, he says, trying to sound confident but nonconfronting, I'm an archaeologist, this body was found on my dig, what might be irrelevant to you might be important evidence to me. That means that if this body's going to be examined I need to be there.

As he speaks another detective approaches. The two of them exchange glances.

What's going on?

This bloke here's the archaeologist who found the body. He reckons he should be there for the examination.

We're not likely to find much, whoever he is he's been there a long time.

David opens his hands in a gesture of impatience. Doesn't that mean it's my territory then?

Yeah, the second detective replies, I suppose you're right. He looks to his colleague. I can't see any harm in it, can you?

The first detective shrugs, knowing his authority is gone.

Sure, he says, walking away.

II

Claire

Very deep is the well of the past. Should we not call it bottomless?

THOMAS MANN,
Tales of Jacob

*T*wenty-four hours later, David sits in the hot air of the police station, flicking idly through an old magazine. Intermittently he catches the eye of the woman at the front desk, who smiles, and he smiles back absently before returning to his magazine. The policeman next to her stares steadfastly at the battered paperback he is reading, turning the pages with agonizing slowness. Although it is early the air outside is already hot, and in here it is hotter. When he arrived the woman at the front desk apologized for the heat, saying the air-conditioning was out of order, a state of affairs David suspected from the note of annoyance in her voice was not uncommon.

The waiting room is empty, and several times men in uniform appear at the glass doors to the rest of the building. Each time David looks up expectantly, but each time they walk past him, the doors to the street silently sliding open as they step out into the glare of the city streets. After a while he stands, walks to a long photo framed on the wall to his left, disinterestedly studying the ranks of officers who stare out of it at him.

His eyes ache from lack of sleep, and he finds himself dreading the drive back south that awaits him later today or this evening.

Suddenly from behind him he hears a voice, the soft lilt in the accent familiar, and he turns, surprised.

David, the voice says, I thought it must be you.

Claire?

Who else? So, you've been digging up bodies.

Yeah, I . . . um . . . He shakes his head, trying to regain his poise. Finally he laughs, admitting defeat. I didn't expect to see you. Not here.

Obviously, she says, the gentle irony of her tone so familiar.

Not sure what to say next David hesitates, each of them watching the other, then both of them are speaking at once.

I—

How are—

You first.

No you.

Both of them laugh again. OK, says David, I'll go first. How have you been?

Well. And you?

Good. I thought you'd gone overseas, with . . . um—

Paul. As she speaks her eyes move away, avoiding David's gaze.

Paul. David sees the shift in her manner as he repeats the name, but almost as quickly it is gone again.

I came back, she says, her eyes meeting his once more.

And Paul?

She shrugs. Some things just aren't meant to be. Again there is a moment's hesitation, a sliver-thin crack in her skin, the way she pauses before she speaks, that makes David wonder whether her indifference is real or feigned. Then turning back the way she came she opens the door for him, leading him down the long corridors with their linoleum floors and governmental smell.

Following Claire down the stairs to the basement labs, David feels the ground shifting beneath him, her connection to a part of him he'd tried to bury drawing the past up from below, leaching into the present. She walks quickly, and he has to hurry to keep up.

But what are you doing here?

Autopsies mainly. Aren't many people with my qualifications, so they take me on a part-time basis. Rest of the time I spend doing private work.

David remembers Claire's academic prowess; lawyer and doctor, knowledge coming to her easily, seemingly without effort.

Nice.

Not usually. Anyway, I hear you found this one on a dig.

Mm-hmm. But it's a different vintage from what we're looking for.

Opening a door she turns to look at him, her eyes meeting his. Still looking for your ship? she asks, her voice lower.

David nods, and for several seconds neither of them speaks, Claire holding his gaze for a half a second longer than is comfortable. He feels the challenge in the inquiry, but he does not look away. So much unspoken between them.

You're never going to let it go, are you.

David knows the words are a statement rather than a question, and does not reply, and she releases the door and heads
on, as if she had not expected it to be answered herself.

Are you all right? he asks, and she turns back to him and
laughs, quite suddenly.

Of course, she says, and looks away again. You don't need to
worry about me; you should know that.

For a moment there is silence, then Claire continues.

I suppose finding bodies is pretty much par for the course
for you.

David smiles wryly, their former ease reasserting itself. Not
ones the police are interested in . . . although surely this one's
on the cusp anyway.

Turning to one side Claire opens a door, letting him pass
through it before her. We're not going to get into some kind of
demarcation dispute here, are we?

He looks at her, sees from her expression she is joking and
laughs.

I hope not.

It's funny though.

What?

The way that in the end we're in the same line of work.

David looks at her curiously.

What do you mean?

Trying to coax secrets from the dead.

Before he can reply he realizes they are there. In front of
them the body is arranged on a metal slab, still enshrouded in
its blanket. It lies in the center of the room, the small space
turning on this axis of silence. This room, with its clean white
walls and cold metal, is a place given over to death, a cold

church for services in which the fluid life of the body is reduced to a series of knife strokes. David shudders, arrested in his movement by the presence of the body. Behind them the heavy door swings shut, enclosing them. The air within smells of antiseptic, formaldehyde. Overhead the fluorescent lights whine.

David looks at Claire, who stands to one side, pulling on rubber gloves, still curious about her last remark. A young woman in a police uniform enters with a camera. Claire smiles at her and introduces her to David. As she shakes his hand he studies her face, wondering how this woman, little more than a girl, must feel, spending her time capturing images of the dead, recording these stark particulars of death. Claire hands him another pair of gloves. Take these, she says. From the younger woman's expression it is impossible to know.

As David pulls on his gloves Claire crosses to the body, flicking on a tape recorder and stepping into the bright circle of light that falls upon the slab. David watches her, listening to her cool, calm voice cataloging her movements. Her voice is low, slightly accented, the Hindi of her parents coloring her words, an echo of ankle bells and sandalwood. She remarks upon his presence, smiling at him as she does. Then, taking a pair of forceps she peels back the blanket, remarking upon the brown stains that cover it, its Army identification and serial number, gently revealing what is beneath.

Freed from its cocoon the body lies twisted, arms at its side, legs straight, but the line of the neck, back, shoulders, hips, legs unnatural. The memory rising unbidden, David finds himself reminded of the twisted shapes of dried eel tethered to a shining metal hook in a market somewhere. Looking closer he sees the head twisted too far sideways, wisps of hair still clinging to the scalp. Fragments of sallowed skin stretch across the bony outlines of the face, yellowing bone protruding at the cheeks, eyebrows, jaw. He feels it filling his mind, while Claire moves around the body, her voice low, methodical, speaking for the benefit of the tape recorder, not David, the photographer circling quickly, efficiently behind her, the camera clicking and whirring. The neck is impossibly thin, windpipe and esophagus writhing beneath the surface like grotesquely corded veins, disappearing into the yellowed collar of a shirt. A dirty brown stain covers the shirt and jacket almost to the neck, spreading down into the crotch of the pants. David, although no stranger to death, feels a stillness pass through him, but then Claire turns toward him, interrupting his thoughts.

Any preliminary opinions? she asks, stopping the tape with one finger.

What? he starts, then shakes his head, deferring to Claire. It's your examination. He takes a step back. To his surprise, the thought that this man has been lying beneath his feet, unseen, for years has unsettled him.

This one's so old I think it's more up your alley than mine, Claire remarks, bent over the body. David looks at her, trying to determine whether this is a challenge of some sort, but her expression is unreadable. When she says nothing more he shrugs, stepping forward and around so he is facing the body. A paper-thin lid still covers the sunken socket of the left eye; the right stares blindly.

Male, he says, judging from the clothes and the suit, but

we'll need to get the clothes off to be sure, Caucasian, blond or light brown hair, five foot ten to six foot tall. Hard to know how old; we'd need to look at the teeth and the skull plates to know that.

She nods. I'll go with that. Delicately she lifts the jacket open with a pair of forceps, exposing the stained and perishing material of the shirt and tie. Sand trickles onto the slab, the grains bouncing and scattering. Looks like he was shot, so that's probably our cause of death. Want to take a punt on how long he's been there?

David fingers the blanket meditatively. He's in pretty good nick, but the site we found him in is very dry. The sand could have mummified the remains. The suit's twentieth century, but I couldn't say more than that.

The army blanket?

That's odd, isn't it? It makes me suspect it was during the war, which would mean he's been there about fifty years, but I honestly couldn't say.

Shall we undress him?

David nods, and Claire reaches for a pair of scissors. With some difficulty she begins cutting the cloth away from the body, the skin tearing away with it in ragged strips.

Within minutes the body lies naked, the clothes laid out neatly for further examination on long silver trays. Beneath the dried skin patches of broken bone mark out four bullet wounds. One high, just beneath the throat and to the left, a second just to the right of the left nipple, the third in line with the first, but lower, beneath the sternum. A crescent moon of death. The right wrist shattered by the fourth, the tiny bones broken almost to powder, the bones of the hand only attached to the arm by skin and shriveled tendon. As David watches, Claire probes the wounds with a metal instrument.

Almost definitely gunshot was the cause of death, she says, turning the instrument in the middle hole. This one would have penetrated the heart. Death would have been almost instantaneous.

The photographer's camera snaps it up. Standing back to take in the totality of the form in front of her, she surveys the body.

No distinguishing marks or features, no visible scars or tattoos, she says for the benefit of the tape recorder. Then she looks up at David.

I don't know there's much more we can learn from the body itself. Shall we examine the clothes?

David nods.

The trousers reveal nothing. In the left pocket of the jacket, however, there is a piece of yellowed paper, folded, which Claire removes carefully, laying it down on a metal tray. David stands beside her, his heart beating fast. She looks at him and he nods, and slowly they unfold it, the paper threatening to crack and part as they do so. It is a letter, smudged ink crawling across its face, blood staining it, watery ghosts of words reflected onto opposing surfaces. For a long moment the two of them stare at it, straining to make sense out of the jumble of ink and blood.

THE LETTER IS unreadable, the shapes formed by the ink having faded or smeared beyond recognition. No address, no signature at the bottom. The paper dry and brittle like ancient skin. Yet once these smears and blurs were symbols, charged with the task of passing meaning from their author to another; another who found this meaning plain, or ambiguous, its content wonderful or tragic or banal. But now that meaning is lost, together with the identity of the author and its recipient, what they meant to each other, how they met, their loves and dreams. Perhaps this man whose body lies dried and twisted on a metal slab beneath the city, exhumed from his sandy grave, wrote these words for another, but their progress was deflected by the violence of his death. Perhaps they are the words of another, written to him; perhaps they are the reason for his death. Yet all that remains is a piece of paper, words blurred beyond meaning, a body.

AFTERWARD THEY WALK through the long corridors, Claire just in front of David, leading him. Their speech is quiet, low, and as they walk, David watches her movements, trying to remember how it was when they were together.

Claire and David met the year after Tania died, brought together by friends. A summer dinner party, the not-so-subtle maneuverings of their hosts. After the dinner the two of them had walked home through the warm streets together, half drunk, talking, and David had found himself relaxing into their tentative liaison, Claire's undemanding presence giving him room to unfold the battered vessel of his heart. In the dark outside her flat she had taken his hand, and David had felt her lips on his cheek, and his body had trembled so violently he thought she must feel it, must know. So much tangle and bruise inside of him. But she had said nothing, just smiled and squeezed his hand, his skin remembering the cool pressure of her lips, fingers, as he navigated the orange-lit streets to his home.

After that night, their orbits brought them together, their bodies and hearts falling into each other, each seeming to fill a need in the other. David's need consumed him, defined him, his heart brittle, cracked already and threatening to fall asunder at any moment. Her presence, her cool and undemanding intimacy, the fact of her body, all of them allowed him space to explore his grief, to move outside himself. Slowly he began to find his way home to himself, to understand the gulf that gaped at the center of his being, as if he were a traveler returning to his birthplace, only to find the remembered home empty and abandoned. Sometimes in the night she would hold his face to her thin body while he wept, and slowly, gently, he began to heal. Then, slowly, without warning, she had moved on, leaving him without explanation or recrimination, the formula that plotted her course moving her on, away, and David had watched her go, also without recrimination, and slowly each had become separate again, the nights and days they had spent together fading, slipping out of reach, until it was as if they had never been more than friends.

But Claire herself was a cipher to David, then and still, now. For all that she gave him, he had never understood what it was that he had given her, for she had always kept something closed from him, a space within herself that he could never penetrate or chart, her presence mysterious, an undiscovered country, but still it had drawn and held him with a silent motion, tidal, as if within her there was a gravity, a depth, a moon that pulled at the deep water of his cells then passed away, out of sight, as silently as she had come. Months after at a party, her cheeks flushed with drink, she had told him she was in love, and as he looked at the way she held herself, the carelessness of her movements, he had known she was telling the truth. But as she pressed her lips to his cheek he had also seen that something had changed within her, that she had surrendered that space he had sensed within her, and he had drawn her close, held her one last time, suddenly afraid for her.

LATER THE TWO of them sit in Claire's office, the faded piece of paper imprisoned in the transparent amber of an evidence bag on the desk between them. David gazes out the window over the park outside, the motion of people along the paths, the clusters in the pools of shade. The glare of the sun penetrating even through the tinted glass.

Are you heading back down tonight?

David turns, jolted out of his reverie. Hmm? Oh yes, probably. It's a long drive.

He shrugs. There's a lot of work to do and not much time. Funds for digs are hard enough to come by as it is, funds to search for mythical shipwrecks are even harder.

Any luck this time?

There's an anomaly on the magnetometer readings we took, but it's probably too small.

Could the anomaly have been the body?

No, the anomaly's larger than that, there's something else down there, something bigger.

But not big enough?

David shakes his head. No, probably not.

For a while they are both silent. Finally Claire speaks.

David?

Hmm?

Were you angry with me?

No. Maybe at the time.

But not now?

He shakes his head. Not for a long time. Why?

Instead of answering his question she looks away, her eyes hidden, distant.

I'm sorry about Paul. I liked him.

So did I, she says, her few words bearing a heavy burden.

After this there is a silence, broken eventually by David, who clears his throat, the rough sound shattering the tension of their closeness.

I should go.

Claire turns back to him. It was good to see you.

You too, she says, then leans forward, her guard dropping for just long enough for David to see she does not want him to leave, not yet.

The ship, you're still sure it's there, under the sand?

David nods. Why?

As quickly as it was there, Claire's openness is gone, she is cool, hidden once more. I don't really know. I was thinking about that man we just examined. She pauses for a moment then continues. I mean I don't suppose we'll ever know who he was, or even what happened to him. Except that he was shot. I don't tend to think too much about the past . . . not if I can help it . . . but it's a mysterious place, isn't it? We know so little, and it's only when we come to try and understand why something might have happened that we realize how poor and cheap our tools of understanding are. Forensics; memories; the law; but in the end they're all just matches we're striking in the darkness. But your ship, if you can find it then it's something concrete, isn't it, something to hold on to.

She finishes, her words faltering, and David realizes this is as close to a confession as he has ever heard from her.

I sometimes think that when . . . if . . . I find it, then I'll understand, but I wonder whether I'm fooling myself, whether all I'll have is more pieces in a puzzle I can never complete. So maybe you're right, maybe we'll never know why he died or even who he was. But if you knew, do you think it would make a difference, would you understand even then?

Claire smiles. David can see that this line of reasoning is already becoming part of her armor.

Perhaps. You're the historian, what do you think?

He waits several seconds before replying, looking for the words.

Who knows. Knowledge and understanding are very different things. Different countries, different tongues.

III

Footprints

There are maps now whose portraits
have nothing to do with surface.

MICHAEL ONDAATJE

There is a map, known as the Dauphin Map, which shows the existence of a vast landmass lying to the southeast of Java and south of Timor. While this landmass, which bears the name Java la Grande, cannot be found on any of the maps with which we are conversant, there is something about the shapes described by the arc of its northern coasts that is immediately, irresistibly familiar. Looking closer, this familiarity only grows, as other features, a scattering of islands here, the curve of a headland there, suggest themselves from out of its detail, none of them perfect, but all familiar, their coincidences echoing first of all across the northern coasts and then eastward and southward down the line of the coast.

What is surprising about the Dauphin Map is its antiquity. Our history relates the story of Australia's discovery as a series of unconnected landfalls, some by misadventure, some by design, a continent that was slowly retrieved from the obscurity of myth by men like Jansz and Hartog, or the unfortunate Tasman, whose path took him into sight of the island that now bears his name, but not the continent off which it lies. These tentative discoveries revealing little more than the existence of a vast and barren wilderness, the true outlines of which remained unknown until Cook charted the eastern coastline at the end of the eighteenth century. All explanations ignoring the fact that this continent's original inhabitants had lived here for a hundred thousand years and maybe longer. Only white men, European men, discover. The darker peoples dispossessed not just of their land but of their history, just waiting to be "discovered." Or worse.

But the Dauphin Map predates Cook and Banks by a quarter of a millennium, having been begun some time before 1536 as a commission for King Francis I of France, as a gift for his son Henry, the Dauphin. The dates are uncertain, the evidence of heraldic features confusing; on the one hand it bears the Arms of France as they were before 1536, on the other it bears the Royal Arms of Henry as King Henry II, not as the Dauphin. From the letter of commission and the Arms of France we know it was begun before 1536, but when it was finished and whether alterations were made later is less clear.

Likewise its authorship cannot be determined with certainty. Historians have traditionally attributed it to Pierre Desceliers, one of the greatest of the school of cosmographers and cartographers who gathered in the French port of Dieppe in the sixteenth century, but this too is largely a matter of convention, for the map is unsigned. But the fact that the commission for the map came from the King himself, as well as the style of the map and its somewhat flamboyant disregard for accuracy, all point to Desceliers. But there is no solid ground for this belief, only guesswork.

All we know for sure is that it was begun some time before

1536 for the Dauphin. Two hundred years later it came into the possession of Edward Harley, Earl of Oxford, by whose name it was known for a time before being stolen upon his death in 1724. Its whereabouts for the next half a century or so are unknown, but eventually Daniel Solander, the astronomer the Royal Society charged with observing the transit of Venus on Cook's great journey of 1769, came upon it, recommending it to the young Joseph Banks, Cook's botanist. Banks in his turn showed it to Cook, who the Royal Society had secretly commanded to search for Terra Australis Incognita, and it is certain the map accompanied Cook on his extraordinary voyage.

What credence Cook gave to the map is not known, but perhaps the concern Banks gave to its preservation might tell us something, for he charged the British Library with its keeping in 1790. Of course by that time Cook was more than ten years dead, slain in the shallows of a Hawaiian beach, but the map survived him, just as it had its makers, as it had King Henry II and Edward Harley, and as it would Joseph Banks.

The map itself still rests in the Map Room of the British Library. A wall map, it is surprisingly large, the paint and ink faded by the centuries, yet the detail and beauty of its execution barely diminished. At some point it has been folded into uneven thirds, and then again in half, and great fissures now crease its surface, disturbing the shapes its maker cast forth across its surface, breaking apart the beauty of its lines and hues.

In many details, even of the known world, it is imprecise, accuracy sacrificed for decorative purposes. Not that this should come as any surprise; mapmaking in the sixteenth century was not the precise business it is today. Then, as now, there was a tension between the demand for detail and the intended use of the map. Just as they do today, maps existed for various purposes: the map you would use to find a house or a street is not the same map you would use to understand the location of Antarctica in relation to the land beneath your feet.

And, just as they are today, maps were instruments of power. Places do not bear the names given them by their original inhabitants, but the names assigned by those who came later, the indigenous languages giving way to the language of the colonizer; the center exercising power over the margins, privileging official names over local ones. Political disputes over borders are resolved to the satisfaction of the cartographers or their rulers, areas rendered barren by ecological devastation or overfarming are hidden away, dry lakes shown full, dead rivers left snaking across valleys rendered deserts by dams and irrigation.

In the sixteenth century, when the Dauphin Map was made, maps were used as ornamental repositories of power. They granted their owners claims over territories, even if the claims were not enforceable; the map extended the grasp of its owner, lord of all he surveyed. As an instrument of the state the map was decorated accordingly, its aesthetic value as important as the symbolic reach of power it bestowed upon its owner.

And the maps of Desceliers were no exception. Historians have noted his tendency to embellish, to exaggerate, indeed to invent whole lands, magicking them out of the air. In this manner he conjured an Antarctic continent which merged with the mysterious landmass to the southeast of Java, counterbalancing the top-heaviness of the known lands of Asia,

Europe, America, and inhabited both by strange peoples and imaginary creatures.

But regardless of his less meticulous tendencies, the Dauphin Map indubitably shows a land, bearing the name Java la Grande, which bears too great and too immediate a likeness to Australia as charted by Cook and Flinders to be easily dismissed as a figment of Desceliers' vivid imagination. And the Dauphin Map is not alone in this. There are other maps, maps made by men lacking Desceliers' flamboyant tendency to invent and embellish, maps by Jean Rotz, Nicolas Vallard, Le Tetsu and Nicolas Desliens, all colleagues of Desceliers at Dieppe, all sober men of skill and integrity, which show again and again this Java la Grande, peopled with strange creatures, and giving detailed and comprehensive names to bays and inlets and headlands, Portuguese names unfamiliar to the modern eye, but names for a coastline that bears an uncanny resemblance to the coast we know as our own.

Perhaps all of them were deceived, perhaps the land they drew was a fiction. (But what is a fiction that turns out to be true?) Or maybe there is more here than we imagined, a hidden past, a secret history.

For behind the whispering voices of our history books there are echoes of earlier journeys, of secret maps and a race to control the world between two countries, Spain and Portugal. And the invisible trails of tiny ships of wood and iron lost on an ocean of unimaginable vastness. Lost in the shifting patterns of time.

$\mathcal{D}$avid noses the four-wheel drive outward from the city, slipping free of the tangle of vehicles and fumes and heat, falling outward into evening. As he drives the sky outside turns bloodred, streaks of high cloud arc gold across the sprawling landscape like ribs, the sun falls silently into the horizon. The music on the stereo so familiar, his favorite tape, the words of the songs, their tunes encoded deep in his brain, tiny ribbons of molecules spiraling through the darkness. Outside the road slips by, familiar now, cars jostling for position, darkness filling the landscape. The dusk is long, silent, like an ending, a space where there is no more time. Like death. In the last light, David's mind begins to wander, slipping free, shifting out through possible worlds.

Unbidden the memory of the body's face returns, the eyes, one lidded, the other open and staring. The mouth choked with sand. The skin, drawn tight on the bones like paper, thin and brittle. In the darkness David listens to the hum of the road, the sound of his own breathing, his mind turning on the mystery contained in the twisted form of the body, all trace of identity wiped away, swept clean by the brutal anonymity of death. Unconsciously he tightens his grip on the steering wheel, tenses his shoulders.

As a student David had spent a summer working on an archaeological dig in Jordan, the long days spent breathing the dusty air of a forgotten world, working until his back ached and his hands were raw and his eyes filled with dust. For a student the rewards were sparse; a shard of pottery, a scratch of charcoal, a bundle of papyrus that crumbled with the slightest movement of air. There were other students on the dig, and amateurs who had paid for the privilege, and at night they would all gather in the long tents and talk and drink and smoke the cheap Jordanian hashish before retiring to sleep in readiness for the predawn start. As the weeks went by the others grew bored, and restive, and even David sometimes found himself listening to the complaints of the worst of them, a German student, with sympathy.

Then, quite by chance, he was the one to unearth a jar, the full curve of its unbroken form emerging slowly beneath his brush, deep cobalt blue against the pale sand. The supervisor had stood back and watched, attentive lest the jar be damaged, but David was not prepared to relinquish his find, working closely, carefully until the jar lay fully exposed. Then the supervisor had stepped forward and moved it gently, and as he did, David saw on its underside, near the base, a flaw in the glaze, a fingerprint baked into the blue curve of its surface. This remnant of an unknown life long ended.

Later that night he had watched the team photographer record the day's finds for the Jordanian Government, waiting until the jar appeared. As she bent to the camera, he took her arm, halting her. Without speaking he had turned the jar until the fingerprint was in view, then motioned her to continue. He remembers the photographer's dark eyes regarding him curiously, her intrigued nod as he asked her to make him a copy, the quick click of the camera as it caught the moment, freezing it in place, arresting it in memory. For many years afterward that photograph, the fingerprint visible in its lower right-hand corner, has occupied a place over his desk, a clue to a puzzle with no answer, a constant reminder of the shroud that obscures the past from our gaze.

And now there is the body, its parched lips clasped tight on its secrets. And Claire. The ambiguity of her parting kiss, her lips on his, so briefly he hardly felt them. The immediacy of his isolation clear in that moment. His need.

IN THE DARKNESS outside the landscape changes, unseen, the broken coastline with its thick greenery and the wide bays with their parabolic arcs of sand subsiding, giving way to scrub and finally sand arching silently into the distance, shapes rendered whole by memory. Two hours past midnight now, the road is silent, other cars appearing only rarely; a distant glare becoming a rush of night air that shakes David's four-wheel drive then they are gone, anxious to be past this empty place. Finally David's headlights pick out the gate, its metal sign warning motorists not to proceed. David pulls in toward it, opening the door into the cool night air. The breeze off the sea moves through the grass, the creak of the gate loud as he opens it. Something unseen rustles in the grass to one side of the track, its motion startling David.

Through the gate he drives on, winding into the dunes.

Without thinking he finds himself examining them as he passes them, searching for the elusive clue that may reveal the ship he is searching for. As always he tries to pierce the secrets of the sands, trying to imagine how it was, the past hovering unseen in the air, encoded in it like a ghostly X ray of broken bones. A shattered wrist. Once, two summers before, he had seen a figure on the hills, indistinct, shimmering in the sun's heat, known it was watching him. He had stood, and as he had it had moved away, vanished, its movements slow and labored, as if burdened by great age or injury. Surprising himself, David had pursued the figure, angry, the realization that he might be being watched out here, making him feel somehow soiled, but when he had reached the place where the figure had been standing the sand was unmarked, as if no one had been there. Caught in the grip of his sudden fury he had stood there on the dune's summit for a long time, swaying in the ocean wind as he stared around himself, looking for an indication that what he had seen had been real, but there was none. Then, as quickly as it had come upon him, his anger had ebbed away, and he had turned, stood staring out over the hills to the line of ocean in the distance, feeling himself beginning to fade into the emptiness of this place, his presence leaching into the silence of the shifting hills, the murmuring waves.

After half an hour's slow drive he reaches the base camp, the cluster of brightly colored nylon hemispheres indistinct in the darkness. Conscious of the fact the others are sleeping, he stops some distance from the collection of tents, closing the door behind him carefully. Outside the sealed cabin of the four-wheel drive the air is cool, salt water misting hazily landward, diffusing the moonlight over the white sand, and as he walks toward the tents he feels himself waking up, his need for sleep dissipating in response to the night air, the sense of space. As he approaches a figure steps out of the larger tent in the middle, navigating its way through the others toward him. Its outline bleeds into the hazy dark but David knows who it will be. Anna. Nearly at the tents now the figure stops, waits for him.

What happened?

David sighs. Not much. Whoever he was he was murdered, but it was a long time ago. Anything here?

She shakes her head. Not a thing. The cops have been asking questions, but my impression is it's all a bit perfunctory. They haven't let us do any more digging since the other night.

David feels a sudden rush of anger. Shit, he says, under his breath. Did you tell them how tight a schedule we're on? Anna nods, and for a second or two neither of them speaks. Finally Anna asks, How did he die? her voice low.

He was shot.

Do they know who he was?

No.

David knows she is waiting for him to tell her more, that she knows he is holding back. Finally he succumbs.

Claire was there.

Claire? Your Claire?

David nods. He tries to make out Anna's expression in the darkness. He has never been sure how she felt about Claire, Claire's distance seeming to make Anna's matter-of-fact directness almost loutish, drawing her out and making her louder and more blunt, as if Anna felt the need to fill the space Claire created with sound and movement. They had spent a lot of time together in the year after Tania's death when Claire and

David were together, and although Anna was always friendly, David was never sure that the friendliness wasn't for his benefit. But there was something more, a tension beneath his and Anna's friendship, something almost . . . sexual?

I thought she was overseas, with . . . what's his name.

David laughs. Paul; I forgot as well.

Oh, she says, signaling her desire to know no more, but David cannot help himself and continues.

They broke up. She's back alone.

A silence . . . And?

And what?

Claire; how was she?

Something makes David hold back. Fine, he says.

Then the two of them stand in the darkness, each not looking at the other. Both knowing a boundary is nearby, reluctant to approach it. Finally David steps forward, reaches for her arm, then, thinking better of it, retreats, saying, It's late. We should get some sleep.

I suppose.

David steps around her toward the tents. Then, on impulse, he turns, touches her shoulder, and she looks down at it, her expression unreadable.

See you in the morning?

Anna's voice betraying nothing. Sure.

Undressing in the curved chamber of the tent David listens to the sounds of the sleepers around him. Much later he wakes briefly, hears footsteps outside, and wonders if they are Anna's, if she has been standing there in the darkness alone all this time.

*A*fter Tania died, David's friends had rallied to him, endless offers of meals, chaperoned evenings, activities. He'd sat through them, his wounds distressingly near the surface. Slowly the offers had declined in number, his presence filling any space he was in with a pain that was almost tangible. Her death so stupid, so unnecessary.

hen David wakes it is already hot, the air in his tent oppressive, sweat pooling on his chest. He wakes slowly, his head and eyes aching from lack of sleep. When he emerges from the tent the others are already awake, gathered under the tarpaulin, some working, most just sitting, talking, reading magazines and cheap paperbacks. When they see him they look up, and Anna stands, watching him cross toward them, pulling a singlet on as he does.

I've already told everyone what you told me last night, Anna says as he steps under the tarpaulin. She flashes him a cheeky grin. Sorry.

Seeing her smile David knows she has decided to ignore their momentary collision of the night before.

No problem. Why are you all still here?

One of the others calls out from above a magazine. The cops are up there, they won't let us onto the site.

Still? David looks around, his tiredness rapidly transforming into annoyance. Jesus. Did they say how long they were going to be?

No.

One of the others laughs sardonically. At least they seem to be doing something today. Yesterday they didn't do anything all day.

Except stop us doing anything, another retorts, and there is a rumble of assent.

David shakes his head, knowing that this is his responsibility now. All right, he sighs, I'll talk to them.

As he turns to go Anna steps forward. Want a hand? she asks. David shrugs. Sure.

They walk together over the dunes toward the dig. David walks with his eyes ahead, not speaking, trying to gulp back his ill temper. As they crest the hill he sees several police cars parked on the slope beneath, surrounding the site of the discovery. Yellow plastic tape flutters in the breeze. He looks at Anna, who meets his eye, her steady gaze an assent to his mood.

At the bottom of the hill they are approached by the detective who had agreed to David's attendance at the autopsy. David walks toward him, Anna hanging back. The detective smiles in a friendly way, and David wonders whether his manner is designed to deflect the anger David is sure he is exuding.

You're back.

Mm-hmm, David nods. And you're still here.

The detective turns and looks at the site behind him. Yeah, I know. Sorry about that but things are taking a bit longer than we expected.

David folds his arms. Any idea how long you're going to be. We're on a pretty tight schedule.

The detective looks at David, his eyes narrowing as he assesses David's manner. I appreciate that, Dr. Norfolk, but these things take time.

So, how much time?

The detective sighs. Hopefully we'll be out of here later today.

Good.

The breeze shifts around them, the light of the sun on the sand suffusing the air. Then the detective clears his throat, shuffling his feet in the sand. You're looking for a ship that's supposed to be buried somewhere under here?

David is uncertain how to respond, unclear whether the detective's interest is genuine or just professional courtesy. Finally he decides he may have misjudged the man, and that his question is genuine.

Portuguese, yes.

Any luck?

Not really. There's an anomaly under this site we're interested in.

It's probably too small though, adds Anna, looking sideways at David.

David glances from the detective to Anna and back. But— he begins, aware of the annoyance in his voice—it's the best lead we've got. And we're nearly out of time.

The detective looks at him dispassionately, and David has the sense he is adding this information to a vast file in his head.

As I said, we're doing our best. But I promise, we'll be out of here a.s.a.p. As the detective speaks David realizes he is telling the truth.

Thanks.

Almost as an afterthought the detective clears his throat and asks, Have you spoken to the old bloke down in the shack?

David and Anna exchange glances.

No . . . Shack?

There's a place in the dunes about three kilometers down the coast from here, he says, turning to gesture. I haven't been there myself but one of the local blokes went there yesterday to make some inquiries. He was saying the bloke had been there for about a thousand years, but he also said something about the old bloke having been looking for a ship himself. Said you guys had made him think of it.

Thanks, says David, a bit uncertainly.

No problem, I hope he can help you. As he speaks the detective turns to walk away. But then he hesitates, looking back. Oh, and don't be surprised when you see how he looks. Apparently he's a bit of a mess.

DAVID REMEMBERS THE shack. Near the opening of a creek, at the southern end of the sandhills, where the drifting sand and marram grass give way to limestone cliffs, low scrub. But he has never seen its owner, never spoken to him.

*K*now anything about this shack? David asks.

Anna pauses before answering, considering. Not really. I think I know the place he's talking about. Think it's worth a look?

David shrugs. Can't hurt.

He is aware of her eyes on him as she speaks. Want me to come with you?

No. It's probably nothing.

HALF AN HOUR later David stands at a gate a hundred meters from the shack. The sun overhead is high, the day white hot. Grasshoppers hum metallically, the heat singing in the air in a high-pitched whine of space. And emptiness. The metal of the chain binding the gate closed burns his fingers, and he works fast, untangling it and crossing inward, swinging the gate shut behind him, then, step by step, along the shimmering surface of the track.

The shack's crumbling form swells up from the sand, a creaking mass of tin, bleached wood. Rust bleeds down it from innumerable wounds, the shifting sand held back by sheets of corrugated iron staked in place. The windows so filthy they let nothing escape. The green door peels in the shade of the veranda. An ancient station wagon is tethered nearby. A screen door hanging on loose hinges shifts in the breeze.

At the door to the shack David pauses, not moving. Finally he reaches forward, opening the screen door, and knocks on the green door behind it, the peeling paint sharp beneath his knuckles. At first there is no reply. David is about to knock again when he feels it. Not a sound, more a sense of movement from within, a knowledge that there is someone inside. He lowers the hand that he had been about to knock with, hesitating, then lifts it again, pushes the green door gently and peers into the dim interior.

Hello?

From somewhere inside there is a voice, thin, wheezing. Who is it? it asks, followed by a bout of coughing. A television blares. David steps inward, following the voice.

My name's David Norfolk . . . I'm an archaeologist. From the dig in the sandhills . . .

His voice halting, waiting in each pause for some kind of confirmation from within, but none comes. Inside now, David blinks, his eyes adjusting slowly to the dim interior. When there is no reply he steps forward, moving toward the sound of the television. The air in here is close and unpleasant, surly with the smell of urine, unwashed body, a hundred years of cigarettes. Coughing comes from the door on his left, and David steps into it, trying to appear as unthreatening as possible.

Hello? he says again, shading his eyes from the light filtering through the smeared window in the opposite wall. A figure sits in a chair, the light falling on its legs. A black-and-white television flickers through the pall of cigarette smoke. As David's eyes grow accustomed to the dimness he sees the face of the figure, barely suppressing a gasp of surprise. A massive snarl of pink and white burn tissue covers his scalp, forehead and cheek; a puckered, shiny furrow of scarring extending downward through it, across the distorted line of the nose and left eyebrow, beneath one milky white eye stares blindly from behind its drooping lid, before continuing onward, around the shattered stump of the left ear and into the neck of his filthy shirt, almost as if half his head has been lifted away by some titanic blast and later grafted back in place by a cack-handed Frankenstein. His bald head is spotted with deep stains, liver spotted and bruised with age, while his neck and the back of his head are crisscrossed with white traceries of damaged skin. His breathing is loud, rasping, in the small room.

The police have already been, he says. I said I don't know anything about it.

David is caught between staring at the man's injuries and looking away. I know, I'm not a policeman, I'm an archaeologist, working on an excavation near here. I wondered whether you might know something that would be useful.

I know what an archaeologist is, he snaps, his voice collapsing into wheezes.

I'm sure you do, I didn't mean to be rude.

The old man hawks, the noise derisive, lifting the cigarette he is holding to his mouth and drawing back deeply, an act that only provokes another spasm of wheezing coughs. As he does David sees several fingers are missing on his right hand. The old man snorts bitterly.

It's not pretty, is it. The words a statement, not a question. David looks up, startled, to find the old man looking up at him, his one good eye staring, his expression almost cruel.

I'm sorry, I—

Don't be stupid, you think I'm not used to people looking at me? he says, his voice flat, his good eye still fixed on David.

David, realizing this is a question with no right answer, ignores the remark, asking a question instead. Do you mind if I ask you a few questions?

What about?

The ship we're looking for. One of the police told me you've lived here for a long time. I thought you might know something that could help us.

The old man doesn't reply, just looks past David as if he isn't there. David finds himself growing irritated with the old man's game. Unconsciously he allows his weight to shift to one foot, gradually assuming a position of impatience. Finally he sighs, annoyed, but before he can say he is leaving the old man looks back at him.

Tell me about the ship.

What do you mean?

You said you were looking for a ship. Tell me about it.

Unsure of the spirit in which the question is asked, David hesitates. It's a wreck that's meant to be buried somewhere along this piece of coast. I . . . we . . . believe it's Portuguese, from the early sixteenth century.

The old man watches him speak, and David, warming to his subject, continues, more certainly now.

There are a lot of historical accounts, records made by locals and visitors to this area who claim to have seen it prior to about 1860, but after that there's almost nothing. We think it was covered up when the sand began to drift around the middle of the last century.

You think it's still there?

David nods, and the old man clears his throat phlegmily. I know the stories you're talking about.

As he speaks David is struck by the sense that the words are not addressed to him but to someone else.

Do you believe them?

Would it make a difference if I did?

David shakes his head, conceding the point. Probably not.

A sudden spasm of coughing rocks the old man. David steps forward. He sees the discolored rag the old man uses to cover his mouth is stained with fresh blood, black phlegm. Reluctant to reach out and touch the older man David kneels, placing a hand on the arm of the chair.

Are you all right? he asks, knowing the question is a stupid one.

The old man doesn't reply, just moving his head in a tight shaking motion. Finally the spasm passes, leaving him looking shaken and weak in its wake.

Do you want me to get a doctor? David asks, and the old man shakes his head.

So he can tell me I'm dying? We're all fuckin' dying all the time, he says, his voice bitter. Then he laughs cruelly. It just takes some of us longer to realize it than others.

David remains kneeling in front of him. Are you sure?

The old man brushes the question away with his ruined hand, changing the subject. You want to find the ship?

Of course. Why?

I might be able to help you.

You know where it is?

The old man shrugs. I knew someone who said they did.

David's hand closes on the arm of the chair, tensing. Who?

It was a long time ago. He's dead now.

What did he tell you?

It's not that simple. Things were different then.

I don't understand.

The old man looks up at him. Don't you? He pauses. It's a long story. Maybe you should come back tomorrow, when I'm less tired. There are things I can tell you.

David fights the desire to demand he tell him now, stepping back and up. And you'll tell me then? he asks, his heart shaking in the cage of his ribs. The old man just looks at him, unspeaking. Then, as he turns to go, the old man coughs again, then stops. David turns back, surprised by his sudden stillness.

I saw you, the old man says, something in his tone making David freeze.

What?

I saw you; in the hills.

David looks at him, trying to read the expression on the man's ruined face. When? he asks, but even as he does he knows. The mirage, two years before. The old man wheezes.

You remember.

David nods. Why did you run away?

The old man shrugs. You haven't asked me my name, he says.

David realizes the old man is telling the truth and blushes. I'm sorry, I didn't . . .

The old man waves the shattered hand dismissively, the cigarette nestled between the stumps of the first two fingers.

It's Kurt. Kurt Seligmann.

As he says it David realizes he has heard the name before, but not where.

Kurt, he finds himself saying as he steps out of the room, feeling his way into the name, I'll see you tomorrow.

OUTSIDE THE SHACK the sun is still straight overhead, dazzling David as he emerges into the heat. He walks slowly, allowing his eyes to adjust to the brightness, his mind still inside, with Kurt. He is feeling his way into this new intelligence, this man who claims to provide a clue. The familiarity of his name. David's shadow crawls inward toward him, vanishing as the sun rises higher.

APPROACHING THE SITE, David sees the police cars have gone. Relieved, he walks slowly along the ridge of the dune behind the site. Beneath him a hole has been dug in the sand. At its center he sees a rusty stain, twisted shapes. His heart beginning to beat faster, he runs, sliding in the sand, down the hill toward the small knot of people near the hole. As he approaches, Anna steps out toward him, brushing sand from her hands onto her shorts.

What is it? he gasps. What have you found?

Anna sighs, wiping her brow. Farm machinery, she says. Fucking farm machinery.

*W*hen David began it was different. He was a pattern finder, a historian, charged with the task of sifting the past for organizing structures, causal patterns. His original doctorate was *An Enquiry into Conceptions of Society and the European State in the Age of Exploration, 1400–1600* and for two years he burrowed through dusty manuscripts, looking to understand the past, order it, make it comprehensible. Never able to reconcile the purpose of his work with his growing sense that the past was shifting, uncertain, that any attempt to bind it in place was doomed to failure, its sprawl as uncontrollable as it was unknowable.

Then that morning in the library in Lisbon, the sun streaming through the windows, catching in the dust that danced in the air as it was released from the books. He was reading a journal kept by the Portuguese chronicler de Barros, a personal journal, its dusty paper brittle, stained with age. Deciphering and translating the faded handwriting as he went, he found a marginal note that puzzled him:

I am told this day that Mendonça, the commander who so distin-guished himself in the battle with the Mir at Pacem, is to be sent to search for the Isles of Gold. That this should be decided when there is still no sign of de Cueva, who made from here on a similar mission less than two years ago, seems to me imprudent. But we are forced by the threat of the traitor Magellan to take risks we might prefer not to, the search for these southern Isles of Gold being much on the mind of my lords these last months.

THE NAME DE Cueva was unknown to him, but that of Men-donça was not. Mendonça was the commander of a doomed expedition some believed had explored the eastern coast of Australia in 1521. Yet here was de Barros, the greatest chroni-cler of the time, making note of another, earlier, expedition. His mind buzzing, he took out pen and paper and transcribed the words, noting their place as he did.

Back in his apartment David read and reread the note. The words echoing in his mind, he searched his notes, the indices of every book in his small room for the name de Cueva, but found nothing. Finally he rang a friend in Sydney, waking him from sleep. In Sydney it was late, and the friend knew little. But no, he had never heard of de Cueva. David had put the phone down, walked to the window and gazed out over the city lights. History, events unseen and long forgotten, were about to change his life's course. Irrevocably.

That night in the camp the team are restive, the disappointment of the machinery, the disruption of the body and the police, the heat, combining to leave them defeated. If asked a month before, not one of them would have said that they expected to find the ship, but all of them felt its pull, all of them had allowed it to enter into the mood of what they were doing. In all their minds the ship had been there, ghostly, flickering silently in a silver nitrate dreamscape of sand and bleached light, and now, now that imagining has been shattered, spooled off the reel in a sudden convulsive movement of dark borders and melting celluloid, they want to leave, to return to their lives. Too many possibilities crowding into this space around them.

Anna touches his arm and he turns to her, startled, realizing he has been lost in thought.

David?

Sorry, I was miles away.

She smiles wryly. Miles away where?

Now he is asked David realizes he doesn't know. He slides

upright in his chair. Nowhere really, he says, trying to dispel his mood of distraction. He pauses, looking at her. You OK?

Anna shrugs. I suppose.

Pity about the anomaly.

She laughs. That's rich, coming from you. I've been the one counseling caution for the last month.

David nods, laughing now too. I suppose you're right.

For several seconds the two of them laugh, a sardonic amusement uniting them.

Anna is the first to stop, her eyes moving to the can of beer she holds with both hands.

This is the end, isn't it? she says, and David nods, knowing she is not really asking, just seeking confirmation of what she already knows.

Unless something new turns up, we're not going to get funding again.

David doesn't continue, knowing he doesn't need to.

You didn't tell me what happened with the old guy.

David looks at her, startled. In the disappointment of the afternoon he had forgotten his visit to the shack.

I'm not sure, but I think he knows something. He says he knew someone who said they knew where the ship was a long time ago.

Do you believe him?

David shrugs, remembering the shattered face and hand, the foul air. Perhaps. He seemed pretty strange though.

Strange how?

Strange strange. Crazy. He's all smashed up, as if he'd been caught in some kind of explosion.

How do you mean?

As he speaks David finds himself remembering the twisted features of the corpse on the slab, not Kurt's.

His face is scarred; here—he indicates—to here, and his hand is half gone.

Anna looks fascinated. Shit, she says, then remembering why she is interested she shakes herself and continues.

So what did he say?

Not much. I said I'd go back tomorrow.

Who is he?

I don't know. His name is Kurt Seligmann. I thought it sounded familiar but I couldn't think where from. You know it?

Anna shakes her head. Nup. Then she opens her arms a bit, smiling. But who cares, maybe he'll become the find we need to keep this thing going.

David chuckles. Maybe. Then he laughs outright. Look at you. I thought you were meant to be the skeptic on this team.

Maybe I'm just a closet optimist.

Maybe.

As fast as it came, their amusement fades. Jesus, David sighs, what a fuckup.

ANOTHER TWO BEERS and David slips away. For all his cheerfulness with Anna he is worried, his need for the ship aching inside of him. While they were talking he saw she wanted it too, but not like him. For him it is not something he wants, more something he needs, something that is already part of him, aching in the darkness like a limb severed years before. Phantom but real. Outside it is cooler, and he crosses to the tent where the charts and supplies are kept, flicking the light on as he enters. Beer fills him in a warm fug as he spreads his work before him: charts, maps, magnetic scans, trying to lose himself in their patterns.

For a long time he sits there, alone, the harsh glow of the electric light, incandescent white, shivering as the power from the generator slips and plays. Outside the sea wind sweeps across the sand, ruffling the long grass, the sounds of the others drinking and laughing, scraps of music filtering in from outside. The thin canvas of the tent wrapping around this bubble of light like a skin.

Suddenly his mobile rings, its electric trill loud in the quiet dark. David grabs at it, urgently, trying to silence it.

There is a pause, then Claire's voice, soft, tentative. David? Were you asleep?

No.

That's good. Sorry to call so late.

Don't worry. Is something wrong?

Not really. I just thought you'd want to know I've made an estimate of how long our friend had been down there.

David lifts his eyes to the darkness of the door. How long?

I'd say somewhere between forty and sixty years.

David nods to himself. That's about what I would have said. So what now?

Probably nothing.

What do you mean?

They're not likely to bother investigating a murder from fifty years ago, particularly not when we can't even identify the body.

Should I be surprised?

No. There's nothing for them to go on. He could be anyone. Besides, whoever did it is likely to be dead.

Or forgiven?

You don't think fifty years is long enough?

For a moment David's eyes fill with the motion of the murdered man, his body spinning backward, arms scratching at the air as he slips down through the treacherous air, toward . . . what?

I suppose. David pauses. If I find anything else shall I call you?

Do you think you will?

I don't know. Maybe.

Have you found something?

David hesitates, the image of Kurt's ruined face intruding suddenly. He shakes his head, trying to dispel it, annoyed with himself for such simplistic suspicions.

No.

What is it? Claire asks, and David realizes she has heard the hesitation in his voice.

I don't know. Nothing; it's been a difficult day and I'm tired. How're things with you?

Good. For a moment she pauses, and when she speaks again her voice is different, less formal. David?

Hmm?

It was good to see you the other day.

You too.

Will you call me when you get back?

The request, or at least its tone, surprises David. But he agrees, feeling her need. Sure.

Thanks. I should go.

Me too.

The phone clicks off, and David lowers it to the table. He feels suddenly alone. For several minutes he sits where he is, not moving, then he stands, walks out into the darkness.

The tents billow as the wind breathes into them, warm sleeping lungs. A woman's voice comes from the main tent, clear and loud. Turning away from the camp David walks slowly down toward the shore, the sand slipping around his feet, cushioning him as he goes. Near the water the air is misty, the ocean rolling ceaselessly in and out. Standing here David cannot help but be awed by the sweep of ocean before him, its shifting endless landscape. This shore little more than pebbles cast up out of the sea, even the sand lime sand, grown deep in the ocean, a silt of shattered bones, the brittle cages of prehistoric seashells. This land so ancient, yet so impermanent.

Turning now he looks back at the rolling forms of the hills, indistinct in the darkness. In the dark it is possible to imagine these hills two hundred years before, a low wilderness of scrub and grass, the silent ghosts of its people. Two hundred years seems barely time enough to do anything, yet in this time men like him, pale-skinned, have swept away the world that was here, made a new one. He closes his eyes, trying to imagine the hills as the Portuguese would have seen them, low, unmoving, before men and their cattle eroded the grass, set the sand free to drift and move. Even the landscape not immune.

AND LATER, ALONE in his tent, David dreams of the corpse, its shrunken face, and of Claire, her hands cool, their imagined motion jolting him awake. The wind rippling like water across the nylon roof.

The next morning David goes back to the shack, drawn to it. Instead of driving he walks the three kilometers along the beach. No longer any need to hurry, he feels the impetus is gone in all of them this morning. As he walks the wind blows cold on his skin, having turned in the night, shearing across the Tasman from the frigid waters of the Southern Ocean. The sun's rays perversely hot. Earlier he had stood at the folding table, listened to the others discussing whether to give up the search tonight or tomorrow. He had stood there spinning his spoon around and around in his coffee, not turning back to them, not listening. The milk will not unstir. Everything is falling apart.

No one answers the door so David lets himself in. Inside it is dark. He calls out, and when there is no answer again he presses on into the room he had been in the day before, his heart rising in his throat as he goes.

Kurt is asleep on his bed, his body curled in on itself so that for a moment David thinks he is dead. A long moment, then David clears his throat, announcing himself. Kurt stirs abruptly, looking around with the wild flailing of an animal cornered.

Who's there? A terrible frailty in his angry demand.

Me, David Norfolk. At the sound of David's voice he sees him straining to focus in the half light.

Who?

The archaeologist. From yesterday, have I disturbed you?

An angry noise. *Pshaw.*

Shall I come back?

Why?

You said yesterday that there was something you knew that might help me, told me to come back, so I have. Do you remember? As he speaks David feels the edge of anxiety in his voice, the words coming faster, pleading to fill up the space left by Kurt.

When there is no answer David steps forward. As he draws closer he hears Kurt's labored breathing has slowed, and it occurs to David that he may be asleep, but then Kurt smiles, a lopsided grimace. Watching the struggle of the damaged side of the face to match the movement of the other David realizes half the face is palsied. The old man laughs, a low sound, and not kind, David thinks.

You're the one looking for the ship, aren't you?

Mm-hmm.

Again the laugh. I'm sorry, my memory plays tricks on me these days. I remember now.

If it weren't for the polite words David would have thought there was malice in the laughter, a glint of something cruel.

I said I'd tell you about the ship, didn't I? David's heart quickens, breath coming short.

Yes.

I can't . . . A burst of coughing . . . I need to know what you know though. Do you believe it's there?

David looks at Kurt, weighing the question up in his mind. Avoiding his professional caution he answers simply. Yes.

Kurt doesn't reply, just nods.

And you?

Perhaps. Yes. We got so close.

We?

Fraser and I. Veronica.

David shakes his head. I don't understand; these are the people you said thought they knew where the ship was?

Even at the beginning I wanted her.

David realizes the old man is wandering. Kurt, please, you were going to tell me about the ship.

Kurt looks at him, suddenly aware. The ship, that's right, you wanted to know about de Cueva's ship.

At the sound of the name David feels his stomach twist.

De Cueva? How . . . ? he begins, his voice cracking as words fail him. This name, de Cueva, a secret knowledge the other man cannot possess. The room suddenly still, the old man's words lying between the two of them in the stinking air like a bomb. A ticking in his head, the endless silence before the explosion for minutes, hours, days. Then David's words low, terrible.

How do you know that name? The old man not speaking, not moving. Tell me, please. David's voice coming through clenched teeth. Desire for the ship almost sexual, eating at him, coiling low in his abdomen. Tell me. He fights the desire to lean forward, to seize the old man and shake him, to jar his words free with force. Tell me.

Kurt twists away, his head falling on one side, his voice coming strangled through his throat. David is almost in tears. Please, tell me.

No.

Please . . . David realizes the older man has left him, wandering away into some labyrinth of his mind. Chambers turning inward from the seashell coil of the ear, a tangle of memories moving in sheets of meaning through the brain. A sudden convulsion runs through his body.

David takes Kurt's arm, trying to calm him with the pressure of his hand. Kurt! he says, Kurt! but the old man doesn't reply. His head moves from side to side, his voice coming in short breaths, muttering, peaks and troughs in it like waves. A sudden cough issuing in a gurgling wet choke from his chest. David reaches up, grasping the older man's face and turning it to his, and as he does he sees his good eye is open and staring, its faded surface glistening, rheumy liquid running down from it across the sunken cheek. Reflexively he pulls away, Kurt's hand scratching at the space his body has left in the air. Regaining his composure he reaches out again.

Who's there? Who is it? the older man moans. Who's there?

David takes the waving hand in his, surprised by its thinness. His hand closing around it, enfolding it, like a child's or a woman's.

It's me, it's David.

Who?

David, he says again.

No, moans Kurt. No. David realizes Kurt cannot see or hear him. A stain spreading across the sheets, the rank smell daubing the room.

Please, he says, moving closer, his concern overwhelming his revulsion at the state of the sheets. It's all right, you're safe.

Kurt moans again, and David strokes his cheek. The skin beneath his hand is burning hot. Suddenly he realizes Kurt is dying. Not some time in the future, but soon, perhaps even now if David cannot help him.

Shhh, he says, still trying to calm Kurt, who whimpers in fear or pain. Shhh. His chest rises slightly, and again the wet sound issues from inside him. David flinches, but as he does he feels a resolution urging itself upon him.

He knows what he must do. He must call a doctor.

*T*he doctor comes quickly once he is called, and David is relieved to discover that he knows Kurt. David hovers behind him, watching anxiously as the doctor administers an injection—pethidine—and organizes antibiotics. Under the doctor's ministrations Kurt's distress seems to lessen, his muttering slowing and fading. Between the two of them they lift the old man's wasted form from the sheets, peeling his soiled pajamas from his body. When they lift his body from the bed the smell rises in a wave, and David has to turn his face away, gasping at the sharp tide of bile that floods his mouth, his shoulders shuddering involuntarily. Turning back, jaw set, he looks to the doctor apologetically, but the doctor makes no sign that he has seen, continuing the unpleasant task of wiping the worst of the filth from the old man's legs and back efficiently, with a detached, almost clinical composure. The two of them work side by side, the piss and shit and blood that stains everything leaching out onto their hands and skin, until finally, the worst of it done, the doctor politely relieves David, dispatching him to find clean bedding and pajamas.

Throughout the operation Kurt lolls and shivers, his scabbed hands pushing at theirs, deflecting them, complicating the already difficult task. At first David finds the intimacy of cleaning the older man's buttocks, the shriveled penis, almost unbearable, but gradually, as the operation proceeds in near silence, punctuated only by the doctor's brusque instructions and Kurt's groans and vague protestations, he finds it easier, less confronting. He allows the warm sponge to linger on the terrible scars that continue across the body, down one side of the rib cage and hips to the leg, where other, longer scars seem to indicate surgery of some sort. Seeing him pause the doctor looks up, grunts, The war, then continues. On the older man's back are two pitted ulcers, one five centimeters across, the other smaller, the exposed meat red beneath them, their crusted edges releasing a stink of corruption. The doctor dabs at them with antiseptic, dressing them, and administers an intravenous shot of antibiotics.

This done the doctor turns his attention to David. The man's manner is odd, suspicious, and suddenly David realizes how peculiar his presence here is. He stumbles, trying to explain what he is doing, but it is clear from the doctor's expression that he is only half convinced. Slowly though, and grudgingly, the doctor seems to accept that he is who he says he is, and that his reasons for being here are legitimate. Finally David asks him how long Kurt has been sick, the nature of his illness.

The doctor looks at David over his glasses, an attitude that makes him look rather stern, but kindly, and David wonders if it is an expression he has learned over the years to reinforce his advice to patients.

Cancer, he says. In the lungs originally but it's spread now. Inoperable. He didn't do anything about it until it was too late, and he wasn't interested in radio- or chemotherapy. Didn't want to go into a hospital. I had enough trouble getting him to drive the fifty kilometers for the tests in the district hospital. I told him then, when he was diagnosed, that it would end up like this if he didn't put himself into a nursing home, but he refused. People round here are like that, they like to die at home.

The doctor hesitates on the last word, glancing around the shack in a way that expresses his perplexity at such a decision.

So what now?

I don't really see any alternative to hospitalizing him. He needs constant care and attention, and there's no one out here who can . . . His voice trails off, his manner indicating the surroundings as if they are all the evidence he needs. David nods agreement.

How long has he got?

The doctor shrugs. I don't know. Weeks maybe. No more. Possibly less.

David feels a space yawn inside him. The ship.

Taking David's silence as a request for more information, the doctor continues, his eyes on the sleeping Kurt. His mind's pretty much gone as it is, poor old bastard. It almost seems wrong to intervene.

David's mind races. You knew him well?

The doctor shakes his head. No. No one did. He was living up here when I was a child, but even then he was eccentric. Never came into town more than once every few years. Stayed out here in these hills, watching over them. He snorts. When I was a kid I thought they were his. You know, that he owned them. Me and the other kids used to follow him. His wounds fascinated us.

For a long while there is silence between them, then David clears his throat. If I were to stay here with him, look after him, would that be enough?

The doctor looks genuinely surprised. You? Why?

David smiles. I don't know. It seems wrong for him to be taken away. You heard him before, he doesn't want to go. He smiles, trying to disguise the lie.

The doctor shakes his head in vigorous disagreement. He needs to be somewhere where he can have constant supervision, and you can't provide that.

You could visit.

I could, but he needs more than just visits from me. He needs full-time nursing help, someone who can administer painkillers and antibiotics, someone to bathe him and dress the ulcers on his back, at least daily, maybe more often.

The doctor removes his glasses, watching David's expression for a sign that his point is being made.

It's not that I doubt your motives, Dr. Norfolk, just that you're simply not equipped to handle this on your own. He needs someone who knows what they're doing. A professional.

The doctor allows this last point to sink in.

You said yourself people round here often prefer to die at home. What do they do?

They have family, they get a nurse in, but you're not family, I can't just leave him here with you.

David looks at the doctor, the set expression on his face, and realizes he must change his approach. Look, he says, starting slowly, this might sound crazy, but I think he has the location of this ship we're looking for locked away somewhere in his head. If you take him to a hospital they'll just sedate him and I'll never know. If you leave him here with me, I can look after him and he might, he just might tell me. I can't tell you how important this is to me.

The doctor watches him, and David sees from his expression that he is considering it.

Finally he clears his throat. You'll need to get someone in to help you, he says, and I'll have to be sure Kurt agrees. It's his decision after all.

David smiles. I've got a friend, he says, a doctor, she might come.

The doctor grunts disbelievingly. A doctor? They'd want to be a good friend. I might be able to arrange a nurse.

David shakes his head, realizing now that he has suggested it he doesn't want a nurse, he wants Claire.

Let me try my friend first.

The doctor shrugs. It's your decision. He gestures at David's mobile. Call me later today and tell me what you've worked out.

DAVID STANDS IN the shade outside the shack and dials Claire's number. It rings twice, three times, then she answers.

Claire Sen.

Claire, it's David.

Hi, she says, her tone softening. As she speaks David suddenly realizes how absurd his plan is, her voice bringing the reality of it home to him. What's up?

I've got a problem and I wondered whether you might be able to help me.

More bodies?

He laughs. No, not bodies. It's a medical problem.

Hmm. Her voice low. Not suspicious, but cautious. David wonders if he is overestimating the tenuous link between them.

I've found a man, an old man, and I think he knows where the ship is.

There is a pause. But?

He's sick, dying, and they want to put him in a hospital to die. And . . . David falters, unsure of how to explain his certainty he will learn nothing there . . . I don't think he'll tell me anything if he's in a hospital.

When Claire says nothing he knows she has realized where this is heading. I need someone to help me look after him.

Why are you asking me this, David? Claire asks, her voice not distant, but hurt.

Because I need to know what it is he knows and you're the only person I trust enough to ask.

David, I've got work to do here, I can't just up and run. Besides, you need a nurse, someone who knows about palliative care, not me.

David watches a hawk circle overhead, considering his response. All right, he says, I understand.

But look, says Claire, this weekend, I haven't got plans, I could come down, see you and this man. We could talk about it then.

Friday night or Saturday morning?

I could be there late Friday if you gave me directions. But David? I'm not promising anything.

David nods. I know.

*A*nna arrives just before dark, her car roaring in to the small area around the shack, tires sliding on the gritty surface. David meets her on the veranda. Her face is unreadable as she approaches.

Thanks for coming, David says as she steps up onto the veranda.

No problem, Anna replies, peering past David into the house's interior. This is the place, huh?

He's asleep. The doctor gave him an injection.

Anna looks up at him. So what's the deal? What makes you so sure he knows anything?

To his surprise David realizes she is angry at him, and the realization makes him suddenly cautious.

He knew de Cueva's name.

So? He could have read it somewhere. It's not a secret.

I know . . . David pauses, considering. He has not thought of this possibility and is momentarily embarrassed. I don't think he read it somewhere, he says at last, I think he learned it from somewhere close to the source.

Where? Anna demands. You found it in Lisbon. He would have had to have done the same.

There might have been other sources.

Like what?

David shrugs. I don't know. But I'm sure he knows something.

At this Anna seems to give up on this particular line of investigation. Instead she looks around her at the desolate landscape.

So you're going to stay here alone with him and try and wring the information out of him. As she says this David realizes how off beam this must look.

I won't be alone, he says.

No? Who'll be here with you?

A nurse. He pauses. Or Claire.

Anna shakes her head, says nothing.

Anything I find will be our discovery, though, he says, it's part of this dig.

Anna looks at him coldly. Jesus, David, listen to yourself. You're staying out here alone with some crazy old man, watching him die, and you're talking about who's going to get the credit for the research. It's desperate, David, I know it, you know it, the whole bloody department will know it. We both know what we've found out over the last few months; that there's no ship here to find. Maybe we've got the wrong patch of coast, maybe it's buried too deep, maybe it broke up and eroded. Jesus, maybe it was never here, the point is that it's not *here to be found*, and we both just have to accept that. I have, so why can't you?

Listening to her David hears a voice of reason. He knows

this search has become an obsession with him, but he also knows that is irrelevant. The ship is here, he knows it. Anna and the others are happy to have done magnetic analyses, analyzed vegetation patterns. The inconclusiveness of their evidence telling them there is nothing here to be found, but none of this matters to David, only the ship, his unspoken knowledge of its physical presence matters to him. But listening to Anna now he knows arguing with her is pointless, so he chooses to acquiesce.

I will. If nothing comes of this I will, but I have to know. If there's any chance he knows something we can't let it slip through our fingers. But after this I agree, we should give it away.

Anna looks at him coldly. Both of them know he is lying.

Will you? she asks. I don't know.

I promise, he says, his voice soft.

She nods. I brought your things, and the cleaning stuff you asked for. Will you call me if you need something?

Sure.

And you won't come back for the party tonight?

I can't leave him alone.

I'll call you tomorrow.

David nods. Thanks.

AFTER ANNA HAS gone David goes back inside. The house smells less stuffy now that the doors have been opened, but the wind entering is cold. Kurt is lying in his bed, sleeping, his breath rasping in and out, and for a long while David stands watching him in silence. Outside the daylight drains away into a colorless twilight and finally night. Slowly David becomes aware the house has become dark, and he searches for a light switch in the kitchen, away from the sleeping Kurt. Now, in the gathering silence, he slowly realizes the enormity of what he has done, and a panic begins to grip him. He considers ringing Anna, Claire, if only to hear another voice, but the need in him strangles the desire. From the room next door he hears Kurt groan and cough in his sleep, and slowly lowers his head onto the scarred surface of the table.

*D*eep in the night he wakes, Tania's presence so strong that for almost a minute he cannot locate himself, cannot find his way to where he is, when he is. The dusty smell of the mattress, the shafts of moonlight drawing a web around him. His heart beats like a train. The old man; Kurt, his house. The scent of her sweat like a tattoo on his skin. All that is left of her.

*F*riday passes quickly, David working hard cleaning the shack. The task begins in the room where Kurt sleeps, David working around his bed, one eye on the sleeping man, watchful. Kurt's sleep discordant, disturbed, his erratic wheezing and gurgling making him seem constantly on the point of wakefulness. In the beginning the task is easy, old packages and empty containers, dirty plates: things undoubtedly rubbish or in need of cleaning. But eventually the task becomes slower, as the debris in the room becomes less easy to categorize. On the mantel he finds an old photo of a man David recognizes as Kurt, but younger, still intact, his arm around a tall woman in a loose floral dress. The photo unframed and facedown, the paper curling and yellowed with age and cigarette smoke. Both of them smiling, but the woman holding a cigarette and looking sideways, out of shot, making the photo look unrehearsed. Kurt's eyes on the photographer, staring, earnest, no hint of foreknowledge of his fate. David picks it up, turns it over, looking for a name, a date, but there is nothing. He turns it back over, looking for something, a clue perhaps, a fixed point in the tidal hugeness of the past. The woman's face is unusual, strong and high boned, a wide mouth and dark eyes, but beautiful, in an unconventional way. Her dark hair cut short, straight and almost boyish. David wonders where they are, the background seems to be a city street, but the buildings do not look like an Australian street. Looking closer he sees women in wide conical hats, black coolie trousers, a rickshaw. Banners hang downward from the buildings illuminated in Chinese script. He smiles, replacing the photo where he found it, enjoying momentarily the inconclusiveness of the evidence.

Later, after the doctor has been again, David retires to the kitchen table, spreading his papers on the surface. The wood smells damp, David having scrubbed it, trying to remove the layer of grime that had permeated the unpolished surface. Alone now, he retreats into the labyrinth of mirrors his research has constructed. So much paper, so many words. The snaking lines of maps. The scraps of evidence like shards of something shattered, its shape only dimly guessed, and David fumbling like a blind man to repair it.

Tonight, though, he is looking for something different, something less than half remembered, more than half forgotten. A flicker, the pulse of a moment. Page after page moving by, skimmed and then discarded. Then, quite suddenly it is there. An old photocopy of an article in the *London Journal of Archaeology*, 1937, by Dr. Fraser McDonald. "Possibilities for a Portuguese Discovery of Terra Australis: A Lecture; Proceedings of the British Archaeological Society," and there at the end, a postscript: "The assistance of Kurt Seligmann is acknowledged with gratitude." David flicks between the photographs, a portrait of McDonald, tall, blond, dapper in donnish tweeds. The chemical smell of the photocopy on his fingers. Beside McDonald another face, a younger man, smiling for the camera in a jacket and tie. The face rendered in a smear of ink and shadow, but recognizable, if barely. The man from the photograph on the mantel. Kurt.

David's heart almost audible in the quiet kitchen.

DAVID REMEMBERS MCDONALD, the man whose pioneering research laid the groundwork for David's own. He remembers him as much for the stories that surrounded him and his treatment at the hands of Peter Kirkby and the then head of the Department of Classical Languages and Archaeology, Digger Colmer; the way McDonald had been hounded and ridiculed, his work sabotaged. The way he killed himself in 1942.

The sound of a car in the darkness outside jolts David from his thoughts. Glancing at his watch he sees it is just before midnight; he has been sitting here, motionless, for nearly four hours. His legs are cramped as he clambers to his feet, and he moves awkwardly as he rushes down the short passage to the front door to greet Claire.

She is standing by her car, looking uncertainly at the shack as he opens the screen door. When she sees him she smiles, a little nervously David thinks, and steps forward with a bag over her shoulder.

Thank God, she says, I was worried I had the wrong place and was about to wake up some holiday makers in their seaside hideaway.

He laughs, Right place, and steps forward to take her bag. How was the drive?

Good, she says, leaning forward to kiss his cheek, her manner businesslike, I didn't get away from work until after six so I made good time. What is this place, David? she asks, looking around, uncertain.

Kurt—the old man I told you about—it's his place.

It's appalling.

From her tone David realizes this has not got off to a good start. I know, he hears himself saying. But he doesn't want to leave.

Claire stands, staring at him. Then David is reaching for her bag, ushering her forward.

Come inside and we'll talk.

Once they are inside he shows her the room where Kurt lies sleeping, illuminated by a reading lamp turned backward to the wall, a yellowing eggshell of light spreading over the cracked paint of the wall. Claire crosses to him and looks down, her eyes traveling briskly from his shattered face over the tidy bed, his shrunken body. David is aware the room smells faintly of cleansers. She looks up at David briefly, then back at Kurt, her eyes pausing on his ruined face. Finally she walks back to the door where David waits.

He's very frail.

I know. But he refuses to leave. I've agreed to care for him.

Do you have any idea what that's going to be like? the edge in her voice tightening the muscles in his neck.

He didn't want to go into a hospital. He wants to die here, and there's no one else.

Jesus, David, have you discussed this with anyone besides me or did you just decide?

It wasn't a matter of deciding, I just had to.

For his sake or yours?

David doesn't reply, knowing she is right. Finally he shrugs, trying to change the subject. Have you eaten?

Claire shakes her head. I'm starving. David smiles, gesturing toward the kitchen.

There's food out here. I saved some.

Seated at the table Claire eats slowly, chewing her food and looking around the room.

This place is pretty terrible. It looks like he's lived here for centuries.

At least there's electricity.

Claire grins spontaneously for the first time.

That's not saying much. Power's usually seen as pretty basic. As she speaks she meets his eyes, and his gaze holds her there for a moment too long before she looks down at her food. Her eyes look hunted suddenly, something like fear crossing them.

Who do you think he is?

David grabs the papers he has pushed to one side, flicking through them as he speaks.

His name's Kurt Seligmann. He was an archaeologist of some kind in the 1930s . . . here, he says, pushing the photocopied picture toward her. Claire looks down at the proffered page, chewing carefully on a crust.

Is this yours or his?

Mine, David says, and Claire nods.

So he actually might know something.

Mm-hmm.

And the body?

I don't know. What do the police think?

Claire shrugs. Nothing. It was all too long ago.

In the next room Kurt moves in his sleep, moaning quietly,

the sound silencing both of them. Claire is the first to speak again.

Could he have done it?

I don't know. Maybe . . . As he speaks David remembers the glint in Kurt's eye, the flat sound of his voice . . . Yes. But capacity and culpability are different things. Anyone could have done it.

There is a pause and then he continues. Anyway, it's not the killer I'm after, it's the ship.

Claire watches his face as he says this, the bunching of the skin around his forehead and the top of his nose, the closing off of blame.

Later, the two of them sit on the slope of the hill over the ocean. Theirs the only human presence for miles. Overhead the sky vaults into infinity, gray clouds sliding over the swirling band of the Milky Way. The only sound the movement of the air and water. Finally David speaks.

Why did you come?

I don't know. I've been asking myself the same thing. I don't think I know the answer yet. Not sex, if that's what you're asking.

A twinge inside him. No. Or at least not completely.

She looks at him and grins, both of them aware of how close they can be. Do you mind me being here?

He turns to look at her. She is sitting very close. Still formal, but easier within herself. More certain.

No. I like it.

Good.

You said he was an archaeologist. How much more do you know about him?

Not much. When I was first getting interested in this stuff my supervisor introduced me to Bill Norman. He was an emeritus lecturer in the department, but he'd been around the University since before the war. He told me about Fraser McDonald and his work on the Portuguese discovery. David's eye is caught by the sudden motion of a falling star. He touches Claire's hand and points. In the luminous moonlight he sees her smile.

It's beautiful, isn't it?

David nods. And quiet.

What happened to him?

Who?

This lecturer.

Bill died a couple of years ago. I went to the funeral.

No, the one he told you about.

McDonald? From what Bill told me it was a terrible story. Apparently his colleagues and the Professor at the time hounded him and made his life a misery. Did dreadful things, ridiculing him in front of students, denying him promotions, all kinds of things. And eventually he killed himself.

For a moment Claire is silent. Jesus.

I know.

And the old man was a friend of this McDonald?

I think so. I found a photo of them together.

And what's he told you?

Not much. Just enough to make me think he knows more than he's letting on.

Why don't you just ask him?

It's not that simple. If I just ask him he denies knowing anything. But then he'll let something slip. I think I'm going to have to come at this sideways, by stealth.

Do you think he's senile?

Perhaps. It's hard to tell. He's very confused.

As he speaks David is aware of Claire watching him. But when she puts out a hand, its touch on his shoulder surprises him and he turns. Her eyes clear, steady as he meets her gaze.

He's an old man, she says, her voice low but definite, so he cannot think there is equivocation in the words she is going to say. And he's very sick. You've got to understand that for people in his condition things change; the boundaries between what's memory and what's imaginary blur. Every day must be like a waking dream for him, so when you come along, needing to know, really needing to know, your need is quite capable of becoming part of his world.

Is that really what you think?

She doesn't remove her hand. It's one explanation. I just want you to be careful. For your sake as well as his.

Gently David reaches out and covers her hand with his own.

Have you ever watched someone die before? she asks.

He shakes his head, feeling Claire's eyes on him. His heart loud in the quiet evening.

Only Tania.

She says nothing, her silence an acceptance of this fact.

When she speaks again her tone is different, its patterns distancing her from what has just passed between them.

It's late, she says, and I don't know about you but I've had a very long day. I need some sleep.

Five minutes later David is watching her spread sheets on the bed he has slept in for the last two nights. Without words he knows he is not going to be invited to join her. See you in the morning, he says, and she turns in the half light.

You too, she says, and David lingers for a moment before turning. The sand and the sea whisper around them.

THAT NIGHT DAVID dreams of the ship, the hummocked surface of the hills. The landscape so familiar he could navigate it without light, each tussock, each rippled slope so much a part of the fabric of his memory he sometimes wonders where he ends, these hills begin. His knowledge of the hills more reliable than his memories of Tania. These last six months he finds he is forgetting her, that he cannot recall her face to mind without effort. Last week he could not remember the color of her eyes. Unprepared to let go of these memories; they and his grief the only things left to him now of her, held close, hoarded. The ship so close he can smell it.

*B*eneath the surface there are always secrets, rootlike traceries of veins and capillaries, shifting webs of allegiance and deceit, skeletons wrapped tight in the earth, the labyrinthine motion of water beneath our feet. The heart of a lover. The present a shimmering skin, a meniscus of possibilities, drawn tight between the unseen future, the unknowable past. And in that ghost of a moment we turn around ourselves, sometimes looking, sometimes choosing to believe, but always left with nothing but whispers and suspicions, staring at footprints whose maker we can never know for sure.

IV

Mercator's Projection

Mercator's Projection: *(after Gerhardus Mercator 1512–1594)*
*First used in Mercator's famous World Map of 1569, of which
only four copies remain, Mercator's Projection is one of several
methods commonly used in cartography to project points from a
three-dimensional spherical surface onto a two-dimensional plane.*

*A cylindrical projection, so called because it treats the points on
a sphere's surface as points on the flattened surface of a cylinder,
Mercator's projects the three-dimensionally curved lines of latitude
and longitude onto a two-dimensional grid (or "graticule") of
straight lines at right angles. In this way the area bounded by a
pair of parallels and meridians is treated as identical regardless of
their location on the sphere's surface, a cartographical sleight of
hand that overlooks the convergence of the meridians at the poles on
the surface of a globe and the resultant reduction in the size of such
areas the closer they are to the poles on the globe's surface.*

*As a result, while accurate over small areas, Mercator's Projection
causes oddities and distortions when used over larger areas. In recent
years there has been considerable debate focusing upon the political
ramifications of the distortions inherent in such maps, in particular
the manner in which Europe appears to be larger than South America.*

*A*nd again we return to the maps.

While the northern and northwestern coastlines of this shadowy Java la Grande seem to our eyes unmistakable as modern-day Australia, the further one follows them south the more tenuous the resemblance becomes. To the modern mind the coast of Australia arcs southward and east, from the tip of Cape York down the long fall of the Queensland coast, then slides back under, south by west again, toward Bass Strait, and finally back west across the truncated stump of the continent where once low hills ran all the way to the north coast of Tasmania. Instead the coast of Java la Grande continues southeast, then almost due south, before a new crick sends the line of the coast running due west to a point from which it drops away, south by west, eventually merging with Desceliers' imaginary Antarctic landmass. So despite the detail the maps offer us, their crabbed shorelines and scattered islands, their alluring promise of a secret discovery (again that word, let us be cautious of it) collapses under its own weight.

Or does it?

Certainly Matthew Flinders allowed these discrepancies to convince him to dismiss claims the Portuguese explored the eastern coast of Australia. But Flinders was a navigator and cartographer, a man who trusted maps with his life. Flinders' attention to detail, his exquisitely accurate charts, his life of duty, are all the marks of a man who believed what he saw. For Flinders, accuracy was a narrow thing, truth was what he could see, touch, measure, the possible merely the actual. A cold and mean philosophy. But the truth is often more slippery than Flinders would have liked, reality deceptive, the actual merely one of an infinite range of possibilities. And implicit in the process of using one map to discredit another (as Flinders was) is an assumption that one map is "right," or at least righter than the other. The map that is "right" is usually the most recent, or the most detailed, or the one produced by the most reliable source.

Yet maps, like any other representation of events or things, are just that: representations. Not reality, merely facsimiles, stitched together with gathered evidence and made whole by our trust in them. For representations can manipulate and distort; lie, disguise, skimp on detail, slant the evidence. Lead us astray. And if one map is suspect, surely all are?

Perhaps the answer is both yes and no. For just as statistics can be reported in different, even contradictory ways, so too can maps be drawn in different ways and still be true.

To understand this we must return to the oldest of sciences, geometry. (As Socrates said, "Let all who enter here study geometry.") The geometry we learned in school, the geometry of triangles and circles, is Euclidean, an idealized geometry.

(Idealized because Einstein's General Theory of Relativity tells us that space is not only real, but curved, and never susceptible to the rigors of Euclid's world.) Euclidean geometry is a deductive theoretical science, an abstract world unto itself, where the rules of existence are all the product of five axiomatic truths. Of these five the fifth is the most troublesome, but it is not the one that will concern us here (except in its negation). What concerns us here is the first of these axioms. This first axiom is axiomatic because of its dependence upon two primitive terms, "point" and "between," and defines a straight line as the shortest distance between two points.

In a two-dimensional plane this is an uncomplicated notion. Between any two points there will be only one shortest distance and therefore only one line. But on the surface of a globe, where the surface is curved, things are not so simple. A straight line does not and cannot exist, and there can be more than one shortest distance between points. Perhaps the easiest way to understand this is to picture the Earth itself and take as your two points the poles. Immediately you will be able to see that between the two points there is an infinite number of lines that can be drawn between the two points, all of which are the same length, and all of which are the shortest distance between the two points.

Once we understand this, the complexities of mapping the Earth's surface onto a two-dimensional chart should be clear. Because our two dimensions cannot accommodate this profusion of lines, our map will distort the facts. The question for cartography thus becomes not how we are to represent the facts accurately, but how to distort them the least.

And there can be different solutions to this problem. Witness the profusion of maps of the Earth's surface that exist. Broken ellipses, the polar regions divided into pointed strips and flattened, like the peel of a vast orange, cut into eighths and flattened. James Gall's orthographic equal area projection, with its lines of longitude and latitude intersecting at right angles in a rectangular grid, which preserves the relative areas of landmasses, but drags them out, drawing the continents south and north into long ragged strips. Or the sinusoidal projection, which presents the world in a curved diamond, and carries with it a whiff of Persian elegance, the scent of hot winds. And there are others, many others, but all are responses to the question posed by the shift from three dimensions to two. How is distortion to be minimized?

Perhaps the map we know best is Mercator's. In this, the lines of latitude and longitude form a grid of squares, which, although distorting the continents, has great value for navigators. Because it is a grid, compass bearings are truly represented, and the compass course is the two-dimensional straight line between two points. Thus at sea, a navigator may plot a rhumb line, which will intersect the lines of the grid at the same angle, and this angle will represent the compass bearing.

The sextant, the navigational instrument that allowed Cook and Flinders to make their detailed charts of the Australian coastline, was not invented until the early eighteenth century. Two hundred years earlier, in the period from which our maps date, navigation was far less rigorous. Sailors were confined to the use of the astrolabe, a notoriously inaccurate instrument; to guessing the time from the position of the sun and stars; and to estimates of distance. Some were better at this than others, but even for the best navigators it was a hit-and-miss affair. And although the idea of a spherical world was spreading, the practical ramifications of this notion, particularly for navigators whose experience was in general confined to the Mediterranean and the east of the Atlantic Ocean, were yet to be fully understood. The notion that the meridian lines converge at either pole was largely unconsidered, and instead they were represented in a gridlike fashion, the meridians straight and parallel.

Perhaps then the wonder is not that the maps made by these early mariners were occasionally inaccurate, but that their maps made sense at all. Nevertheless their mistakes are illuminating, for, if we return to the Dieppe maps, and redraw the grid, taking into account the distortion inherent in not understanding this convergence, then project it in the manner developed by Mercator, the bulging continent of Desceliers' map shrinks and re-forms, twisting in a piece of geometric metamorphosis into the Australian continent as charted by Cook and Flinders, and more lately familiar from satellite photographs.

So the enigma of the Dieppe maps reasserts itself, for as ever, appearances are deceptive. Trust in maps is like trust in love; little is what it seems.

hen David wakes the light is filtering through the window in the small room next to Claire's. Outside there is a clamor of gulls, the gentle roar of the sea. Rising, he walks carefully from room to room, checking that Kurt is sleeping, then opening Claire's door quietly. Inside, her bed is empty, the sheets loose on the mattress. Curious, David walks to the door, looking for her. Outside the cool air lies in shadowed pools on the sand, the dawn orange in the east. Depressions in the sand lead away toward the beach. From further inland magpies warble their morning song. Pulling on a singlet he walks after her, wondering how long ago she passed this way, the sand cool beneath his feet, a petrel hurling itself into the air in a flurry of wind and commotion as he steps forth, flinging itself upward and away.

As he crests the last ridge of dune before the beach, he sees her step from the water, her skin dark in the soft light. Watching the long curve of her back, the dark nipples, he remembers the taste of her against him and his tongue swells, an ache inside of him. Walking quickly she crosses to a bundle of clothes and picks out a towel and dries her skin, pulling a loose dress over herself before attending to her hair. David does not approach, simply watches. She dries her hair slowly, deliberately, then pauses, looking back out over the water, the swell rising and falling. A cluster of birds mark out the progress of a school of fish, appearing and disappearing as the water's surface rolls in, out. He stands there unobserved, silent against the sky, watching, then turns and goes back the way he came.

BACK AT THE shack, Kurt is awake. David hears the change in his breathing from the door and enters the older man's room quietly, clearing his throat to announce his presence. Kurt turns to him, his eye looking straight through David as if he is a ghost.

Who's that? Is there someone there?

It's me, says David. David, you've been asleep for a while.

What's going on? Why are you still here?

David sits down carefully, placing a hand on Kurt's arm as he does. I'm looking after you. We discussed it with Dr. Flew, remember.

Kurt turns away. No, he stammers. A pause, then he says it again. No.

David swallows hard, an intimation of the difficulty of what is ahead for him making his breath catch. Kurt, he says, it's all right, I'm here to look after you.

Kurt rolls back toward David but he doesn't speak, his eye wandering across the wall over David's shoulder, fixing on points in the empty space of the room for no discernible reason, his mouth moving in a low mutter.

For ten, fifteen minutes they sit like this, Kurt's hand opening and closing on David's arm. Twice he looks up, his eyes wide and waking, but the questions he asks reveal his mind is still lost. Strange questions about the Pope, the Emperor of Japan. David listens to his ramblings until he, too, glances over his shoulder, apprehensive. Finally Kurt's grip on David's arm slackens and a shadow passes behind his eye.

You're here because of the ship, aren't you?

David nods.

I remember now. What makes you think I know anything?

You knew de Cueva's name. And I know who you are.

Kurt twists to look at him, but the effort clearly pains him, and he subsides back onto the bed with a groan.

What do you mean?

I found your photo, in a journal. You were young then.

Kurt shakes his head. What journal? I don't understand. David sees his mind is slipping away again.

With Fraser McDonald.

At the name Kurt stiffens, but for an instant David sees a path into the fractured maze of his mind. He leans forward, trying to hold it steady.

Kurt, listen to me. I need you to tell me about Fraser, and about the ship. I need you to tell me everything.

Kurt's hand tightens around David's arm. It was so long ago, he says, and as he does David sees a tear forming in the corner of the old man's ruined eye, glistening.

I know, but I need to know. I need to know so I can find the ship. From the beginning.

Kurt nods. From the beginning, he says.

.   .   .

THE FIRST TIME I saw him he began by asking a question.

Why study archaeology? Fraser asked. Perhaps it's not unusual to begin teaching this way, to ask why we learn, but once it had been posed he did not move on to answer it himself. Instead he looked up into the sloping rows of students, searching our faces as if he was genuinely looking for an answer. Years later I was to learn that the question was indeed rhetorical, a way of engaging the students that Fraser had developed, but then, then I was dazzled. Like the others I sat there watching him, almost angelic with his white shirt and blond hair, and seeming only barely older than myself, hypnotized by the fluidity of his movements. There was an energy about him, a grace, that gave him a beauty that was almost overwhelming, and because of that beauty we granted him power over us. Later I was to find that this had always been the way with him, this beauty, and the only people who could resist it were those who were threatened by it.

When no one answered he lifted his hands, opened them, then closed them tightly as he continued.

Perhaps if I ask it this way you might see an answer more easily. When we speak of archaeology we normally mean the process of excavation and reconstruction that is a necessary part of research into ancient civilizations. What then is the benefit we derive from this process of excavation?

The class shifted uncertainly, a murmur passing through it. I looked around myself, wondering who would speak first. Finally a serious young man two rows in front of me lifted his hand. Fraser's arm flicked out, cracking in the air.

You!

For knowledge, I suppose.

A twinkle. Ha. Too easy! Someone else?

Another young man, nearer the front. To understand the evolution of the race.

A pause. Perhaps. He moved away, appearing reluctant to dwell on this suggestion. Suddenly I felt my arm go up unbidden, and as it did he turned to me, pointed.

You!

I blushed, feeling the eyes of everyone in the hall on me, but when I spoke my voice was clear. And loud.

Because if we can understand the past we can make sense of ourselves.

He paused, watching my face. Why do you say that?

I don't know. It's just, what other reason could there be? We read the classics, study history. All that learning is so we can understand our world and ourselves.

He didn't answer straightaway. Instead he pursed his lips together and clasped his hands as if in prayer. Then, after several seconds, he spoke, his words slow, as if he was considering each before he uttered it.

Coleridge said knowledge of the past had the potential to be a lantern to guide us into the darkness of the future. But he also said that our passions blind us to that potential, so the light that experience gives us shines only on the waves to our stern. But this does not have to be. Archaeology can guide us into the past, and its scientific methods allow us to see beyond our passions. Archaeology is a tool to understanding ourselves, the lantern we shine into the gray dawn of the future. He paused, looking at me again.

Thank you, Mr. . . . ?

I cleared my throat. Seligmann.

He nodded. Seligmann.

Then, as quickly as it had come, the searchlight of his attention was gone.

WHEN CLAIRE RETURNS it is fully light, the heat beginning to soak through the tin roof. Kurt is sleeping and David has returned to his papers, spreading them once more across the pitted surface of the kitchen table. He hears her come through the front door, pause outside Kurt's room, then step into the kitchen. Her hair has dried wild with the salt, but she is smiling, relaxed. She stops when she sees him at the table. A moment of silent candor between them. Then David folds his arms, grins cheekily.

I see you've discovered the amenities.

It was either the beach or the bathtub, Claire replies, crossing to the sink. And I didn't like the look of the bathtub.

David turns in his chair, following her. The bathroom is a tiny, windowless extension through a door behind him, little more than a grimy sink and a filthy, chipped enamel bathtub. What light penetrates the once-clear corrugated plastic that covers part of the roof only serves to highlight the gloom.

I was going to clean it today. As Claire begins to run a glass of water David motions to another tap, higher up, which leads to a narrow copper pipe over the sink.

Use that one, it's rainwater. And watch out for wrigglers.

Claire examines her glass mock-dubiously, holding the clear water up to the slanting sun from the window. Satisfied, she leans back on the sink and drinks in large gulps.

He's sleeping, she says between mouthfuls.

David chews the pen he is holding. He was awake before. I think he started to make sense at last.

Claire looks over the rim of the glass, interested now. Really? What did he say?

Not much, but he was making sense.

She lowers her glass to the sink. Really?

You sound surprised.

Not surprised . . . I . . . David, I meant what I said, last night.

About what?

About you and him, about what he says. The painkillers I'm giving him will make him lucid, but they affect the mind, make things seem real that aren't. He may think he remembers things he's only imagining.

I know that, says David, his voice sharper than he intended.

But Claire does not recoil from the annoyance in his tone. It's not just him I'm worried about, she says.

What do you mean?

I know how important this is to you, but please, be careful. Make sure you hear what's being said, not what you want to hear.

David does not reply, suddenly afraid of acknowledging her concern. Both of them feeling this space between them. This needing.

Her words hang unanswered between them for several seconds, until David, trying to regain something that both know has slipped, slides out of his chair, stepping away from her almost without thinking.

What will you do today?

Claire shrugs. I don't know. Read. Swim some more. The beach is beautiful.

Empty, too. This part of it's too far from the roads for most people to bother walking to and the surf's better to the north, so not even the surfers come here much.

You'll have to stay here with him.

You shouldn't feel that you need to wait around though.

As he says this Claire regards him carefully, her eyes guarded.

I won't.

David hears from her tone that while her reserve has returned, the brittleness of the night before seems to be gone. This knowledge relaxes him.

Then, her tone lower, she continues.

David, while I was on the beach I thought about what you asked me last night—her words are halting, as if she is not yet certain of what she is saying, or as if she fears that what she is going to say will lessen her, weaken her—about me staying here, helping you look after him. And I've decided I will, at least for a day or two more. I won't promise after that, but for now I'll stay. Is that good enough?

David nods, his heart clattering. That's fabulous. I understand—

She holds out a hand to stop him.

No, you don't. And don't try to. Something breaks in her voice. Please.

*I*nstead of bringing them closer, Claire's offer to stay seems at first to push them apart. She spends the afternoon reading on the veranda, twice coming in to administer painkillers to Kurt, then returns to the beach in the late afternoon to swim again. While she is away David works quietly in the kitchen, attentive and absorbed, but somehow detached from what he is doing, his whole body alert to any sound from Kurt's room, his eyes flicking up, listening, each time the old man coughs or wheezes or moans. At dusk Claire returns, her hair wet with the sea. As she enters, the sound of a voice comes from the room where Kurt lies. No words, just the low murmur of the old man's voice, the widening circles its wandering path describes. At the door she pauses, trying to make out what is being said, but cannot, so pushes the door open. The voice stops, David looking up at the sound of the door. Ignoring the doubt that she suddenly feels she forces herself to smile, mouthing, "How is he?" across at David. David opens his hands, encompassing Kurt, his illness, the room, the hills, everything, his wry expression counterpointing the breadth of his gesture, inviting her amusement at his expense. His generosity allaying her doubts, she grins, and without speaking both know something new has replaced the afternoon's fractious geometry. Buoyed, Claire mimes eating, and David gives her the thumbs-up.

Claire hesitates a moment too long, wanting this moment to last, but it is gone almost as soon as it came, David returning his attention to the old man, leaving her standing in the doorway. The murmuring voice beginning once more. After a moment or two David glances up, sees her still standing there, and smiles, this time distractedly. Pulling the door behind her she hesitates, trying to hear what the old man is saying, remembering David's claims of a newfound lucidity, but she cannot make it out.

TEN MINUTES LATER David hears her car pull away across the packed sand of the track. Beside him Kurt is silent, Claire's interruption somehow having broken the spell that has held the two men these last two hours. Listening to the old man unsettles him, such is the intensity of his recall, his words a spell whose thrall David finds himself submitting to with the readiness he knows Claire is warning him against. She cannot know what this means to me, he says to himself, cannot understand. But even as he rationalizes this need he hears himself as if from outside, knows she is right to fear for him: this hunger he feels gnawing within is already beyond his control, beyond caution, beyond reason.

Then, without warning, Kurt shifts in his sleep, a low moan slipping from his lips. Barely more than a breath, but enough to startle David from his thoughts, a release he is almost grateful for. Standing, he walks slowly to the kitchen, meaning to transcribe the notes he has taken in the last few hours, but in the kitchen, flicking idly through the mess of papers he has spread across the tabletop, he finds his resolve wavering.

Two hours before he levered open the windows, letting the fresh air from the sea flood in, the sun falling in moving rectangles across his work on the desk, then over, onto the floor. Now, though, it has gone, and the room is filled with a deep blue light. As Kurt's breath rises and falls in the next room, David crosses to the windows, then turns and walks the length of the short passage to the front door. Through the tattered flyscreen he can see his four-wheel drive, its white paint lit by the colors of the sunset. On the roof just above the windscreen a gull is perched, wings half unfurled in the breeze, bobbing and swaying. As David watches, the gull turns and begins to make its way down the slippery glass of the windscreen, its feet splaying out as it strains not to slip. Its progress is slow and deliberate, and David finds himself suddenly wondering what has made the gull choose this path. Why does it want to go from the roof to the bonnet? For a moment the utter unknowability of this overwhelms him. How, he finds himself wondering, can we ever know anyone? All of us condemned to these solitary shells of bone and sinew. And skin. David swallows, the space Tania left gaping raggedly within him. For a long while he stands at the door, motionless, watching the gull, which now stands on the bonnet of his car, learning the patterns of wind and air that pass over it. Finally it spreads its wings and rises, borne on the wind, and soars out of sight into the failing light. Alone again, David glances at his watch, suddenly aware he is anxious for Claire to return.

*A*ll evening Kurt's ramblings wander in circles, names and places shifting, recurring. Sometimes he will stop, confused, looking around himself as if to say, "No, it wasn't like that," as images collide and overlap, stories merge into each other, patterns coalesce out of the whole. The frameworks of reason and evidence that order David's desire, contain it, beginning to collapse; the ground beneath him becoming less certain, shifting and subsiding as his need overwhelms him. The murk of history rising all around him, infecting him.

I REMEMBER THE first time I saw her. 1935. My final year at university.

Her?

Veronica.

He looks at David, his good eye clouded. But that came later, didn't it? David knows that it is not him that he can see, but the past.

Is that you, Fraser?

David shakes his head. No, it's me, David, but it's all right, everything's fine.

What were we talking about?

The ship, de Cueva's ship.

The ship? Slipping over the line into sleep as he speaks.

*S*omewhere in the space after midnight, David wakes with a start. He strains for the sound that woke him, but there is nothing. No voice crying out, no motion nearby; but then he hears it, a shift in the old man's breathing, a choking desperation. His heart racing he spills out the side of his makeshift bed; gathering shorts onto his legs he moves quickly through the darkened rooms, the silver moonlight spilling through the windows, seeping under the door. The whole house adrift in a sea of shifting light and darkness as the moon and the wind wash about it.

In his room Kurt moves spasmodically, his arms stretched upward to the ceiling. The sight of this shadowy figure clamoring silently to a heaven of dirty plaster momentarily arrests David, holding him back, before he breaks free and hurries onward, grasping the old man's arms, trying to lower their tiny weight to the sheets. Kurt's face contorted in a mask of pain, tears on the crabbed lines of the cheeks. But no words, not a whisper, just the tortured rattle of his breath, the cloying texture of his lungs passing the air painfully through them.

Kurt, he whispers, holding him. What is it? What's wrong?

No answer, just a jerking movement of the head, a pulling away. Behind David, Claire has appeared, and is fumbling with the desk lamp. David looks up at her pleadingly, wanting her to take this situation, control it. She crosses to him, interposing her body between the two men. Her thin hand on Kurt's brow, her skin dark against his mottled pallor.

His fever's no worse, I think it's just a dream or a hallucination. I—

Before she can finish Kurt has turned to her, grasping at her free hand, pulling at it. Please, he is saying, help me.

She stays still, allowing his hand to grip her, and David is aware of the containment that sustains her.

How, Kurt? she asks. What do you want us to do? Are you in pain?

A shake of the head. No, no pain.

Then what?

The past, he says. The past. So much I'd thought I'd forgotten.

Claire looks at David beside her. Do you mean the ship? she asks, her voice soft, the professional distance in it not cold but kind.

No, he says, Veronica, his eyes opening wide as he stares at the two of them, I saw her, in here.

There wasn't anyone, says David, reaching out to cover the hand that is still grasping at Claire. No one's been in here but us.

But I saw her, clear as life, over there by the window.

You had a dream, says Claire.

No, no dream, I'm sure.

David begins to say something dissuasive, but Claire silences him with a glance.

But it's all right now, she's gone, and she won't be back.

Are you sure? His voice like a child's.

I'm sure. You should sleep now.

Kurt nods, allowing his head to fall back onto the pillow. Claire glances at David, and smiles reassuringly. The tension in Kurt's body lessens as he lets sleep reclaim him.

I get so confused.

I know, it's all right though, we're right next door.

Good, he says, then there is a silence for several seconds. When he speaks again his voice is quieter.

Have you ever been in love? he asks, and as the words move into the quiet room David looks at Claire, the dip of her cheek as she faces the old man and not him, the print of her pillow still marking her face.

Yes, she says after a long while, I have.

So have I, says Kurt, his voice almost dreaming. So have I. But it was a long time ago; another world.

As his words trail out his mouth falls open, slackening with sleep. Claire doesn't speak, doesn't move away. David watches her, realizing she is far away from here. He wonders who she is thinking of, what it is that she is carrying in her.

But it was so long ago, she says, letting her words echo his.

I barely remember.

IN THE HALL outside Kurt's room, neither speaks, their bodies moving in silence, rhythms meshing in the close dark. The pulse of their blood. Too close now, they hesitate. David feels a corner of her body, the skin of her arm on his chest, a motion of hair. An expanse of back. Two worlds colliding, collapsing into one, their territories and oceans flickering, transforming, then the warmth of her breast beneath her singlet as she turns, the sterner pressure of the nipple. Her breath on his neck, faster, the warm damp of her lips on his chin, his jaw, and then suddenly she is pulling away, her body repelling his, slipping out of reach.

No, David, we mustn't, she is saying, a passage of warmth in the darkness.

We mustn't.

*T*he next morning David is awake at dawn, neck and eyes aching from lack of sleep. A whining pain in the base of his head. In Kurt's room Claire is sitting with the old man, one of his hands clasped in hers. David stands at the door, one hand massaging the knotted muscles of his neck, trying to loosen them, reluctant to enter, to approach her, the events of the night before still too close. Claire turns to him, waiting for him to speak.

You're already up.

She nods curtly. I had to give him his painkillers. He's resting now.

David hesitates, hearing the reproach in her voice. Has he said anything?

He was talking about Veronica again.

Oh.

Do you know who she was?

No, not really.

When David doesn't continue Claire turns away, back to Kurt. His labored breathing heavy in the quiet room.

Go and swim, you need the wash, she says at last. I'll wait here with him. David nods, turns and leaves.

In the water he allows the cold surf to push him inward and outward, letting the sensation of rise and fall calm him. A deep, submarine movement around him, echoes in the blue water. His muscles falling into place, loosening. On the shore, the breeze cool on his skin, the sun hot, he dries himself, thinking of Claire the night before. The words that do not seem to be passing between them. Their confused embrace in the hall in the darkness arriving inevitable.

*B*y the beginning of the sixteenth century the Portuguese empire covered half the planet. In ships barely larger than modern yachts, mariners from this tiny country on the periphery of Europe set forth on journeys which spanned the globe. South, across the mouth of the Mediterranean to the Canary Islands huddled close to the bulk of the African continent. Then outward, into the Atlantic, passing the perilous Cape Bojador in a long descending arc west, then east, back to the African coast and on, south to the Cape of Good Hope. Westward, across the vast Atlantic, to Brazil. From the Cape of Good Hope eastward into the blue waters of the Indian Ocean, to Goa, Sri Lanka, India, then east again, along the myriad coasts of Southeast Asia, to China, then on, north again, perhaps as far as the Bering Straits and the Siberian Arctic. South from Goa, to Java, then Timor, and then away, off the edges of the maps, perhaps to the shadowy continent of Java la Grande. The land the British two hundred years later called Terra Australis. The Great South Land. Australia.

This expansion took place for many reasons but its central

rationale was commerce. The European Renaissance, which was beginning to take root in the city-states of Italy, required a constant input of gold and precious stones, as well as spices, used in the preservation and flavoring of food, many of which were worth more than their weight in gold. But commerce and conquest are always bedfellows, and these great voyages of exploration became the vanguard of a vast wave of European expansion, conquest, and colonization, a process that was to transform the world with extraordinary speed.

*N*ineteen thirty-five, my final year of university. The day my life changed, setting me on a path that led to everything that was to come. The day the seeds of disaster were sown, for all of us.

I was in a lecture with Kirkby, one of the history dons, popular with the students for his pacey lectures, his jibing wit. We'd slid sideways from Magellan into a discussion of the discovery of Australia in the age of the explorers. Another student had asked about maps he had seen reproduced in old books, maps that showed a shadowy place south of Timor, a place that might or might not have been Australia. Kirkby was enjoying the digression, but as he spoke I found myself growing anxious, his words erasing my past.

There are some, he said, glancing stagily to the doors at either side of the hall, even some within this university, who have allowed their desire for an early discovery of this continent to override their faculty for skepticism. They take the sorts of maps you mentioned and try to use them as grounds for the existence of such a discovery. Do not be taken in! These

French maps—for French they are, not Portuguese, begging the obvious question of why the Portuguese let the French commit their discoveries to paper in their stead—show nothing more than a cartographer's fancy, a speculation. A mirage. And they raise more questions than they answer. Why did the Portuguese not continue south from Timor if they knew this continent was here? Why do later maps not show the same fictitious land? Why are the Portuguese themselves silent on this matter? And most damning of all, why is there no other evidence for such a discovery? The answer is that the Portuguese were never here; that the maps are a mirage, and that those who make these claims for them are either gullible, or worse, should know better.

Listening to Kirkby I felt myself aching to interrupt, a memory that had haunted me for years echoing in my mind, somewhere beneath the level of hearing, a memory of pain and fear and cold, as so many of my memories were, but one that had a root here in the present. I raised my hand, and Kirkby turned my way.

You have a question?

I cleared my throat. You were saying there's no proof, I said, but I'm not sure that that's right.

Kirkby laughed, his tone inviting the rest of the hall to join in. I felt my ears redden.

You feel you have some? A lost Portuguese journal perhaps? Again there was laughter.

I shook my head. Where I grew up, down south, near the Victorian border, there's supposed to be a ship buried in the sandhills. They say it's been there longer than anyone can remember, and I remember some people used to say . . . Here my voice faltered and I looked around for support but found none. Swallowing hard I continued. They used to say it was Portuguese.

As I finished I saw a moment where Kirkby's humorous exterior slipped, and just for an instant something flashed within, something less kind, but then, as quickly as it had come it was gone, and he laughed again.

This is history, young man, not folklore. The audience laughed enormously.

And then I said something that was to change my life.

It's not a story, I said, my voice clear and loud. I've seen it. For several seconds there was silence, then Kirkby shook his head, dismissing me.

Moving from the realm of fantasy back to the real world, he said.

*B*ut I had seen it, I was sure of that now. It was as if Kirkby's words had snagged something buried deep within me and dragged it surfaceward. A memory, or perhaps less than a memory, a shard, a fragment. Something that had lain hidden for years. And now it had been exposed to the light I found it had a power of its own, drawing me to itself, driving me to worry at it, expose it. Scratching away at those hidden places in the catacombs of my mind until I was a boy again, eight or nine, bumped from orphanage to orphanage, foster home to foster home, until I came to rest here, in these lonely hills on this forgotten coast. The wind whistling icy across the gray water, slicing across my bare legs, levering open the tears in my sweater. My breath coming ragged, gasping, as I ran and ran, my face a swarm of bruises, angry, my back layered with welts, the skin tight on my bones. Running not because there was anywhere to go, but just to get away, to escape, from the orphanage's narrow beds, from the boys who beat me, from Father O'Donnell and his daily thrashings. The wind turning to rain as the sky darkened, casting up the sand in violent squalls, abrading my skin, my thin clothes plastering themselves to my body as the storm tore across the coast. My flight turning to terror as I lurched and stumbled through the churning darkness, falling to my knees as the wind grew stronger, the hail bruising me, the lightning immersing the world in sheeting cataclysms of light, transforming the hills into a nightmare landscape of blue-white sand and racing shadows, the stink of the ozone strong in the air. Thunder detonating inside of me, all around me. Another explosive flash throwing me to the ground, my sobs lost in the howling wind, then another, and then I saw its great bulk heaving itself out of the sand that spilled from its spars like water, the screaming wind slicing it free from the grip of the hill, its broken shape like the belly of a dinosaur. My thin hands clinging to the sand that moved like a living thing beneath me as I crawled slowly toward it, eyes clenched shut against the storm, until its form enveloped me, cradling me as I crawled deeper and deeper into its darkness, into its refuge.

When I awoke it was morning, a thin light filtering into the jumbled space that I found myself in, the broken timbers protruding unevenly on every side. My skin blue and pimpled by the cold. A blanket of sand lapping around my body, covering me, filling the shelter until there was barely room to stand. My clothes heavy I pulled myself free, crawling toward the light that issued from a space in the dark vault of the roof and slithering my thin body out into the rain.

Outside I found myself in the lee of a dune, the skeletal form of the ship half submerged in its breaking wave. Slowly I walked the length of the structure, watching as the sand flowed steadily down, covering what remained of the deck.

Rubble spilling outward into the basin of the hill, shards of wood, a carved door, the rusted shape of a cannon. At the far end a hole gaped in the shell of the hull, and I stepped forward into it, lowering my head to enter the darkness. A stale smell of damp in the air. Inside a space larger than the reach of my arms, lit only by the hole I had entered through. The sound of the wind outside, the creaking of the wood, the whisper of the racing sand. A sudden movement in the darkness, as if something was stirring, and I turned, seeing for the first time the white dome of a skull, the dark sockets upon me, the shock sending me stumbling back, out into the light and the rain, then away, stumbling and running through the drifting sand, away from the ship and its ghostly secrets.

LOOKING DOWN DAVID sees his hands clenched tight. Four semicircles of blood on the inside of each palm. Opening them out he looks up, knows Claire has seen.

THREE DAYS LATER, Fraser approached me in the library. He stood beside the table where I worked, looking down at me for several seconds before he spoke.

Excuse me, he said at last, you're Seligmann, aren't you?

Although we had never met, in the two years since that first lecture I had become familiar with him. Nevertheless I was surprised when he approached me and spoke my name. My surprise making me uncertain, nervous, but when I nodded, he smiled. I was surprised at how friendly he was, almost boyish.

I hear you told Kirkby some story about a Portuguese shipwreck during a lecture the other day.

When he said this I felt myself blush, and ashamed I looked down, wondering why he had chosen to humiliate me like this.

When I didn't reply he continued, prompting me.

It was you, wasn't it?

I nodded.

Was it true? Hearing the tone in his voice I looked up, wondering if I was mistaken about his intentions.

Yes.

Maybe we could go somewhere and talk then, he said.

And like a fool, I stood and followed him.

*I*n the kitchen, two hours later, David watches Claire move around the room. There is much between them that is unspoken but in the daylight they are uneasy with each other, fractious. Each circles the other, uneasily trying to define the space in the small vessel of the shack. Twice David has tried to steer their talk toward Claire and both times she has replied tersely, diverting him. Each time the conversation has failed, then begun again, falteringly. It frightens David, this new movement of emotion so close to her surface. The Claire he remembers is liquid, possessed of a deep stillness, a cool certainty.

She turns from the sink, a glass of the tank water in her hand. Two wrigglers oscillate in the clear suspension. David watches their movement, one question turning over and over in his head. Why is she here?

*A*mong these Portuguese mariners who were the vanguard of European expansion was Christovão de Mendonça. History tells us little of him, but the scraps and rumors that remain tell us he was a man of some position, certainly by birth, but also due to his skills as a soldier and seaman. De Barros records that he captained one of the ships in the armada of Jorge de Albuquerque, a fleet of fourteen vessels that set forth from Lisbon in the middle of the year 1519 against a backdrop of escalating political tension between the expanding Spanish and Portuguese empires.

Initially this fleet had been assembled by the King of Portugal, Manoel I, to improve Portuguese security in the Far East in the event of Spanish attack. Yet Albuquerque's progress was more than usually troubled, and by the time he reached Goa he had been preceded by another vessel bearing new orders that diverted his fleet from its original destination and divided it.

These orders came as a result of news in the Portuguese court of the departure of Funão Magalhães, the man our history calls Magellan. Magellan, Portuguese by birth and a navigator by profession, had abandoned the Portuguese court several years earlier after falling into disfavor with King Manoel, and journeyed to Madrid, where he had petitioned King Charles of Spain for the vessels needed to undertake a circumnavigation of the globe. And so, equipped with five caravels, Magellan departed from the Spanish port of San Lucar de Barrameda on 20 September 1519.

News of his departure, when it arrived, galvanized the Portuguese court, forcing them to take drastic measures to prevent Magellan's mission from succeeding. Central in the minds of the Portuguese was the interception and annihilation of Magellan's caravels, but simultaneously another mission was begun, one whose goals were less definite, one that might hold within it the answer to the riddle of the Dieppe maps. For Mendonça was ordered to search for the Isles of Gold.

*T*oward dark Kurt wakes again, falling from a fretful sleep into a restless, difficult waking. No recognition in his eyes. His skin gray and clammy, his hands worrying at the blankets, his twisted body trying to pull itself free of the bed, as if it could slip its moorings and drift outward one last time. Claire and David kneel beside the bed, trying to comfort him as he pulls the blankets back again and again. Finally Claire turns to David, tells him they are going to have to sedate him, leaving him to comfort Kurt while she draws the liquid from the vial, David pinioning Kurt's arm as she injects it.

IT TURNED OUT that Fraser was the credulous colleague Kirkby had been alluding to. He had spent several years in London studying the maps, and he was convinced that the Portuguese had indeed traveled to this coast two hundred and fifty years before Cook. As he explained himself I heard a passion that excited me. Listening to him I wanted to believe.

I didn't know much, just the stories I had heard as a child, a memory that could almost have been a dream. But he listened to everything I had to say, his tall body falling backward into the chair in his office. Occasionally he would interupt me, make me clarify something, but for the most part he just listened. If it had been anyone else I would have been suspicious, wary of being taken for a fool, but not with Fraser. There was something about him, an ease within him that made me comfortable.

When I had told him everything I knew he stood and walked to his window, silent, his back to me. Outside the rain was falling in a steady mist, obscuring the spires of the buildings. The chimes of the clock rang out once, twice, a dozen times, their tones muffled by the drift of water. It had been raining for two weeks, every day, throughout the night, soaking the ground until it had begun to give way like sponge underfoot, until clothes had begun to molder, surfaces in the dark room I rented across University Road slowly becoming damp to the touch, fabric not drying. That morning on the way to Fraser's office I had seen the bitumen beneath my feet was beginning to crack, fissures running outward from subsidences like veins through flesh. My shirt clinging to my skin, damp, warm.

I don't know how long he stood there, with his back to me, nor did I care. I felt wanted, needed even, and I wanted this moment to last, wanted it to go on forever. As I watched his back I knew there was something else, something he wanted to tell me, but of which he was unsure. Finally, though, he turned, ran a hand through his hair, and cleared his throat nervously. These gestures so removed from the confidence he had shown all morning.

Seligmann, he said, crossing to a cabinet behind his desk, there's something I need you to see.

I stood, following him, watching him turn the key in the lock. Inside were a stack of notebooks, bundled papers, and a small case. Fraser glanced at me and I drew closer, so close we were almost touching, aware I was being shown something few others had seen.

Here, he said, drawing forth the case and handing it to me. I took it, turning it toward myself, surprised by its weight. Fraser's initials, *F. J. McD.,* engraved in the brass of the latch.

Open it, he said. It's not locked.

I let my fingers stray onto the tarnished catch, the metal cool beneath my skin. A gentle pressure, then the smell of wood and leather spilling forth as it opened.

Inside were several objects, each wrapped in cloth. I looked up at Fraser and he nodded, gesturing toward them. I lifted the first, slowly unwrapping it to reveal a sliver of ancient wood, dry and heavy, its reddish hue faded but unmistakable. My breath rushed outward in a convulsive sigh. Fraser smiled at me.

Mahogany, he said, and I swallowed, resisting the impulse to snatch up the other objects in the box, tear the bindings from them.

And the others? I asked. Fraser grinned, taking one himself and unraveling it to reveal a blackened coin, its face scarred and cracked, as if by fire. He hefted it slowly, then handed it to me and I took it, turning it over and over in my hand, allowing my fingers to trace the markings on its surface. The remnant of a date, A.D. *1514.* Fraser's eyes on me as I felt a sudden joy take hold of me, our sudden intimacy liberating me into laughter. I grabbed at the others, opening them to reveal more coins, a camber of green metal, the spider tracings of some elegant script arcing along one edge.

I'm pretty sure it's part of a bell, Fraser said, and when I looked up in surprise he reached for it, his finger tracing the script along its rim.

This is Tamil, he said. Bells like it were made in Goa and used on Portuguese ships in the early sixteenth century according to Barbosa.

Where did you get it? I asked, and Fraser smiled, his finger still resting on its elegant carving.

I've had them for years, he said. They belonged to a family friend, a colleague of my father's. Been in their family for years. I saw them when I was a student, and when no one could say where they came from it got me to thinking.

And?

Nothing. But it was these bits and pieces that got me interested in the maps. And in your story.

I stood there, absorbing the implications of what he had said. Our moment of joint excitement had faded, and I was feeling wary once more, unsure of myself.

You think they could come from the ship I saw?

Perhaps. There are a number of reports from that area of a reddish ship lost among the dunes. Sealers say they saw it in 1809, there's mention of it in a survey from the 1850s, and even Marcus Clarke gave an account of a visit to the wreck of a Portuguese caravel in a letter he wrote in 1868, although he said there was nothing to be seen but a line of broken spars in a sea of sand.

Sensing a qualification I hesitated, turning the coin over in my hand.

But . . . ?

But anything that was there was covered up years ago. That's why your story is so exciting. You've *seen* it.

I wonder what I would have done then if I'd known what was to come. I'd like to think I would have stood and walked away, but it's hard to be sure. Fraser had this way about him, a generosity, that he extended to all those around him. He had a way of overriding objections, of making things happen, and it drew me in.

So at that moment, after the hours we had spent together, when he suddenly glanced down at the fragment of the bell in his hand and swore, fumbling for the watch in his pocket, I was confused, and when a moment later he invited me to lunch, I agreed, although I knew I shouldn't have, that I couldn't afford it. That I was somehow overstepping the marks that covered the ground in the University, defining the space between the students from good families, with big homes on the North Shore and holiday homes in Bowral, and students like me, with nothing but our scholarships to our names.

At first though I assumed the worst. As he pulled the watch from his waistcoat, the gold chain oddly old-fashioned on such a young man, I almost dropped the coin in my rush to put it down, stammering an apology.

If you want me to leave . . .

When I spoke he looked at me, momentarily baffled, then just as quickly as it had come the expression faded, his face creasing in his good-tempered smile.

Don't be stupid, Seligmann, he said, looking back out over the rain, It's not you, it's just . . . are you hungry?

I stood uncomfortably, not meeting his eye, unsure what was being asked of me. I suppose . . . I said, and Fraser grinned, taking this as a yes.

Splendid. Then you can help me through lunch with my sister and the dreary Veronica.

Who? I asked, confused, the speed with which the intensity of the previous moments had passed startling me. In time I was to learn this was one of Fraser's greatest strengths and greatest weaknesses, this ability to shift his mood and attention so utterly, to keep his passions in boxes to which they could so easily be returned. Now, though, he shook his head.

Never mind, he said, his eyes searching the room, hands slapping his pockets.

Have you got an umbrella, Seligmann? I seem to have misplaced mine again.

Still mystified, I produced my umbrella, and his eyes lit up. Good show! Mind if I share?

I shook my head and followed him away down the corridor.

BY THE TIME we arrived both of us were wet down opposite sides from the rain and the shared umbrella. Fraser paid for the cab and led me toward the restaurant, which was down a small street in the city. Inside, it was like no place I had ever been before; its clientele was clearly men from the banks, lawyers, and stockbrokers, and ladies out shopping at David Jones for the day. Following Fraser in the door I was suddenly uncomfortable, aware of my shabby clothes and worn shoes, angry at having allowed myself to be brought here. Fraser thrust my tattered umbrella at a waiter, who I was sure sneered at it, then set out across the floor, me following in his wake, smiling at everyone in an effort to hide my embarrassment, until we suddenly came to rest. Two women sat at the table in front of us, a third place sat empty. As we arrived one of the women at the table stood, and Fraser leaned into her, kissing her gently on the cheek. I knew immediately she was his sister; the blond hair, the wide curving mouth, the creasing at the corner of her eyes.

You're late, she declared, as she disentangled herself from his greeting, but Fraser didn't reply, instead brushing the water from his shoulder with one hand, causing a fine mist of droplets to scatter across her arm.

As the water struck her she cried his name, her tone tart, but her eyes laughing.

What? he asked, looking up, and she tried to look stern.

You know perfectly well, what; you're a beast.

Me? A beast? No.

You are. First you're late, then you come racing in here and spray me with water. Look at me, I'm dripping!

Fraser grinned, enjoying the attention.

Throughout this exchange I stood behind him, shifting uncomfortably from foot to foot. Feeling her eyes upon me I turned to the other woman, and she looked up, meeting my inquisitive gaze, and for a moment I had a glimpse of a thin face, short dark hair, green eyes, then the blond woman was in front of me, pushing Fraser away, offering me her hand.

I apologize for Fraser, she was saying. He's notoriously rude. I'm Jane McDonald.

Unsure what to say I took her proffered hand, shook it. I was still grasping for a reply when she continued, indicating the other woman, And this is Veronica Marshall.

Again a hand was extended and again I began to speak, but once more I was cut short, this time by Fraser.

I'm sorry, old man, he said, turning back to Jane and Veronica. This is Kurt Seligmann, a student of mine. Very bright fellow.

I took Veronica's hand uncertainly, allowing her to control the gesture. Feeling my tentativeness the corners of her mouth creased upward in a half smile.

Charmed.

I smiled back nervously, uncertain whether she was being polite or whether I was providing some private amusement, but she held on to my hand a moment too long, her eyes holding my gaze steadily, direct, frank. As she released my hand she turned back to Fraser.

You should have told us you were bringing a guest. We've only three chairs.

Fraser glanced around, trying to spot a chair within easy reach, and in that moment I stepped forward, trying to halt the progress of this inevitable day.

It's all right, I really can't stay anyway.

Fraser looked round to me. What? Don't be ridiculous, Kurt, it's just a matter of finding . . . as he spoke his eyes fixed on what he'd been looking for . . . a chair. Triumphantly he seized it and pulled it toward the table.

Here.

I shook my head, although I could feel my resolve faltering. Really, I . . .

Then from beside me I felt Jane touch my arm. Please, she said, stay. Turning to her I saw the look of kindness in her eyes, and took the chair I was offered.

Brilliant, said Fraser, seating himself beside me. I looked up at his radiant face. I owe you lunch anyway, he said, and grinned, the expression spreading like a light across his face.

Throughout I felt Veronica's eyes on me, watching, but when I turned she did not look away, the green eyes steady, her wide mouth creasing upward at the side, enigmatic.

I remember the way I sat there, rigid with embarrassment, terrified that I would somehow disgrace myself, use the wrong fork, or spill my wine. Reveal myself in some unsuspected way. The other three chattered happily, trading playful insults, while I sat in silence, envying them their grace and elegance, their quick wit. All three of them revealing only the flawless exterior of the wealthy. Gradually, though, their attention turned to me, the silent guest. Veronica fixed me with the same direct gaze as before, her eyes guarded, but this time I saw something else in them, something that seemed remarkably fragile.

You're very quiet, Kurt, she said, sipping her wine, and I coughed slightly, feeling my ears redden.

I'm sorry, I said, looking down at the tablecloth.

Why are you sorry? We're the ones who've been ignoring you. She shot Fraser an unreadable glance. Blame Fraser; he's always dragging people along to things and then leaving them to fend for themselves.

Her voice was surprisingly pure, a richness to it like the clear sound of a bell.

You're a student of Fraser's?

I nodded, nervous, and she laughed, a strange, almost masculine sound.

If you're worried about money, Fraser will pay. He's got more than he knows what to do with.

Hearing his name, Fraser looked over. What?

I was just telling Kurt lunch is on you.

Of course it is, Fraser said, smiling. We can't expect students to have money, now can we?

I blushed. Thank you, but I really can't, I said, going to rise, but Fraser stopped me with a wave of his hand.

Don't be stupid, old man, he said, then cocked his head on one side as if observing me keenly. You're a scholarship student, aren't you?

Afterward I realized he meant nothing by this remark, but at the time I wished the earth would swallow me up. Yes, sir, I said, nodding slowly, my eyes on the table in front of me.

Thought so, he said, stuffing a piece of bread into his mouth. And don't call me "sir," my name is Fraser.

Slowly I found myself relaxing, their good-natured bullying and insistence I enjoy myself beginning to have effect. By the time we had finished eating I was surprised to find I was actually enjoying myself. Then, unexpectedly, Veronica turned her attention back to me.

Seligmann, she said. That's a German name, isn't it?

Surprised at the question I nodded.

Are you?

What?

German?

I shook my head. My parents were. I was born here.

As if satisfied by my answer she picked up her glass, but her eyes remained on me.

Are they alive?

My mother died when I was very young.

And your father?

I looked away. He died during the war. As I said this Fraser and Jane turned to me. Veronica nodded.

You should count yourself lucky. My father wasn't killed, although he might as well have been. Instead they stitched him back together and left him to die slowly in a vets' hospital.

Veronica! Jane exclaimed, and Veronica turned to her coolly. What?

You know! said Jane, her voice annoyed, while Fraser shook his head.

I really don't understand why you feel the need to do this, to provoke, to say things that are so bloody unnecessary. I'm sure Kurt doesn't want to hear about your father.

Nodding, Jane agreed with her brother. Fraser's right, she said, although not as severely.

I listened to the exchange around me, my eyes downcast. I couldn't tell them the truth, couldn't describe my father's pain and humiliation in the internment camp, the heat, his gray face and shaking hands, the horror of the midnight trips to the filthy latrines with him as the disease progressed. Of my father lying still in the hard narrow bed in the stinking heat, mosquitoes ignoring him and clustering on my soft pink skin.

So instead I looked down, said nothing, and for a long moment there was silence at the table. When I finally raised my eyes, Fraser was looking away, Jane was staring at Veronica, and Veronica was looking ahead defiantly. As I looked up she met my eyes, and I had a sense of an alliance being formed.

I'm sorry, she said. You probably don't want to talk about it.

Relieved, I smiled. That's all right.

I hope you won't hold it against me.

Swallowing hard I shook my head. No, I said. Never.

OUTSIDE, THE RAIN had broken at last. Fraser and I walked up Broadway, cars slipping by, carts passing more slowly, the air fresh, the smell of the wet asphalt mingling with the scents of petrol, warm manure, as the pavement began to dry beneath our feet. He had taken the umbrella, and was absentmindedly poking at the cracks in the asphalt. Finally he turned to me, smiling.

And what did you think of Veronica?

I grinned involuntarily, almost sheepishly. I thought she was rather nice.

Rather nice! Veronica! With all that huffing and puffing about equal pay and the repression of women. It's bad enough listening to her, but she even got Jane started after a while. And you think she's rather nice! I don't know, Seligmann, I just don't know. From his smile, I couldn't be sure whether he was serious or not, but his mood was infectious. I followed him, enjoying his closeness, his energy.

Who is she?

A friend of my sister's. She's an opera singer, he said, grinning. Then he stopped, looking back at me. I slowed, coming level with him.

Do you like opera?

I don't really know, I said, shrugging.

Then come with Jane and me on Saturday night. It's *Butter-fly*. Modern stuff, but good. Mother was going to come, but she's still not well, so there's room in the box.

For a moment I didn't answer, casting about for a reply, and before I could speak Fraser had turned away again.

Veronica's in the chorus. You'll get to hear her—how do they say it?—strut her stuff.

I just nodded, allowing myself to be drawn along.

When Kurt's voice finally slows and stops it is dark, the light in the room absent an hour. A piece of tin flaps in the evening wind, a creaking, lonely clatter. David and Claire stand, and David is suddenly aware the muscles in his legs and neck have locked tight. Sitting so still, so long. Claire crosses to Kurt, stands over him while she lifts his hand, measures the shallow flicker of a pulse. The tight rattle of the old man's chest loud in the quiet room.

When she is finished she crosses to David at the door.

Did you know all of this?

Most of it. Fraser—realizing he has begun to call this man he never met by his given name, David hesitates, correcting himself—McDonald wrote a paper in 1937 setting out his anecdotal evidence for a Portuguese wreck on this section of coast, but he made no mention of a sighting by a contemporary . . . David's words slow, watching Kurt's wasted form shifting beneath the sheets, then he adds, his voice lower . . . By a friend. And they didn't have the diaries—

The diaries?

The relics he said Fraser showed him; they must have been the ones Townshend says he took from the wreck, but without the diary entry they wouldn't have been able to link them to this location. Nor would they have known de Cueva's name . . .

So?

That means they must have found something else later on that told them that the ship they thought was buried here was de Cueva's, maybe something independent . . .

That's good news, isn't it?

Probably.

And the relics; the coins and the bell?

David shrugs. Who knows? Lost, long ago, no doubt.

What about Fraser's work, his maps and notes?

Gone too. No one knows where. And believe me, I've looked.

In the silence that follows flows a moment where their bodies almost touch, then they are in the hall, separate again. Both knowing how close they are.

MUCH LATER, DAVID and Claire are sitting outside on the back of David's four-wheel drive, smoking a joint David has rolled. David has turned the car so they can look out over the ocean, where lightning plays among the clouds silently, lighting their distant mounds and turrets in great snaking barbs of light. A tape of Claire's plays over the speakers inside the car. Claire passes the damp tube of dope back to David, who takes it, feeling again the dry skin of her hands. She notices his attention and lets her hand rub against his again. Surgical soap, she says.

Loosened by the dope, David laughs out loud. What?

Surgical soap. It ruins your skin. No amount of moisturizer seems to make up for it.

You have lovely hands.

Claire giggles, then catches herself, suddenly aware she is sounding girlish. Something loosening between them at last, but still only a truce. Everything else still aching like a bruise.

Thank you. But that's a terrible line.

It wasn't a line, says David after a long pause.

Right, she says, her voice playing at being sarcastic, but not looking round, not wanting to meet his eye. Over the ocean, lightning sends sheets of white fire rippling through the heaping weight of the clouds.

This is an amazing place, she says, her voice lower. It's like you're some tiny piece of wood, or wreckage, cast up on the edge of the world.

David hands the joint back to her, and she draws back on it, holding the burning smoke in her lungs. He watches her straining to hold in the smoke, her eyes bulging, but she catches his eye and bursts out laughing, the smoke pouring out in a rush.

What? she demands, laughing.

Nothing.

Tell me.

David takes the joint back. It's so remote, he says, drawing back. Imagine what it must have been like for those men, lost here, no hope of ever returning. I wonder sometimes what must have gone through their heads, what they really thought they were doing. Were they just sailors doing a job, or soldiers of God, or what?

What do you think?

David shrugs. I don't know, really. A bit of both. I know so little about them. Part of it was money, the Isles of Gold and all that, but in the end, who knows? When I'm here, though . . . sometimes I feel like it's so close, like I could almost touch them, as if the half a millennium between us is no more than a membrane, a flicker of an eye. Like I could wander into their time just by taking a wrong turn.

Or vice versa?

I guess. I suppose that's why I like it here; this place is close to them, as if it connects me with them, ties us together.

Do you think that's what he's doing here? asks Claire, inclining her head toward the shack.

Maybe. He's like a riddle.

As he speaks David becomes aware of Claire's eyes on him.

What?

Do you believe him?

Of course, he says. Why wouldn't I?

Claire allows her head to fall against his shoulder. The smell of her hair against his cheek.

No reason.

For several seconds both of them sit like this, still, not speaking, exploring the possibilities in this moment of contact. When Claire speaks again she does not look at him, her voice soft.

Do you still miss her?

David shrugs, looking away, over the sea.

I suppose. Not really.

Once again Claire covers his hand with hers. Turning back to her, David sees the damage she is carrying, the way it colors her movements. Her need so like his own.

From Malacca, on the Malay Peninsula, de Barros tells us Mendonça struck southeast. His route cannot be known for certain, but it seems possible, even likely, that he passed through the Indonesian archipelago and into the Arafura Sea, then eastward into what is now Torres Strait, passing beneath New Guinea and above the north coast of the Australian continent to Cape York, and then south, along an unknown coast skirted by a vast reef.

Meanwhile the efforts of his countrymen to halt the progress of Magellan were proving futile. Having rounded South America, passing between the mainland and Tierra del Fuego through the strait that now bears his name, Magellan had already entered the ocean that he named the Pacific by the time Mendonça left Pedir. And as Mendonça sailed out of the pages of history, Magellan's journey continued inexorably onward, eventually reaching the islands we today call the Marianas, where the Spaniards made port, half starved and exhausted from months of bad food and little water. In Guam they fought a battle with the natives, who were notable for their aggressive acquisitiveness, leading Magellan, in an ironic counterpoint to the history of European expansion, to name the islands the Ladrones, or the "Islands of Thieves." And in Mactan, in the Philippines, Magellan himself perished, slain in a confrontation with enemies of a local king. Finally, almost two years to the day after they departed, Magellan's ships, now under the command of Sebastian del Cano, returned to Seville. The Portuguese mission to stop him had failed.

When Mendonça returned from his secret mission is not known. But we do know he returned, limping back to Goa, two of his three ships lost, to the news of Magellan's success and the Portuguese failure to halt him. But with him he brought news of a new world to the southeast, together with portolan charts and records of the coasts of this land. The details of these charts are lost, as are the official reactions to his discoveries. What little we know tells us they were charts of a fertile continent to the southeast, a land hitherto unknown.

From here we hear little of Mendonça, and although in 1524 he presented his discoveries to King João in Lisbon, and then later became Governor of Ormuz, he continues to be little more than a historical footnote, an aside.

And while we can trace the future history of the man Mendonça, in rumors and commissions and the dusty reams of paper with which they detailed their times, what happened to his charts and records? Where did they go? And how did they come to be known to the French cartographers at Dieppe? The answers to these questions are even less certain, shrouded in the obscuring veil of time.

What we do know for certain, or as certain as any story can be, is that Mendonça sailed from Malacca in 1521, and later returned, with charts of lands unknown.

But before Mendonça there was de Cueva, whose two ships sailed out of Goa in 1519, and vanished into the vastness of time.

*T*hat night Claire comes to him in the space after midnight, silent, moving on bare feet through the dark. The skin of her feet warm against the floor. Outside, the moon is beginning to rise, casting slivers of light across the liquid hills, the clumping grass. The world humming in the secret motion of night. In front of her David's face lies half in shadow, his mouth slightly open. An eyelid flickers. Dreaming in an uneasy sleep. Her hand on his face jolting him suddenly awake. Both of them exhausted from lack of sleep, nerves like wires.

David? A tremor in her voice.

She is kneeling above him, the long arc of her body silhouetted against the shading darkness, her face in deep blue shadow. The scent on her fingertips soft as lizard skin. Without speaking he moves aside, her body sliding into the narrow bed beside him. Her dark skin cool against his. Her heart beating, almost audible. They lie face-to-face, feeling the rhythm of each other's breath. David suddenly afraid to touch her, the fragility of the moment overwhelming him, but Claire is stronger, lifting a hand, brushing his hair away from his face, then slowly, carefully, molding his face with her hands, learning its outlines, its contours.

Shh, she says, and David cannot tell whether she means him or herself. Then her face against his neck, her lips on his throat, cheek, mouth, her lips warm, swollen. One of their faces wet with tears. Her hands drawing him into her, her teeth around his nipple, the tidal motion of their bodies, circadian, gravitational. Later they sleep, still knotted into one, and in the morning, when he wakes, she is gone.

IN THE KITCHEN, just after dawn, David finds her, knees drawn up into herself. She hears him at the door but doesn't look up, knowing it is him.

Claire? he asks, his voice soft.

When she doesn't reply he steps into the room, crosses the short distance to where she is sitting.

What is it?

Claire shakes her head. Nothing.

Tell me. Another shake of the head.

We both knew it was going to happen. It was only a question of when.

That's what bothers me, she says. The inevitability.

*S*aturday night, seven o'clock, and I was waiting outside the theater, my suit heavy and hot in the warm dark. The smell of the salt from the harbor in the night air. Over the low rooftops the silhouettes of ships moored at the wharves, the rearing cylinders of their smokestacks picked out against the hazy night by pools of yellowing electric light. A low murmur of voices. Chinese signs of painted silk hanging from nearby buildings.

In the street in front of me taxis arrived in ones and twos, disgorging men and women who swirled and chattered in shifting groups on the footpath and the stairs, slowly drifting inward, passing me on the carpeted stairs and moving through the doors behind me.

I felt conspicuous, different. Anxiously I glanced at my watch, catching a woman looking at me as I did so, but when I met her gaze she looked away, whispering something in the ear of her companion. A heavily built man with a monocle and a fat cigar clenched in his teeth paused beside me. He half turned to me and grunted. I realized he, too, was waiting for someone. Suddenly there was a hand on my shoulder, a voice speaking my name, and I turned, but too quickly, losing my balance. The fat man grunted again as I brushed against him, and I stuttered out an apology.

I felt myself blushing furiously, and frantically tugged the lapels of my suit, trying to divert attention, tidy myself, whatever. Fraser looked like he was born to wear the suit he was in; tall, handsome, his blond hair slicked back, close to his scalp.

Sorry, old chap, he said. Didn't mean to startle you.

I shook my head, stuttering. It's perfectly all right, you didn't.

Jane laughed. Not even a bit?

At the generosity in her tone I found myself smiling, disarmed. Perhaps a bit.

Well, blame Fraser. He's the one who made us late.

Fraser gave me a grin. I'm afraid she's right, Seligmann. But we're here now, so perhaps we should head in.

I nodded, then stopped as abruptly as I began, afraid I must look a fool, but then aware that it was my jerky movements that made me look ridiculous. Before I can make things any worse Fraser ushered me after Jane, then followed the two of us, half a step behind, up the stairs and into the theater.

I took the seat Fraser offered me, looking down over the audience filing in and filling the seats, my heart beating faster as Fraser and Jane arranged themselves, the space in front of me seeming immense. The noise from the theater rose, voices forming a babble that reflected within the chambered hall.

Then the curtain rose and it began.

THAT FIRST TIME I heard that music, I felt the delicious exultation of sudden understanding, as if the world was so much more than I had ever seen. I remember realizing I had lived in a world of appearances, without ever feeling, or knowing. For three hours I was held there, suspended in the still space inside the music. The refracting melodies and cadences a web of potentials, a state of being that existed outside and beyond the mere sound of the voices, the sweep of the orchestra. Like love. Like a fly caught in amber.

By the time David returned to Australia from Lisbon, he had gathered enough evidence to convince him of de Cueva's mission's existence. Fragments in de Barros' papers; a cryptic report on the loss of two ships on a journey in 1519, in "the waters of the southern seas"; a reference in the annotations to the 1592 edition of Anton Vermeer's *Speculum Orbis Terrarum* to "the three missions of the Portuguese south, past Novae Guinea to the great tract of Terra Australis, a land peopled by savages and strange apparitions, bounded to the east by a reef thousands of leagues in length, and to the south by the icy waters of the Antarctic seas." And, most tantalizingly, an account provided to the Portuguese court in Lisbon of an audience in 1518 between Diogo Lopes, the Portuguese Governor of Goa, and a young captain (who may or may not have been de Cueva) who was convinced of the existence of a land east and south of Timor.

But if the mission had truly existed, then what had become of it? Wrecked? Sunk? And where? On the coasts of Australia? Among the treacherous reefs of the Arafura Sea or on the coast of Papua? Or in Asia, on the coasts explored by Magellan two years later? Or east, on the coast of New Zealand or one of the countless islands scattered across the Pacific?

What literature there was revealed nothing, all attention focusing on Mendonça's mission two years later. So David took a teaching position, hard won, at the University and continued his search, corresponding with others; professionals, interested amateurs, experts on local histories and folklore. Twice there were leads, but neither, in the end, was sustainable.

Then, serendipitously, he was approached by an elderly man, an alumnus and former Justice of the Supreme Court, who wished to make a gift of papers to the University. A telephone call, referred to David by one of his superiors, followed by a meeting, twice postponed.

The third date agreed for the meeting was a hot day at the end of the summer. David, busy with students and course details, was late. He came hurrying down the corridor, juggling books and lecture notes. Sitting outside the office he shared with another lecturer was an elderly man dressed in an unseasonably heavy suit. He sat upright, arms flat on a smallish wooden case that rested on his lap. Seeing him, David pushed forward, struggling to retrieve his keys from his pocket. A passing student turned and asked a question about tutorial allocations. As she spoke David saw the elderly man had turned to face him, his thin face peering through thick lenses without expression. David stammered out a reply to the student, then hurried on to his door.

Justice Townshend? he asked, shifting the balance of the stack of books and papers he carried.

The elderly man smiled gravely. Yes. You're Dr. Norfolk?

Mm-hmm. David jiggled the key into the lock, pushing the door open with one foot. Please, come in.

The judge stood and followed David into the room, the box in his arms. Once inside David dropped the papers to his desk with a thump and turned to face his visitor.

I'm sorry I'm late.

The judge did not reply, his silent gaze managing to give David the impression that he was accepting the apology without excusing David's lapse of manners.

Would you like a cup of tea or coffee? David asked, stumbling over his words. He was unused to men like this, men who bore with them power of a kind usually disguised in the modern world. Men of position and influence, who carried with them a lifetime of privilege and assumed respect.

Tea would be lovely, said the judge, settling himself in an aged armchair David kept in the office for students. He did not seem perturbed by the shabbiness of the chair or the office, a small room sandwiched between the fire escape and the air-conditioning unit, the sound of which was a constant backdrop in the room.

David busied himself with making tea, attempting small talk with his visitor. His stumbling efforts were bolstered by the judge's measured and courteous tones, his skill in transforming banalities and awkwardness into pleasant conversation. The tea made, David passed the chipped mug to the guest and settled himself at his desk.

I'm assuming the papers you mentioned are in the case, David said, sipping at his tea. The judge nodded, and David leaned forward toward the case.

Do you mind if I take a look? he asked, and when the judge shook his head David took the case, turning it over in his hands and examining it.

And the papers inside are the property of a relative of yours who arrived in Australia in 1794? he asked.

My great-great-great-grandfather, said the judge. I hope I had that right.

Near enough, David replied, grinning, finding the judge's remark disproportionately amusing. He was a . . . ?

Surgeon. He married the niece of the Governor and later instituted the first programs for disease prevention among the Aborigines.

David looked up, raising an eyebrow. Really? How interesting. As David spoke he fumbled with the case, which he had discovered had a tiny key, which turned with some difficulty. And the case is from the same period?

I believe so. But these particular papers were mixed in with some other documents belonging to my grandfather when he died. They spent quite a while in a safety deposit box before I found them while I was organizing my own father's estate about ten years ago.

As the judge spoke the key finally turned, and lifting the lid, David found several small bundles of paper, each stained and warped with age, and beneath them a leather-covered folio, bound with cord.

The judge leaned forward, placing one hand over the papers on the top.

May I? he asked, and David withdrew, allowing him to remove the top bundles and take the folio from the box.

I've spent some time on these documents since my retirement. Most of it is pretty run-of-the-mill stuff; interesting, but nothing remarkable.

As he spoke he laid the folio on the desk beside David,

opening it delicately. David watched as the judge turned the yellowing pages, the smell of the ancient paper strong in the small room. But there's something in here that I think might interest you.

David looked up at the judge. Me. Why?

I read your article in the *Alumnus Magazine* last year, about the Portuguese exploration of the coast.

Mm-hmm, said David, his heart suddenly beating faster as the judge stopped at one page, allowing the curling papers to settle, find their own level.

Here it is, the judge said absently, pointing to the page, 17 August 1794, "de Cueva" . . . that was the name, wasn't it? It seems they found a ship and papers that must have been his on the coast after a storm.

David leaned forward, the judge's words echoing within his chest.

De Cueva? You're serious? he said, following the crabbed hand of the judge's ancestor, the faded ink. The judge said something in reply, but David didn't hear him, the importance of what was before him overwhelming him. Evidence.

ALL DAY THE two of them move through the house, the small distance of a room enough to keep them apart, separate. An uneasy motion, both of their bodies humming with desire, their need an ache in their hands and chest. David closes his eyes in the close light of Kurt's room, feels her yawning like a space inside him. Twelve feet away, Claire, in the kitchen, a memory of his hands on her skin echoing, here, at the throat and here, in the small of her back; a shifting of muscles in concert. A vertigo that rises from within.

For two months after Tania died David lived among the remnants of her, the small flat they had shared a tangle of memories. So many pieces of her life, books, clothes, makeup. Finally David gathered them up, giving those he could to friends, stacking the rest into boxes and bags, taping them shut. When he was finished he loaded the boxes into his car, drove to a dump in a suburb he had never visited, and swung them one by one into the towering mountains of refuse. The summer sun hot on his back, sweat running down his arms and neck. His eyes dry. Unloading the boxes without speaking. The job took four trips and a day and a half but eventually the house was empty, her presence purged.

*A*long the front of the house is a narrow veranda, its floor buckled and uneven, cracks gaping between the twisted lines of planks. Near nightfall, David steps out onto it, lowering himself to the boarded floor, letting the clean smell of the ocean wash over him, through him. He sits there for ten, fifteen minutes. Claire left an hour before, driving away in search of food for the evening meal. He wonders where she is now, this instant, whether she is driving the road back from the town, walking down the main street, sitting in her car staring out at nothing. Whether she, too, is thinking of him. There is something about her that frightens him, an urgency, a needing. A vulnerability he recognizes and which he had hoped she would never know. When he finally becomes cold he goes back inside, to where Kurt is murmuring in his sleep.

WHEN THE CURTAIN fell I sat motionless, caught within the music. A shift in attitude, a word, enough to sever my body from the echoes and resonances that held me there. But gradually I became aware the tumult of the applause had died away.

A hand on my shoulder. Fraser's voice speaking my name. Looking at him I saw the face of a friend, the differences between us having fallen away. Jane's gloved hand on my wrist, telling me they were going backstage to see Veronica. Their kindness making friendship come easily.

BACKSTAGE WE PUSHED down narrow corridors stacked high with props, sets, racks of costumes and rope and tools. Chorus members and stage hands pushed past, talking and laughing. Fraser led the way, his expression almost boyish, clearly enjoying himself hugely. He asked for directions, joking with a thin balding man in shirtsleeves and spectacles, and set off down a side passage. Jane and I exchanged a glance, and grinned, his enthusiasm infectious, the two of us having to hurry to keep up as he dived ahead. Eventually he came to rest by a half-open door. From within came the sound of women's voices, sudden giggling, a snatch of song cut short by a barking laugh. Fraser stepped inside, knocking as he went, and Jane and I followed him. As we entered the voices fell, their owners turning to face us. I stared around the half a dozen women in painted kimonos and robes who occupied the long room, their faces and bodies in various states of undress, keenly aware that we were intruding here. Then to my left I saw Veronica, standing by a mirror in a loose gown, her elaborate costume draped over a chair beside her. Seeing the three of us she stepped forward and Jane rushed past me, colliding with Veronica, kissing her cheek and hugging her; this action somehow dispelling the tension that surrounded our entry.

You were wonderful.

Veronica laughed. I was passable.

Fraser came forward and held out his hand. Oh, I don't know, Vee, he says. I thought you were better than usual.

Veronica threw her head back and laughed, trying her best to look offended. And what is that meant to mean?

Jane glanced from one to the other. That's high praise coming from him, she offered, and Veronica chuckled in agreement. I know.

Standing there, listening to the three of them talk and laugh, I felt the distance I had begun to cross toward them open again. Suddenly embarrassed, I moved back toward the door. But Veronica noticed me, her glance halting my progress. Her dark eyes were direct and frank, and I suddenly found myself vividly aware of the fine skin of her neck and chest, barely concealed by the robe, her long slender hand holding it closed.

And what did you think?

Jane and Fraser turned toward me, and as they did I felt a sudden rush of desire. I wanted to stammer out an explanation of the experience I had just had, but my words sounded clumsy and brittle as I tried to order them in my mind, so I just smiled and said, I liked it very much.

At this she groaned, rolling her eyes. Jesus, you're as bad as Fraser here. Tell me what you really thought.

Jane grinned cheekily. Kurt cried, she said, and I felt my ears and cheeks burn. Jane, suddenly mortified, reached out and grasped my hand.

I'm sorry, Kurt, she said, I was just joking. And it's so rare to see men display feeling.

Looking up I saw her eyes were honest, and I swallowed, my embarrassment subsiding. Relieved, Jane squeezed my hand.

I liked it, seeing you really moved.

There was a long silence, the two of us standing like this, linked, Jane not removing her hand, me not pulling mine away. Finally I looked up and met Veronica's dark eyes again, and spoke, slowly, directly, honestly.

I loved it, I said. More than anything I've ever heard before. As I said this she looked away, as if ashamed.

SIX TIMES A day this ritual, the swab on the arm, the gray skin moving with it, loose on the flesh, the intrusion of the needle. Today Claire pauses, the needle resting against the flaccid skin, watching the play of shadows on his ruined face.

You're an addict, aren't you?

He turns his face to hers, a look she knows all too well in his eyes, a look she learned as a doctor in casualty training, a hunger of the soul.

What do you mean? he asks, something cold, almost reptilian behind the words. Hearing the edge in his voice she curses herself for not seeing it sooner, his evasion only confirming her suspicions.

You know what I mean. Was it morphine?

I was injured. This . . . he gestures with his ruined hand at the wasteland of his face. You've seen it, you know.

Claire says nothing, leaving the old man to speak into her silence.

They took it away from me years ago. Flew—you've met him—his bastard of a father refused to prescribe it anymore, notified the hospitals, other doctors. Cowardly little shit called the cops when I went to convince him he was wrong . . . said I was dangerous and threatened to have me put in the nuthouse.

A sudden spasm of coughing breaks the flow of his words, and Claire stands watching, waiting. When the coughing passes he looks up at her, pleading.

I need it now. For the pain.

I know.

Is this some kind of a game, are you punishing me for something?

Claire shakes her head. No, just asking.

You won't tell him?

Tell who?

David.

Hearing the edge of cruelty in Kurt's voice Claire is suddenly cautious, her unease about the old man returning.

Why not?

You're a doctor, what I tell you is secret.

Of course it is. But I asked why you didn't want him to know this specifically.

We both know that's not the point, don't we?

She hesitates, then, against her better judgment, she nods. A distance in her voice, caution.

Perhaps. But tell me this, how long did it go on?

A moment of silence before the old man answers.

Longer than it should have.

Forever.

$\mathcal{T}$he soprano. From the Italian "sopra" or "above," the term soprano refers to the highest category of female (or less commonly, artificial male) voice. Many subdivisions exist within opera houses, and these subdivisions often overlap, especially between countries. For this reason the distinctions are best understood in terms of the character of the voice, rather than its *tessitura*.

Until the sixteenth century the female soprano was rarely used in European music, but from the mid-1500s onward its use became more common, first in madrigals, and later in opera. It flourished in the late seventeenth century because of its suitability for the *bel canto* melodies of the period's Italian opera and the florid music of the late Baroque, and by the early eighteenth century agility, beauty of tone and the ability to ornament an aria were considered a soprano's most important faculties. Nevertheless the nineteenth century saw a shift toward more heavily dramatic operas, a shift that increasingly demanded that sopranos exhibit considerable vocal power as well, leading to the development of the modern dramatic soprano voice.

When Claire returns it is quite dark, the house adrift in the low hiss of the cooling hills. At the sound of her car David moves to the door, standing aside to let her enter. Her eyes on his as she passes him, unsmiling.

Is everything OK? he asks, worried by her long absence, her manner.

Mm-hmm, she replies, pausing by the door to the room where Kurt sleeps. And him?

Quiet. He was talking about opera before, though.

Claire looks at him, surprised. Opera?

It seems this Veronica woman was an opera singer.

Oh.

David follows her to the kitchen.

Was there some problem?

She does not look at him as she unpacks the shopping.

I went to the site where they found the body.

And?

There was nothing there. Just the police tape.

Why did you go?

Finally she turns to face him, her hands bracing her against the sink behind her. I don't really know, she says. But there's something about this we're not seeing.

You think he killed that man?

Perhaps.

David hesitates, incredulous.

On what possible grounds? Because he lived nearby? For Christ's sake, Claire, we don't even know whose body it is.

She lowers her head. I know that, but there's something about this, about him, that's not right. Don't you feel it too?

He's dying, Claire, of course he's peculiar. But it's still no reason to accuse him of murder. If geographical proximity was enough to establish guilt half the country'd be in jail now. I mean, you're the lawyer, not me, you should know better.

I'm not talking about guilt, I'm talking about whether he was involved. They're different things. And anyway, I don't understand why you're so upset about this. Look, do me a favor and just think about this for me. If that body has been here as long as we think it has, aren't you surprised Kurt didn't know? He says he knows these hills like the back of his hand, and somehow, in all those years of walking around looking he never saw a thing?

David shakes his head, surprised at how annoyed he is. That's it? That's why you're suspicious? I don't believe this.

I'm not sure I expect you to, Claire says at last. But do me a favor and be careful.

Of Kurt?

Claire looks away. Just be careful.

Irritated, David turns and walks away, walking the length of the short hall twice in quick, convulsive steps before he enters the room where Kurt is lying asleep, his shallow breathing loud in the quiet tin shell of the house. For a long time David stands there, listening to his breathing, watching the flicker of his eyes and lips, trying to imagine the confused skeins of dreams that wash across his ruined face like clouds. Next door he hears Claire moving quietly. This tension between them frightens him. Both of them needing this too much.

*H*ave you ever been in love? he asks, and David leans over him, straining to hear.

What?

Kurt laughs bitterly. Listen to you, the word frightens you. It wasn't a trick question.

David looks at his feet, ashamed, knowing his demurral was unworthy of him. And of Tania.

I know, I'm sorry. I just wasn't sure exactly what you were asking. If you were asking whether I've ever been in love then the answer's yes, I have.

And?

She died.

For an instant Kurt hesitates, as if this somehow alters things. I'm sorry, he says.

David shakes his head. It was a while ago now, don't be.

. . . How?

An accident. She was asthmatic, we were on a beach, alone, and something set her off. She went for her inhaler and it wasn't there; she must have dropped it or forgotten it, either way it doesn't matter now, what matters was that it wasn't there.

David pauses, his mind replaying the events yet again. Kurt says nothing, watching the memory of pain and impotence play across the younger man's face. When David continues his voice is slower, quieter.

The attack got worse and worse until she could barely breathe. I remember scratching through her things, flinging them everywhere, trying to find the inhaler. Then she stopped breathing altogether. I picked her up, half carried, half dragged her up the beach to the car. We drove to the hospital, and all the while I kept thinking that I was too late, because I knew that if the brain goes without oxygen for more than a few minutes then it doesn't matter whether you can save the body or not. She had her head on my lap, and I can remember stroking her hair, hating myself for having let this thing happen. Afterward . . .

What?

Afterward I would have done anything to make that day happen differently, make her alive again, but there was nothing I could do, nothing.

When David finishes neither speaks for a long time. Then David clears his throat, looks up at Kurt.

And you?

Twice.

When David says nothing he continues, falteringly. Or maybe it was just once, because it was the same person.

Veronica?

Kurt nods. Each time was so different it always seemed

easier to say I was in love with her twice, but I'm not sure it works like that.

How do you mean?

People talk about love like it's something definite, something singular, but it's not. We all love differently, and none of us know how it is for anyone else. Not even the ones we love ourselves.

All I know is that I have been in love twice, twice with the same person, and each time was different. The first time we were like children, hungry for each other, caught up in a game that, although delightful, was still only playacting. All that time I felt that there was more that was not being spoken, but I could not explain it.

But the second time it was like a sickness, a burning in the blood. As if something had passed between us and we had been grafted together. Maybe love is like a disease, an infection, and its method is like a virus, cutting deep into your being.

*A*s that first year went on I spent more and more time with Fraser. Steadily I found myself being drawn deeper and deeper into his efforts to prove the origins of the Dieppois' maps, and as the weeks and months progressed the ship steadily became more and more the focus of these efforts. But simultaneously there was more to it than just the search for the ship, the two of us quickly becoming friends, companions, spending hours together, talking intensely, listening to opera, that first experience of opera rapidly growing into a passion for me, a passion Fraser was more than happy to encourage. One autumn afternoon I walked the length of the crowded second-hand stores in the Haymarket searching for an old gramophone, finally pressing what seemed an immense amount of my pitiful allowance for the term into the hand of a young man who gazed at me with polite indifference, my delight in my purchase failing to pierce his enormous disinterest in all that surrounded him. After that there were many afternoons where the two of us walked to the city, visiting the record shops, selecting the titles from the catalogs, waiting while the

attendants retrieved the wax-papered discs from the racks that
lined the rear of the stores, then standing in the booths feeling
the amazing sounds encoded on the black discs loose themselves into the clear fluid of my spine.

As my friendship with Fraser widened and deepened I found
myself being invited more and more often to the McDonald
home for meals and afternoons and evenings. Happy for an
opportunity to escape my dingy room, the oppressive meals
with my ill-tempered landlady Mrs. Langton and her backward daughter. Gradually I became used to the idea of their
life, comfortable with the rituals of its grandeur. On the first of
my visits I met Fraser's father, a stern and distant man, who
I immediately believed to be what it is said he was: a Judge
of the District Court. Later I was to learn that he was famed
for the leniency of his judgments, his belief in reform and
rehabilitation over punishment, and for several visits after I
watched that stern, unspeaking man for a hint of the unexpected humanity his judgments displayed but it always eluded
me. On another occasion I met Fraser's younger brother, a thin
barrister whose ponderous manner and deep-set eyes made him
appear older than his years. Twice I met Fraser's elder brother,
maimed in the war, who lived in a room upstairs and was usually sleeping. His legs were gone from above the knee, his
right arm from the elbow, but the set of his mouth and his
graying blond hair made it plain that he and Fraser must have
once been very similar. And Fraser's mother, who was a cheerful woman, not unlike Jane, the daughter of a colonel who still
lived in India. Slowly I came to know them all, to move easily
among them, to begin to feel as if I belonged.

And always there was Veronica. Veronica moved among the

McDonald family as if she were one of them, but never relin-
quished her status as one separate, always remaining apart.
Our meetings, which occurred often, were complex things of
distance and caution, for I sensed my vulnerability to her. But
gradually we became friends, an understanding developing
between us, a code of gesture and glance and attitude as we
circled each other warily among the exotic finery of the
McDonald house, like animals or planets, every conversation
taking on cadences and shadows of other, silent exchanges. In
the evenings, walking home from the library or in the quiet
trains across the bridge from the McDonald home, I rehearsed
the textures of her voice inside my head again and again. The
lights within it shifting like opal as it vaulted through the
notes of her parts, my memory giving its tones shape, lingering over its clarity, the colors of its motion. My mouth against
her skin in my mind, imagining its scent, its taste.

And all the while I seemed to be working harder than I ever
had before, struggling to combine study and my newfound
interest in Fraser's work, which I was slowly coming to think
of as *our* work. Late in that first year Fraser formalized our
arrangement, offering me a position as his assistant, which I
accepted without hesitation. But steadily I was drifting away
from the life I had known, the few friends I had made in my
three years at the University falling away without my even
really noticing. Every morning I would arrive early to vanish
into the library, occupying my favorite place in the reading
room, where the morning sun fell across the table in slow-
moving rectangles, often not emerging until long after dark,
blinking and disconnected, then walking slowly home to my
small room, where I would allow the gramophone to pour

forth the vaulting notes I had grown to love, letting them fill the air like a kaleidoscope of color. My life a triangle: archaeology, opera. And Veronica. Always Veronica.

Then one afternoon late in the year I turned down the corridor that housed Fraser's room, a sheaf of paper under one arm, a book beneath the other, to find her standing outside Fraser's door, dressed for lunch. Surprised, I stopped where I was, saying nothing, and watched her lift a hand and knock. Of course I could have spoken out, knowing he wasn't there, but instead I remained where I was, watching her wait outside his door until there could be no question the room was empty. Finally she turned away, sighing, and as she did she noticed me standing silently at the end of the corridor. From her expression I knew this encounter was not one she had anticipated.

Kurt?

Remaining where I was, a fraction too far away for ordinary conversation, I replied, I don't think he's there, feeling my fear of her power over me make my heart beat faster, exhilarating.

Were you meant to meet him?

Ye-es, she said, looking up then back at the door and finally at me again. For lunch.

Oh, I said, knowing Fraser had forgotten.

Will he be back?

I doubt it, he's at a faculty lunch.

For several seconds she stood silently, digesting this piece of information, then suddenly, unexpectedly, she grinned.

Bloody typical, she said. Sometimes I wonder why either of us bothers with him.

Unbidden I felt myself smiling, a shivering delight filling me as I realized not only were we suddenly alone for the first time, but now that we were, neither of us felt afraid of this moment we had skirted around so many times, of the risk both of us felt beneath its surface, the silent disaster of planetary collision, of immolation. Of a single moment's contact.

My words tentative, I began an invitation. Perhaps I could . . . and she looked me in the eye.

You're not busy? she replied, her voice low, not waiting for me to finish.

I shook my head.

Not with that lot? she asked, indicating my books and papers.

No.

A moment's pause as she considered my offer, then she smiled. All right. Both of us knowing what we were agreeing to.

I suggested a restaurant or café, but Veronica declined, whether out of a lack of desire or tactful acknowledgment of the perilous state of my finances I didn't know.

It's a beautiful day, she said, I want to be near the water.

And so, three-quarters of an hour later we were eating fish and chips by the Quay, drinking beer from a long brown bottle. First one bottle, then another, and finally a third. Her appetite for the beer outstripping my own, surprising me. The fat and salt coating our mouths. Seagulls wheeling overhead as we talked, on and on, about opera, Fraser, our work, Jane, politics, the afternoon sliding away.

Somehow Veronica agreed to take me to her afternoon lesson, and together we climbed a narrow flight of stairs in Castlereagh Street, into a long empty room, where an elderly man with a European accent and a goatee shook my hand gravely, politely ignoring the smell of alcohol on both our breaths. I sat where I was told, on a chair beneath the narrow windows, the afternoon sun slanting through the dust, and listened to Veronica work her way through the lesson, her voice rich and beautiful, pacing itself up and down scales, through leaps and turns. As I listened I imagined the feel of her breath on my neck, her ribs a cathedral of bone and air. After the lesson, stopping in the corridor, our movements loose and liquid with the beer, one or other of us stumbling sideways, colliding, our lips somehow meeting, surprise melting into something darker as our mouths kissed and tore at each other in the darkened stairway.

*C*laire draws the needle out of Kurt's arm swiftly, pressing a swab onto the bright bubble of blood. David is sitting in the armchair that he occupies when he is with Kurt, one leg drawn up in front of him, his right hand covering his mouth. Dark rings pool under his eyes.

He'll probably be a bit more lucid for a while now, she says.

David doesn't reply.

You look like you could use some sleep, David.

I'll be fine, David says and smiles, a thin thing, disinterested.

I'll leave you alone with him then.

David nods. Thanks.

Claire touches his face with her hand as she leaves, and in that touch feels their distance.

AFTER THAT, THINGS began to change. Veronica and I spent more and more time together, each of us eager to know more of the other. A constantly escalating game of self-revelation, our words spoken in the half light of her bedroom. My body aching for hers constantly, the smell of her, the feel of her. Her absence a dull pain in my hands, throat, stomach.

OUTSIDE, CLAIRE LISTENS to their voices, the low murmur of Kurt's conversation, speaking quietly, his old-fashioned accent moving its way lightly over the span of his life as the pethidine opens rooms inside of him. Whenever he is awake he is speaking, and whenever he speaks David waits beside him, listening, listening. He is dying, and he knows it. She thinks she understands, has seen this before. All of us approach death differently, and Claire has seen so much of it, as a student, and later as an intern, a registrar, the quiet anesthetized death in the wards in the night, the morning, bright noon, and the long afternoon and the slow dusk. Most deaths occurring in the hours between day and night; dusk and dawn, points of transition. Death in the noisy amphetamine chatter of casualty, choking death, gasping death, broken windpipes and aneurism, sometimes the body shattered almost beyond recognition, some with the look of sleepers, peaceful, quiescent. But always there is this need to gather up the pieces of the life that is fading and pass them on. The talk, the entrusting of these fading fragments, passed from hand to hand like cooling embers. But even cooling embers can sometimes burn.

*B*y evening of the next day things between them are easier again. Over dinner they laugh and talk, leaning close over their food like lovers. Both of them enjoying this moment of peace. But Claire doesn't tell David that three times since their argument the night before she has almost told him she is leaving, that she cannot bear it anymore, and she knows David suspects as much. When they have finished eating there is a moment where the conversation fails again, and first Claire, then David, leans back, away from the other. In the next room Kurt murmurs something and David turns, anxious the old man is awake.

Claire puts a hand over David's. Leave him, she says, he's only sleeping, and David turns back to her. Suddenly she sees the distance in his eyes, the need. She understands for the first time the hold these hills have over him, knows why he does not seem able to imagine leaving.

THE FIRST TIME we came here to look for the ship was in early 1937. Fraser and I drove down from Sydney, along with several students. I was a tutor by then, working as Fraser's assistant while I considered the topic for my master's degree. A strange idea, considering it, when I never had a moment's doubt what it should be. We drove down in two cars, which took an entire day, and arrived after dark. Fraser had arranged accommodation in a bed-and-breakfast in town, which he said was glad of the business outside the holiday season. I remember stepping out of the car in the street, the smell of the wind off the sea. It was exactly as I remembered it, exactly. I stood there in the wide empty street as the others stretched and groaned, glad to escape the cars after such a long drive. For a moment I saw it in my mind's eye, just as I saw it when I was a child, the shattered bones of some vanished leviathan, bloodred in the yellow light of the storm. I felt something move within me, something dark, primeval, something made of lust and darkness and menace. That was when I realized the ship had become part of me. Not then, but long ago, in the storm, when I was just a child.

LISTENING TO KURT, David feels a flicker of recognition. This cold desire, the reptilian hindbrain hunger for the ship, he knows it too. Kurt's breathing slows, the rattle in his lungs rasping wetly. His eyes are closed, so David is not sure whether he is awake or asleep. David closes the book he was reading on his finger and exhales, pushing his hair back off his face. He can feel something coiling within him, an anger that frightens him. He is beginning to suspect Kurt is deliberately avoiding the question of where precisely the ship is, but still he sits here, listening politely, never demanding, except with his presence, the information he knows Kurt is keeping.

*M*uch later Claire shudders, falling from a light sleep into waking. David's head six inches from her face, a deep blue light molding his features. For several seconds she lies motionless, uncertain whether she has been sleeping or not. The house shifting in the wind around her. When sleep does not reclaim her she moves gently, so as not to disturb David, slides her feet out onto the cool floor, stands. She feels restless, but the absence she feels has lessened in the unanchored space of night. Behind her David stirs, and she turns to watch his body shift away from the space she has left in the narrow bed.

Five hours before they had lain, bodies tangled together, David's breath on her neck. At some point she had touched the ridge of his brow and spoken into the darkness.

I noticed something today.

She'd felt the contraction in his brow as he smiled, his breath as he quietly asked her, What?

There's no Bible on his shelf.

A silence, then, So?

You don't think that's strange. Especially for someone of his generation.

I don't know, David had said, and she felt his defenses rising, regretted this choice of topic. And when David didn't reply she had continued, her voice low. Do you believe?

Me? No. His rhetorical question distancing the statement from his inner self. Do you?

Perhaps, she'd said. Then, shaking her head, No, I don't think so.

You've never decided?

I've seen so many dead people, it's hard to believe there's anything after. But I look inside myself and feel like there is something missing in there, a need for something to believe in. And sometimes, sometimes I think maybe that space is for God.

After that neither of them had spoken for a long time, and in that silence Claire had known what she suspected was true, that they both have it, this feeling of absence.

Then, from Kurt's room she hears a low moan, and grabbing a shirt she hurries through. At his door she hears his voice, querulous, demanding.

Who is it? Who's there?

She steps in, moving closer to him, and he turns away in the darkness toward the window. Outside the moon is low and scooped away, crescent.

Do you want the light? she asks, and he shakes his head.

No. I was just thinking.

She wonders whether he is speaking to her or just speaking, but still she replies.

About what?

Fraser.

Your friend?

Still Kurt does not turn to face her.

I was thinking that perhaps in the end it was because his motives were clear. Mine never were. He wanted the ship, and that was an end to it for him. The ship. But mine were confused, shifting. I wanted her, but sometimes, sometimes when we were searching it was really the ship I wanted, and I forgot her. Just as when I was with her I didn't care about anything else, sometimes the ship would crowd her out, as if I only had room for one thing in my heart.

Claire shakes her head, moving closer to his shrunken form.

. . . But that's not wrong, that's normal. You can't let a love consume you, let it eat you up. Do it and there'll be nothing left of you.

Do you really believe that? he demands, his voice thin, turning to face her at last.

Claire pauses before answering. A long time with no words. Finally, Yes.

*I*n the next room David wakes to find he is alone. Falling sideways into her absence in the narrow space of the sleep-out, David speaks her name into the darkness. Kurt's breathing slow from the next room. When she does not reply he rises, crossing the wooden floor in his bare feet. In Kurt's room it is dark, the moon casting a silver contrast into the space. She sits so quietly in the chair that David has come to regard as his own that he does not see her until he is almost at the door. Her shape a handful of sharded moonlight scattered against a deeper shadow. When he speaks her name again she turns toward him, and he sees her eyes gleam in the darkness.

Are you all right? he asks, his hand on her shoulder, a pulse beneath her skin flickering against his.

Fine, she lies. I just couldn't sleep.

*F*rom the diary David discovered the name of the ship on which Townshend had taken his passage to the newly founded colony of New South Wales, the *Berkeley*, built in Portsmouth in 1773 as a collier. In 1789 she had been purchased by the Liverpool Amity Society. Her captain from 1789 until 1794 had been one Hamish McKellar, a Scotsman, who had died of a brain fever in Sydney Harbor not long after his arrival in 1794. Townshend's cribbed hand recorded these details together with his impressions of his new home, his ideas for improvements. In a later entry not long after the death of his wife Townshend wrote of his decision not to destroy the diaries, his desire not to lose anything that might be preserved.

A well-placed fax to the British Admiralty revealed that the *Berkeley* had been sold again in 1819 to one Lieutenant Roger Hawthorne, a former Royal Navy midshipman, whose place of residence was given as Sydney, New South Wales. She was decommissioned in Port Phillip in 1825. Since there was no record of McKellar's papers having been removed from the

Berkeley at the time of his death, David took a gamble and contacted the Victorian Archives, who informed him that they did indeed have in their possession the logs of the *Berkeley*. Within a week David was there, poring over the ancient papers, looking for what he eventually found: a description of a landing after a storm on 17 August 1794, the discovery of a shipwreck.

EVEN NOW DAVID remembers the terrible wheezing of her lungs, gasping for breath, drowning in a sea of air, the feeling of spiraling terror as he searched frantically for her inhaler. The slow walk of the doctor as he approached him in the casualty room, his eyes steady on David, and later, the calm look on her face as she lay in the morgue.

And now he is here, with Claire; Claire, and a faded photograph, a buried ship.

*T*hat first trip I should have known something was wrong, but I was too young, too stupid, to see. I was here as his assistant, helping him look for my ship. As I followed him back and forth through the low shifting waves of the hills the ship slowly slipped away and became his, like everything else . . .

But did you find anything?

Not then. All we could find were stories and fragments of stories. There was an old woman who the townspeople said had seen it as a girl, but she had died two years before, her house emptied by a son from the city. There was an old Aboriginal man who told us he'd seen it, and promised to show us where, but his story kept changing depending on what we said we wanted. Weeks and weeks of these false leads and dead ends, like chasing ghosts. And it was before the marram was planted.

Claire, who is standing back from Kurt and David, takes a step toward them at this.

Marram?

David turns. He means the marram grass that grows on the

hills. They planted it just after the war to stabilize them, stop them spreading inward and destroying farmland.

Kurt grunts, but David cannot tell whether it is in agreement or dismissal.

Before they planted the grass these hills were constantly moving, their patterns shifting and changing like a sea of mirages. You could stand on top of one of the hills on a windy day and watch the sand flow like waves. All our efforts to map the sands, to try and reduce them to lines and patterns, failed. So instead we wandered through the shifting sands, chasing a phantom, navigating by landmarks that vanished in an hour. Our shoes and pockets filled with sand, the crisp sheets of the bed-and-breakfast gritty with it. But Fraser was determined to find the ship. He had staked his reputation on it, declaring that the Portuguese had been here, and that he would find hard evidence of it. So we stayed up here for a month, gathering evidence, sifting through rumors and memories, looking for something solid to take with us, to prove that what we sought was here, somewhere beneath us. In the nights I lay in my bed and dreamed of Veronica, imagining her here with me, wanting her presence so badly that sometimes I would wake and in the moment between sleep and waking feel her shape beside me. And after a month we drove back to Sydney, back to Veronica, taking with us nothing but what we had brought.

As he finishes speaking, Kurt's eyes close, his breathing slowing. David exhales, letting his head slip into his hands.

Jesus.

Do you think it's a game?

Maybe. But he knows something, I'm sure of it.

.   .   .

THE PORTUGUESE CARAVEL was a small ship, a convergence of
European and Arabian design, usually three-masted, with a
rounded hull and high bow and stern. Small, seldom more than
a hundred feet long and twenty-five feet in the beam, the caravel's hull was a fusion of the rounded shape of European cargo
ships and the smaller displacement and carvel construction of
Arabian ships. Its rigging showed the influence of both parents, with a combination of square-rigged sails and the trian-
gular lateen sails of the Arabian dhow. These small ships were
more maneuverable than their European antecedents, and it
was their maneuverability and sturdiness that allowed the tiny
nation-state of Portugal to take the lead in the exploration of
the African coast, carrying them south, beyond the margins of
their maps and into the shadowy realms of the imagination.

KURT OPENS HIS eyes, awake again. David looks up from
his book.

You're awake.

Kurt's voice is weak. Yes. And for once I even know who I
am and where I am. I've been talking about the past again,
haven't I?

David nods. You've been talking about a lot of things.

Kurt chuckles bitterly, but his laugh collapses quickly into
shallow wheezes, then a cough. A lot of things that happened a
long time ago.

I suppose.

Where's your doctor friend?

On the beach I think.

And what's she say?

About what?

Me.

She thinks you're doing fine.

Bullshit! The sudden vehemence of his reply startling David. A spasm of coughing, which leaves Kurt immobile again, eyes half closed. I'm dying, we both know that. How long?

She doesn't know.

She must have some idea. Weeks? Months? A pause. Days?

David's reply is slow to come. Weeks. Kurt nods weakly.

I'm so tired.

David does not reply.

Are you giving me morphine?

No. Pethidine I think.

I didn't think it was morphine. His eyes close, and it is a long while before he speaks again. Are you in love with her?

With Claire? The question is not one he has asked himself before. Finally he shakes his head. No.

I think she is with you.

Why?

Kurt shifts uncomfortably, and David knows his moment of lucidity is passing.

I was once. I . . . A sudden release of breath . . . remember her voice . . . so clearly . . . but I can't . . . picture her face . . .

David leans forward. Why? What made you think that she was in love with me?

But it is too late, Kurt is sleeping again. Aware of another presence, David turns round to see Claire standing behind him in the doorway. I didn't hear you come in, he says, but she says nothing, only turns and walks away.

hen Claire returns neither mentions the events of the afternoon. She examines Kurt in silence, David watching her, looking for a sign as to how much she had heard. David cooks, and Claire opens wine they have bought from the pub in the town. They talk quietly, as they have become accustomed to doing, aware of Kurt's presence in the bedroom, and David begins to wonder whether she came in at the end, but then twice he catches her looking at him guardedly. Later, they sit on the veranda, and Claire leans into David, resting her head in the nook of his shoulder, her skin dark against his.

*T*hat first summer things had already begun to go wrong. Professor Kirkby's paper denouncing our work appeared in the *Archaeological Digest*. What he lacked in logic he more than made up for in rhetoric. All we had was a vision, a hunch. And faith. All through the summer we lived here in the hills, in this shack, Fraser and I. In the days we walked the hills, measuring, taking samples from the sand. Finding nothing. We would walk through the hills and barely speak to one another, except to pass on information. And in the nights we would sit on the veranda and smoke and talk of the ship.

AS HE FINISHES, Kurt's words gutter out, grow slower as he slides back into a state somewhere outside of sleep. Over his shoulder David becomes aware of Claire standing behind him, silent in the doorway.

He's talking.

I've had a look over the medication he's getting and made a few adjustments. He may not make a lot of sense.

He's all right so far.

Claire nods. Good, she says, but as she speaks Kurt moans, low, unconscious, his eyes half opening. One hand grasps at the air, and David, acting instinctively, reaches out, grasps it. Kurt's face turns to David but his eyes look past him, out, through the wall over David's shoulder and away.

Afterward they thought they knew, the old man gasps out, his hand squeezing David's hard, this sudden strength belying his frailty. They thought I'd done it.

David looks at Claire, who is standing close now, and she shakes her head.

Done what? David asks, leaning forward.

Killed him, they thought I'd killed him.

Killed who?

Kurt doesn't answer, looking away now, swallowing before he continues, his voice lower.

I knew they thought I'd killed him. I knew, we both knew, the way certainty looks, the way it takes one and burns inside of you. And they were like that, especially the one with the red hair. Finegan. He was so sure, and he made the others certain, his conviction giving them strength. They would arrive at odd hours, assuming a familiarity with me they didn't have, trying to catch me out. But without a body there was nothing they could prove. And then they sent me north, to New Guinea . . . His voice slows . . . New Guinea . . . after that they left me alone, all except Finegan. Sometimes when I was in the hospital he would call, sit there with his cigarettes, smoking slowly, never offering me one, just to remind me that he thought he knew. Finally he stopped, and I heard he'd vanished, a shark had got him, or they'd sunk him in the harbor. I was almost sad for him, he was so close. Like us.

After this there is a long silence, but just when David is convinced Kurt is asleep again he speaks once more, but slower this time, calmer.

I suppose I should thank Fraser for that, for teaching me to hide. He and Veronica were the ones who taught me how to do it, how to assume that impenetrable disdain of the privileged. He turns, looking straight at David. Never assume the rich are like the rest of us because they're not. They're different, and although they hide it they'll never let you touch them. Never. But I spent enough time with them to learn their sleek, elegant armor of cruelty and certainty. Do you understand what I'm saying? he demands, Do you?

David nods, and the old man sinks back into the bed, his eyes closing.

His grip on David's hand does not slacken for several minutes after he finishes speaking, and for as long as it remains tight, David and Claire wait, silent. When finally it slackens, David lowers the older man's hand to the sheets, turns to Claire. The atmosphere between them is electric. Finally David asks the question both know surrounds them.

What was that about?

Claire shakes her head. I don't know.

David turns back to Kurt, who is sleeping, the ruin of his face lit by the soft light from the window. Did it sound like . . .

A confession? Yes.

But to what?

David turns back to Claire. Neither speaks, both knowing the answer.

*A*nd the maps. Always we return to the maps. Hoping that they are certain, that they do not yield to questioning, and we accept them as true, as solid, as fact. Yet we have seen that maps are as ephemeral and dubious as anything else.

V

An Uncertain Guide

. . . and in trust I have found treason.

QUEEN ELIZABETH I

There are many kinds of betrayal. The betrayal of a lover, a parent, a child. Of a friend. There are the intimate betrayals, of those whom we love, and there are larger betrayals, the betrayals of politicians and priests who use their positions for ill, or turn a blind eye to harm that is done. But these scales of betrayal are not clear divisions: the betrayal of a people by a politician is itself a web of smaller, more personal betrayals, and personal betrayal has a capacity to spread, to grow outward, like a malignant cell. Beneath a clear surface things shift and pull. And burn.

*F*or two days after Kurt's stumbling confession nothing seems right between the two of them. Their bodies come together but the motions are mechanical, without communion. Both know a confidence has been betrayed, perhaps more than one, the ground shifting uneasily between them. David's skin jumps at the touch of Claire's hand, the tight-stitched muscles of his neck stiffening involuntarily. In the night they sleep back to back, Claire's buttocks cold in the crook of his back, her body turned in on itself like an animal's. Twice David almost asks her whether she was there the night Kurt asked him about her, what she heard, and twice he thinks better of it. All the while Kurt lies in their center, not emerging from his delirium as their words and movements describe silent arcs around his murmuring form.

EVERYTHING BEGAN TO go wrong the summer of 1938. The city had settled into that long slow waiting of January, where the heat descends and the city seems to empty, everyone draining away until you feel like you're suspended in a world empty of everything but the heat. All that summer Fraser and I had worked alone in the University. In the year since our first trip down here we had realized we were going about this the wrong way, that without money we would never have the resources we needed to search the area properly. What we needed was evidence that would establish we were chasing more than a fugitive dream, something solid. And we needed it quickly. Kirkby had his eye on the Chair, and he thought Fraser was his only real obstacle. His article in the *Archaeological Digest* the year before had hurt us, questioning not just our conclusions about the maps and the anecdotal evidence but our methods. The mood in the department had shifted away from us, and both of us knew there was only one way to shift it back. Evidence.

Fraser thought we might be able to find what we were looking for in Goa. He had been corresponding with a German academic who was working there, trying to catalog the papers in the Portuguese archives, and there was some suggestion there might be something useful there. The plan was that we would both head up in February and look at what he had found as well as trying to see what else might be squirreled away in the vaults of the Goan archives. I was torn between my excitement at the thought of a month in Goa, the possibility we might find something certain, and the thought of a month away from Veronica. I was so young, so in love with her. So stupid. Every day seemed to brim with possibilities, it was like living some mawkish song. And she was happy too; her career was blooming. That January she was rehearsing Michaela in *Carmen* and the part was consuming her, every time I saw her she was giddy with the work, the music. Her lips sweet with wine or beer or brandy when we met in the small hours of the hot nights, our excitements feeding off each other, hungry. Our passion like a childish game.

Fraser and I were due to leave on January 29. Even now I remember the date. But two days before we were to leave Fraser's elder brother, Lachlan, who had been ill for months with complications from his injuries, died suddenly. Fraser's face gray with shock as he told me. That night Veronica explained for the first time how close the two of them had been and I lay in the hot bedroom trying to imagine Fraser's pain, Lachlan's twenty-two years of dying since the grenade bounced back from the trench wall and tore his limbs from his body, but it was beyond me. Neither of us speaking as we lay in the darkness. The funeral was set for the thirty-first, and Fraser reluctantly told me I'd have to leave without him, there was no question of him missing the service. He would follow a week later on the next ship. Numbly I nodded agreement, wondering how I would do it without his help. The night before I left Fraser and I sat up late, working through our plans while Veronica sat in the next room with Jane. It was late, very late, before Veronica and I found our way to bed, and when I rose in the darkness, my eyes and throat aching from lack of sleep, she held me tight, pressing her skin against my shirt in the dawn light, her cheeks and lips wet on my chest as we said our good-byes.

Kurt pauses, and David, eager to know more, leans forward. So did you get to Goa?

Kurt sighs, his face turning to the window.

Oh yes, I got there.

And?

We found what we wanted.

What? demands David. What was it you found?

A record of the two expeditions. A draft of a letter, pressed between two pages of a journal. Scraps and rumors.

Did you make copies?

Slowly Kurt nods, his gesture resigned, indifferent, as if this conversation is irrelevant.

And what happened to the copies?

They were lost.

How?

Kurt pauses. In a fire. A long time ago, he says. A tear on his cheek.

But what did they say?

They were where we learned de Cueva's name. We found it in a journal, along with a letter, both of which described the bluff, the wreck, gave us his name. They were written by a navigator who sailed with Mendonça.

David nods wildly, feeling this information slot in with what he knows and has guessed.

Of course. That would have been Quiroga. Who was the letter to?

The father of a man who sailed with de Cueva, reporting the wreck, the loss of all the men. The father was a landowner in—

Braga, David declares triumphantly, and Kurt turns to look at him.

That's right, how did you know?

Quiroga retired to become a gentleman farmer in Braga. He wrote a treatise on navigation by the southern stars that was read widely in the 1530s and 1540s, although there are no copies that remain. I knew that de Freni, the man whose estate

Quiroga managed in Braga, had a son who was an officer in the Navy and I'd suspected there might have been some link to de Cueva or Mendonça. I'd actually suspected that maybe he'd been on Mendonça's ships and that was how Quiroga had come to end up in Braga. But I suppose if he was on one of de Cueva's ships that might explain what happened to the son and how Quiroga ended up managing old de Freni's estate.

So you never saw the papers in Goa?

David shakes his head. They've all vanished. God knows where.

Then how did *you* end up here?

Through de Barros; a personal journal.

Kurt nods, digesting this. But how did you make the connection with here?

A ship's log, from the eighteenth century. And just blind luck, really.

IN THE HALL outside Claire is waiting, arms folded.

Well?

David feels the tension in her voice. Well what?

Did you ask him about the body or were you just talking about the ship?

Claire's question merely prodding his own shame at his reluctance to pursue Kurt about his cryptic words the night before.

He was telling me about how he came to find de Cueva's name.

Claire doesn't reply, merely staring back, her eyes angry. Finally David gives in, growing angry himself.

What? he demands, and Claire shakes her head, trembling with fury.

You know, she hisses, her voice low.

I know you want me to hound a dying man about a corpse from fifty years ago, a man who might just know the location of something I've spent the last seven years of my life looking for. But I'm not going to do it, Claire. I don't care what he did, I need the ship. You understand that, don't you? I *need* to find it.

She shakes her head. And what about whoever's body that was out there? What about them?

David sighs in exasperation. Can we please not do this now?

If not now then when, David? You're always doing this, avoiding everything.

David swallows hard, trying to contain his irritation, knowing how much he needs her here.

I don't understand why this is so important to you. How's he so different from all the other bad guys you've dealt with.

I . . .

And then, in her hesitation, David sees it.

It's not about him, is it? he says, suddenly no longer angry. It's about you. And being here with me is only making it worse, isn't it?

Claire doesn't look away, her eyes painful to see. David wants to step forward, hold her, but he is afraid she will shatter from the strain of whatever it is she is so barely containing.

What is it? he asks, his voice soft. Just trust me enough to tell me. Just trust me.

*M*ysteries nest within the Dieppe maps like Russian dolls, each enfolded within the next in a cat's cradle of uncertainty and doubt. And always, just as we think the ground beneath our feet is certain, it shifts, sliding away to reveal more questions. For despite their vast achievements the Portuguese were furtive, suspicious, and guarded their discoveries jealously against the prying eyes of the Spanish. So great was their fear of their rivals that in 1508 King Manoel I enacted the infamous Politica do Siglio. The Politica do Siglio or Policy of Secrecy sought to prevent others from infringing the worlds the Portuguese were discovering by keeping anything that might assist in finding them hidden, compelling captains and navigators who struck east from the Cape of Good Hope to render up their charts and logs to the archivists in the Casa da India immediately upon their return to Lisbon. The penalty for any who disobeyed was death.

How then, if the Dieppe maps are genuine, could the French have come to possess the charts necessary for their drafting? As always when we look into the world of supposition and rumor that we call the past, nothing is certain. All we find are questions, shadows, ghosts. Here, we can say, here are the maps, the etched outlines of what appear to be lands supposedly undiscovered until centuries later. And there, there we can say are Mendonça and de Cueva, men who we have reason to believe may have entered these waters and charted these shores. And if this is true we may suppose without too much fear of contradiction that Mendonça, who certainly returned to Goa from wherever it was he traveled, brought with him charts and logs recording his discoveries. But other than this we know nothing. All we hear are echoes. How did the French come to possess the secrets of the Portuguese, and possess them so thoroughly they were prepared to flaunt that knowledge, embellish it? How did they pass from the vaults of the Casa da India in Lisbon to the chambers of the Cartographer's School at Dieppe?

The answer lies in the wilderness of mirrors that divides nations, the world of espionage and treason, where allegiances come cheap and lives cheaper. For somewhere in this place of grubby dealings and soiled money, where men sell lives and secrets for gold, a copy of a map was taken, perhaps in Lisbon or Goa by a clerk, perhaps by a spy, perhaps by a disgruntled official. Or perhaps French adventurers like the Parmentiers, men who themselves explored the Indies in secret, procured the betrayal of a navigator or officer or clerk, and there, on the furthest rim of the known world, bargained gold for knowledge.

Whichever it is we shall never know, for the only records would lie in the archives of the Dieppois themselves (spies and traitors not tending to document their actions for posterity); archives that history—or the English, who sacked Dieppe in 1694—deny us. But for once there are things we can be certain of. For we may not know who was responsible, but we do know the how and the why. From the inside. For money. For sex. For power.

IN THE SPACE between afternoon and evening Kurt wakes again. David senses the change in his breathing from the next room, enters to find the old man staring at him.

What's the date?

David, surprised by the directness of the question, the sudden clarity in Kurt's eyes, stutters.

What?

The date. What is it?

David glances at his watch and tells him. Kurt settles back into his pillows and makes a sound that could be a chuckle.

My eighty-third birthday.

Claire, who has been listening at the door, steps forward. You're sure?

Of course, he replies, contemptuous.

David and Claire exchange glances. I think this calls for a celebration, David says, rising to his feet.

Claire watches him cross to the hall, turn toward the kitchen. As he goes she feels Kurt's eyes on her, studying her. Unbidden, she feels a tremor run along her spine.

What? she demands, not bothering to maintain her professional reserve now that she is alone with Kurt.

I heard you, he says, his voice slow and weak. The other night in the hall. I know you think I killed him.

Claire hesitates, more surprised than she would have expected by this admission.

We thought you were asleep.

He shrugs, a pathetic gesture.

I suppose I was, at least partly. But I heard what you said. He doesn't believe you, you know, and he won't. He doesn't want to hear it. All he wants is the ship.

A low sound, perhaps a laugh, perhaps a cough, emanates from Kurt's twisted body.

Before Claire can reply David returns with three glasses and a bottle of white wine.

I couldn't find champagne, so I had to make do. Claire? he says, offering a glass to her. Claire takes the glass, aware she is shaking with anger.

And look, he says, holding aloft a small tape player.

What's that? asks Kurt. David smiles.

You'll see. As he speaks he opens the wine and pours glasses for himself and Claire, then pours a half an inch into the third glass and offers it to Kurt. He turns to Claire and smiles, but she looks away, and he turns back to Kurt, unwilling to press the point, and raises his glass.

To Kurt, he declares, and Claire raises her glass in a guarded way. Kurt smiles nastily as she does, but David is fiddling with the tape player and misses their exchange of glances. Finally the tape whirrs and then suddenly a voice swells into the air, rising, rising, its shifts speaking eloquently of an indescribable sadness.

Claire steps over to him. What is it?

Maria Callas. From *Madame Butterfly* I think. Then they see Kurt, lying in his narrow bed, his face turned away from them, tears running down the pitted and sunken landscape of his face. Worriedly, David kneels beside the bed, touching Kurt's hand with his own.

Kurt? he asks, but the older man only shakes his head, not looking over, and then, his eyes looking out and up into the empty sky outside, begins to speak.

IT WAS MY twenty-fifth birthday when they told me. 1938, just after I returned from Goa. A lifetime ago. I had been gone two months, two months spent in the disorienting swirl of Goa, the confusion of the streets and markets. In the end Fraser had not been able to join me at all, his mother having collapsed shortly after Lachlan's funeral, and I had spent the time working alone.

But the hunch that had drawn us to Goa had paid off, for contained in the archives were copies of many documents we might formerly have supposed to have never existed outside the Casa da India in Lisbon. Aided by Kessel, the German academic Fraser had been corresponding with, I had managed to find several papers that confirmed what we both already knew; the existence of a mission to the southern continent in 1519. But I had also found a later record of a wreck on a piece of coastline characterized by low sandhills and dominated by a bluff of sandstone and a freshwater stream. And a name. And now these documents that would vindicate our search, roughly translated in my cribbed handwriting, lay within my cases, enfolded in a dress I had bought for Veronica, the history of a continent wrapped in green silk.

I woke long before dawn the morning I arrived back, waking into the marine quiet of the ocean night. The window of my cabin admitted the constant rumble of the water, the metal of the room pulsed with the deep hum of the engines. In that darkness I let my body imagine what my reunion with

Veronica would be like, the taste of her mouth, the cool pressure of her skin, the brush of her hair against my face and chest. The inner motion of our bodies. I lay very still in that private dark, remembering her, anticipating the future.

By dawn we were in sight of the Heads, and I walked on deck to watch the colors pass over the cliffs, the red rooftops of the city. A child waved from a balcony, and I lifted an arm and waved back. At the wharf I hurried off, expecting Veronica to be waiting for me, but there was no one. Confused, I walked the length of the pier twice, worried I might have missed her, but it quickly became clear she was not coming. I felt a vague disquiet rising in me as I hailed a taxi and drove to her flat, telling myself she had probably overslept, or misunderstood the telegram I had sent, but when I arrived there was only her landlady in a rumpled dressing gown, who regarded me in a way I didn't like and assured me Veronica wasn't in.

Standing in the street outside Veronica's Elizabeth Bay apartment the disquiet I had felt on the pier rose into a kind of panic. Dragging my cases I walked three streets searching for a telephone box, growing hotter as the sun rose higher. Finding one at last I frantically dialed Fraser's number, my closed fist beating a slow rhythm on the wall of the booth as the phone rang tinnily in my ear. After what seemed a very long time the ringing stopped, to be replaced by Fraser's voice.

Hello?

I gasped out his name, barely able to speak, and he hesitated. Not for more than a fraction of a moment, but when he hesitated I knew.

Kurt? he said. Where are you?

I cleared my throat, my voice shaking.

In Elizabeth Bay. Near Veronica's.

When he said nothing I continued. Do you know where she is?

He laughed, but I could tell he was uneasy. In bed? he asked, mock-flippant. It's only just after seven.

My hand drumming faster I looked out the window, watched a bus roar by outside.

Her landlady says she's not there, I said. I thought you might know where she is.

Fraser said nothing; all I could hear was the sound of our breathing. Then finally, when the silence could be maintained no longer, he cleared his throat, the sound loud down the empty line.

Go home, he said. I'll be there as soon as I can.

Before I could reply, I heard the phone click down.

I don't know how long I stood there after he hung up, the receiver clenched in my hand, a terrible vertigo engulfing me, but finally I replaced it, stepped out into the street, and numbly hailed another taxi. Back at my house I fumbled with the lock, wandering into the closed air of the small rooms like a dreamer. In the bedroom was the dress Veronica had worn that last night, when she and Jane had talked on the balcony while Fraser and I had sat planning the trip, and I sat down heavily beside it, allowing my hand to caress its soft material, waiting for what I already knew was to come.

Finally I heard a car pull up outside, then a knock on the door. I opened it to find both of them there, a sickness growing in my stomach. My hands shook when I asked them in, a leaden certainty gripping me.

In the hallway Veronica stood behind him, almost as if she

were sheltering from me, and when I ushered them upstairs to the front room I used as study and sitting room she sat as far from me as she could. Fraser sat with his head in his hands, watching me, his face pale and stricken.

We thought you weren't back until later this morning.

The boat was early, I said. I wired Veronica yesterday, but she musn't have got it.

I looked across at Veronica, who shook her head.

Fraser nodded and looked downward, clearly attempting to compose his thoughts. This was hard for him, I could see that, and I almost felt sorry for him.

Kurt, I . . . we . . . need to tell you something, he said, his eyes meeting mine plaintively, and I nodded, swallowing hard as I looked away from him, out the open doors to the small balcony, and the blue expanse of water beyond the serried rows of tin roofs. In the huge air of the harbor a plane droned slowly across the exploding blue, the propellers burring in the heat. On one side Veronica continued to stare at me, her features composed in a look of pain I had never seen before. I smiled, wanting her to feel at ease, and she smiled back, tenderly. Across from me Fraser was still talking, but I hadn't heard a word he was saying, there was no need. Outside the plane was receding, and I watched as it moved out of sight, Veronica turning to watch it as well. Finally Fraser was quiet, and I just nodded, knowing there was nothing I could say that would make them understand what it was that they were doing to me, and when it became clear I wasn't going to argue, Fraser turned to Veronica and touched her arm. I remember the way he did it. So tender, but distant, like a solicitous parent. She stood, and I showed them to the door, mutely. I suppose I was in shock, but I could think of nothing to say. Perhaps if I'd ranted and raged things might have been different, I might have embarrassed them or jarred them away from what they had convinced themselves to do, but I didn't. I just nodded and said I understood. At the door Fraser shook my hand and thanked me for taking it so well. And Veronica, who had not spoken once, except to say, Hello Kurt, as they arrived took my hand and drew me close, touching her lips to my cheek. I'm sorry, she whispered, her breath on my face. I nodded and let her step away and out the open door.

WHEN KURT FINISHES it is dark. David sits for a long time listening to the old man's ragged breathing. When he finally turns he realizes Claire has slipped out, and he stands to follow her. She is sitting outside, arms folded, watching the moonlight on the pools of grass, the tidal shifts of wind among the stalks. Without speaking he sits beside her.

He's asleep, he says, and Claire nods.

He did it, you know. He killed him. Maybe he killed her too.

David shakes his head. Fraser committed suicide and we've no idea what happened to her.

What about the body?

What about it? You know what I think.

That my professional judgment is clouded by whatever it is that's happening in my own head?

David grins. Something like that. As he speaks he puts a hand on her shoulder and she doesn't flinch, allowing him to draw her close.

It's getting cold out here; you don't want to come inside?

No. What do you think really happened?

If you mean the things he said the other night, about the police, then I'm not sure. I know what it sounded like, both of us do—

It doesn't worry you that he might be a murderer?

David shrugs. I'm not sure. Then he is silent for a long time. Finally he shakes his head. No. All I want to know is what happened to the ship.

Claire nods. He's different with me, you know.

He doesn't know you.

He doesn't know you either. But he is. There's something nasty about him.

Look at him. He's an old man, he's dying. And he doesn't look like he's had a good life. It's hardly surprising he's bitter.

I'm not talking about bitterness. There's something nasty about him. And evasive. He's up to something, David. I mean if he knows where the ship is, why hasn't he told you? Instead of leading you round and round in these endless circles.

Perhaps he's afraid we'll leave once he's told us and he'll have to go into hospital.

That's not it.

Then what is?

I don't know, David, but I'm afraid. Be careful.

Of what? He's an old man.

You're beginning to trust him, and trust can be dangerous.

When David doesn't answer, Claire slides away from him.

Perhaps that danger's something men can't understand, she says, her back to him.

*A*fter that things went from bad to worse. In the department the rift between Fraser and me couldn't have come at a worse time. All summer Kirkby had been working at undermining us and our work, taking advantage of our respective absences to shore up his own position. The seriousness of our situation was immediately apparent to me the day I returned to the University, the way the conversation dropped when I entered the lunch room. I crossed to sit with another of the younger men, Bill Norman. Bill and I were friends then, and even later, after . . . after things went wrong, he was just about the only one who didn't turn away. But Bill seemed distant, as if he was keen to get away, and I was quickly alone again.

Bill gone, I turned to face the sea of impassive faces, and although several of the men in the room looked up and smiled as I looked around, I could feel the wall they had placed between me and the rest of them, and I stood, taking a cup of tea with me, and began the walk back to my small office.

Back in my room I sat very still, feeling my hands tremble as I tried to control my anger. Then there was a knock at the door. I looked up, startled, and was surprised to see Fraser standing there stiffly.

I'm sorry, he said. If you're busy . . .

Still surprised I took a moment to reply. No, not at all, come in.

Fraser entered, closing the door behind him. He seemed edgy, almost agitated, and despite my offer of a seat remained standing, moving nervously about the room. I said nothing, trying to contain the tumult of emotion his presence had stirred up inside of me. For a long time neither of us spoke, but finally Fraser leaned against the windowsill, the sun framing his slim form against the blue sky.

I was rather hoping you'd come and see me in your own time, he said. About the work, but I suppose that under the circumstances it's really up to me.

I shook my head. I'd been intending to come and see you, I lied, I just . . . Here I faltered, unable to express myself without breaking down, something I was determined not to do. I had already wept enough.

I understand, Fraser said. But it's imperative we crack this thing together. I've just had a very troubling conversation with Bill Norman—

I spoke to him just now, I said, and Fraser looked at me quizzically.

How did he seem to you?

Odd.

I'm not surprised. I think Kirkby's really put the wind up

him. I understand he made some pretty thinly veiled threats about the limited prospects for advancement in the Department for those who chose to "tie their flags to the wrong mast."

I sat forward, rigid with annoyance. That's outrageous! Even Colmer can't just ignore this kind of behavior.

But Fraser seemed unmoved. Colmer's not going to do anything. He and Kirkby are thick as thieves, you know that. He paused, as if he was thinking about what he was going to say next.

Kurt, I wanted to come and see you, to tell you what Bill told me because whatever's happened between us I still consider you my friend—

Fraser, I began, interrupting him, but he waved me down.

Please, let me finish. I just want you to understand that for me the work comes first, particularly now, and that I hope we will be able to continue working together despite . . . all the rest of it. But I think Kirkby's going to make it his business to obstruct us every step of the way, and that could turn out very badly for you.

I leaned forward. For me?

Fraser nodded. My position here is secure, but yours isn't. What I'm trying to say is that I think Bill's right, the prospects for advancement for anyone who's tied their flag to this particular mast are going to be very limited and I don't want to see you wreck your career. I don't want to lose you, but I do want you to know that if you were to decide that there were other areas you wanted to . . . move into . . . that I'd support you. And that I'd understand.

Finished, he looked at me, waiting for me to respond. Finally I cleared my throat.

Kirkby doesn't matter, I said. Because we're going to find it.

Together?

As Fraser asked this I realized his concern for me was genuine, and smiling, grasped the olive branch I was being offered.

Together.

Thank you, Kurt, he said. You don't know how much this means to me. Then he stopped, as if there was something else he wanted to tell me. When he began his voice was hesitant.

There's one other thing, he said. We didn't tell you the other day because . . . He faltered. It just didn't seem to be the appropriate moment, but Veronica was concerned you might find out another way.

What? I asked, a feeling of nausea rising within me.

We're engaged, he said, and there was a distant crashing noise. Looking down I saw the teacup I had been holding had shattered, showering tea across the table, blood already beginning to flow.

I'm sorry, Fraser was saying, I really am, but I could barely hear him over the thunder in my head.

IN KURT'S ROOM, the soft rattle of the old man's breath barely disturbing the still night air, David sinks forward, burying his head in his hands. The more he hears the more he begins to wonder if Claire is right, and he has become part of some terrible game. The other players all fifty years dead.

$\mathcal{D}$uring the Second World War soldiers came to these hills, moving through them in grim silence, laying out behind them secret patterns of destruction: land mines, tank traps, barbed wire. These lay hidden just below the surface, the contours of their buried violence recorded in maps placed under lock and key. Locals living in the area were removed, their homes abandoned to the wind, the drifting sand. The entire exercise completed in less than two weeks, and then the soldiers were gone again, leaving nothing but fences forbidding entry to the beaches and hills, grimly rolled barbed wire and razor wire. And other smaller reminders they had been. A baby boy, born nine months later to a local girl, hushed up by his mother's too-quick marriage to the town's new doctor. A scar on the forehead of a local farmhand, inflicted by a tabletop in a brawl.

It was not until 1946 that the soldiers returned to the area to remove the mines. Upon their return there were difficulties, those areas of the sand that were not planted with marram grass having shifted, burying mines deeper, eradicating landmarks. Their maps no longer reliable. A soldier was killed at 10:03 on a Tuesday morning when a mine intended for a Japanese soldier exploded under his foot, shattering his body and flinging it into the air. But the soldiers continued in their work, and the patterns that had taken a fortnight to lay out took nearly three months to unravel.

At the end, the people in the area were told that the job was complete, not to worry. But in 1968 a child holidaying from Sydney stepped on a mine and was maimed and blinded. There was a momentary flurry of excitement, calls for a judicial inquiry, but the panic outside the area quickly subsided, leaving a small boy with his wounds and the locals with a lurking fear of what lay beneath their feet.

*M*idnight, and Claire enters Kurt's room to find David beside Kurt's sleeping form, hands clasped like a supplicant. Her hand on his shoulder makes him start.

I didn't hear you come in.

She smiles. I noticed. It's late.

I know. I'll be in soon.

He's asleep, David. Can't you leave him be till morning?

David hesitates, feeling the force of this silent tug of war. But Claire doesn't budge, and David acquiesces, leaning forward again, pinching the bridge of his nose. Claire watches him impassively.

Headache?

Mmm. He found it, you know, I'm sure of it. The more he says the surer it makes me. And . . .

What?

Finally he shakes his head. Nothing.

But he doesn't have to say it. Claire knows that he has begun to understand he is a part of something he does not understand. Something whose answer lies hidden in the past.

·   ·   ·

KURT IS AWAKE at dawn, his moans waking David and Claire, bringing them into his room at a run. His face is sweating, gray. Claire puts a hand on his face, his skin cold to her touch.

The dosage for his painkillers needs to be increased, she says, he's going to need a drip.

A drip?

He'll still be able to talk, she says without turning around.

Hearing the reproach in her voice David doesn't reply, watching her prep the bag and line, mix the solution. When she looks around for something to hang the drip from he points to a nail on the wall. She looks at it, then him.

Thanks, she says, her face unreadable, handing him the tube. Hold this.

David takes it while Claire opens the plastic cover, connects the cannula to the line. Beside her Kurt is moaning and writhing in the bed. Twice she pinches his arm above the crook of the elbow, then a third, then she relents, swears to herself.

Damn.

What?

I can't get the vein.

David doesn't reply, instead moving forward so he stands right beside her. She turns to him, looks up at him. Her face a mask.

Can I help?

She hesitates momentarily then points at the arm. Hold him in place; it might be easier that way. But be careful, this might be a bit difficult all the same.

Kurt moans and twists as the cannula moves in and out, up and down the arm, searching for a vein in the terrible emaciation of his body. David's hands encircling his arm above and below the elbow without difficulty.

I'll keep him on a constant dose of morphine from here on, Claire says. And the drip will make it easier to keep his liquids up as well.

Finally the cannula takes, its needle point piercing the wall of a vein, and Claire moves quickly, efficiently, sliding the tube into its socket. The morphine spreads in a wave through the old man's body, relaxing him, unknotting the tangle of his features as the pain subsides.

BUT LATER HE is awake again, mumbling and groaning. Twice crying out in pain or anguish. The past seething inside of him.

Nineteen thirty-eight unraveling around us in a shatter. Standing at the back of Fraser and Veronica's wedding, watching them, the backs of their heads. Their lips moving close to kiss at the end of the service. Fraser in a kilt, Veronica in a long white dress. At the reception afterward Veronica stood and sang, her voice full and rich, but I could not bear to listen. Instead I stood and walked quietly to the back. Past the serried ranks of the good and great. Men in dinner suits made in Saville Row, women in dresses worth a month of my wages. No one noticed, Veronica's voice holding the room in a spell of sound. At the door I looked back. Veronica's eyes met mine. Then I turned and kept walking.

Two days later I arrived at Fraser's home, gazed at the splendor of the gifts arrayed in the dining room. Fraser stood behind me, placed a hand on my shoulder.

We missed you the other night, he said. When did you leave?

I looked him in the eye, insolent, angry.

Late, I said at last, I needed some air. And then I smiled and looked at Veronica.

Veronica saw me leave, I'm surprised she didn't tell you.

The moment electric between us, loyalties see-sawing dangerously.

Finally Veronica answered, her face immobile. He's right, I did. I should have told you. There was a pause, and she added, Darling. She refused to look away, holding my gaze. A game had begun.

A SPEECH AT the Historical Society in the winter. July. I caught the train, Fraser arrived by car. Inside the hall it was warm, there were cups of tea from a metal urn. Brewed tannin colored our breath and tongues. The smell of pipe tobacco. Kirkby took the podium to discuss his views on the early European exploration of Australia. As he began speaking, I realized all eyes were on Fraser and me. We were here to be tested, but Kirkby was the one speaking. He started with a joke, and the audience laughed, jostling amusedly in the rows of high-backed wooden chairs, shifting in a comradely unison, men together. I looked down. The chair in front of me bore the University coat of arms on the curved wood of its backrest, painted in outline. At the front Kirkby continued to speak, his voice rising and falling. I barely listened, but I knew from the chuckles around me that what was happening was classic Kirkby. Joke after joke. Suddenly he turned to a board behind him and unveiled a copy of the Dauphin Map, its features rendered in black ink, the illustrations left out for clarity. Over the top, a map of Australia had been superimposed. I felt Fraser stiffen beside me. Kirkby had a pointer, and as he spoke he traced the lines of the two maps. One real, one imaginary, but both representations of a world that may perhaps exist. Laid out like that the two landmasses barely corresponded, Java la Grande hopelessly too far to the west, its outlines a grotesque distortion of the continent's true shape. But as I watched Kirkby's pointer move around the two outlines a second time I looked around frantically, desperate for someone else to see what Kirkby's map was attempting to deny. "There!" I wanted to cry. "Can't you see it? The outline of Cape York, Arnhem Land, the distorted curve of the eastern coast. And if you look closer, you'll find smaller correspondences, islands, bays, reefs!"

But all they heard was Kirkby's voice, all they saw was the manifest discrepancies between the two maps, and as I listened even I found myself beginning to doubt, wondering whether I had been looking too hard. Perhaps I was the one who was mistaken. This fear grew in me as Kirkby spoke, offering alternative explanations, for names, for the patterns of the islands and the bays, words slipping through languages, mutating, changing. He advised us, in the tones of a confidant, of the lack of cartographical rigor applied by mapmakers of the period, their tendency to invent and embellish, their geographical profligacy. All around us the audience listened, rapt. Kirkby's geography lesson had taken them in. When finally he stepped away from the map and slipped his glasses down his nose to examine his papers, his air was that of the friendly schoolmaster, advising his pupils to beware of some foolish temptation, to avoid the tendency to let imagination and desire replace rigor. His eyes did not need to rest on us for us to know his attention was on us. Goaded beyond endurance, as Kirkby must have known he would be, Fraser leapt to his feet, his chair clattering behind him, pushed his way to the end of the row. Heads swiveled, the well-fed faces of the men in the hall taking in the picture of Fraser storming out of this place of calm and rational inquiry. Taking in the image of a man who knew he had been tested and found wanting. I knew immediately that Fraser had made a terrible error of judgment, his pride and anger turning them against us. I looked back to the stage, and Kirkby was standing there with his glasses on the end of his nose, playing at patiently waiting for the disturbance to end, an expression of saddened confirmation on his face. I looked at the men around me, and knew what I must do. Drawing breath I rose and followed Fraser to the back of the hall and out into the night.

By the time I reached the door to the hall he was across the quadrangle, striding through the rain. I glanced down at the profusion of coats and umbrellas by the door, their sheer numbers determining me to run after him, arrest his flight. My shoes splashed and slipped on the wet grass, the rain soaking me before I had gone a dozen steps. I felt like a character in a British film. When I reached him I called his name, but he did not turn, so I seized his arm and wrenched him toward me. His hair hung wetly over his forehead.

Damn him! he shouted. Who does he think he is, trying to make fools of us?

I nodded my head, knowing it was Fraser's behavior that had condemned us. He's an idiot and a charlatan, we both know that, I said. But we can't let him take the advantage.

Take the advantage? It's too late for that. There wasn't a man in there who didn't believe him, we're fucked.

We can prove him wrong, I said. Prove him wrong and us right.

How? By finding the ship? We'll never find the bloody ship.

All we've got to go on is your memories and half a dozen garbled stories! We don't even know we're looking in the right place!

I nodded, slowly, considering. We're looking in the right place, and it's there. We'll find it. And when we do he'll be the one who's fucked.

As I finished speaking our eyes locked, my hand still gripping his arm. Dimly I became aware of my hand clenching his, and released it. The rain kept falling. Finally Fraser looked away, brushed his wet hair out of his face.

Perhaps, he said, perhaps. Then he turned and looked up into the sky, the rain falling in billowing sheets into the glow of the lights around us.

I have to go, he said, Veronica will be waiting, and slowly began to walk away, leaving me there in the rain, alone, knowing that my fate had somehow become linked to this man who had stolen the only thing I wanted more than the ship.

THAT NIGHT KURT'S ramblings stretch out to fill the evening. Alone in the kitchen Claire listens to the soft murmur of his voice, the terrible rasp of his breath. The cough intrudes almost constantly now, the spasms racking his wasted body so badly that she wonders sometimes how David can bear to watch it.

Every day she finds it harder to remain objective about Kurt, to treat him as a patient, and her mistrustfulness disturbs her, taints her. This ever-shifting tension between them. She knows it is open to her to leave, that it would probably be for the best, but she does not. Her feelings for David, her need, both of them make it easier to stay, if only just. But even this closeness to David worries her, doubt niggling and spoiling inside of her. These last months she has realized that she has lost her certainty, her belief in herself. And just as David came to her three years before in need of space, a space to lick his wounds and heal, now she must find her own space to heal. She must find the footing she needs and re-create herself, bend her history into a shape she is able to rule, rather than it ruling her.

As she has so many times before, she takes out paper and begins to write:

Dear Paul
I am not writing to you to remonstrate with you, to tell you that you were wrong in acting as you did. Whatever I felt at the time, the truth is that the right and wrong of it no longer matter—nothing either of us could do would make things how they were again.

As she writes she listens to the words, hears their formality. The distance she has erected between herself and the world. For a long while she sits and regards what she has written. Then continues:

Instead I am writing to tell you where I am. It seems strange to me that two people who were so entwined it was if we shared a heart, a body, could know if the other was waking or sleeping, should now have passed so far out of each other. If I were to take a map of the world I would no longer be able to point at it and say, "There, that is where he is," and know, as sure as I know myself, that I was right. Except that you are still there, somewhere, in that cold northern city. Perhaps you have another lover, a new one, this too I do not know, not any more.
A man has come to me, a man from my past. When we met he was grieving, and there was no room in him for me, so I gave him space, and he gave me—what? Physical comfort? Affirmation? Need? I do not know now, for like so many things that I understood at the time, it

no longer seems clear to me. It is as if there is a line in the sequence of events that have been my life, an equator, and each side is a different world. Before you and after you.

Now things are reversed. I am the one who is broken, in need of a place to recover. There is barely enough room in me for him, but for some reason I have followed him to this place and he cares for me. We have become lovers, but it is a liaison of distance. Perhaps there is a symmetry in this, perhaps there is more.

He is searching for a ship he believes is buried beneath the sand on this coast. He has found an old man who tells him stories which lead him to believe that this old man knows where the ship is. He has also discovered a corpse.

The old man is dying, and I have allowed myself to become his physician, to care for him, but I do not trust him. I think my friend is right in what he believes, but I also think this old man has a price for the secrets he holds, and this he has not yet revealed. My friend's desire has made him vulnerable, and I fear that there is a danger for him in the places he follows this old man. So I listen to him talk, and watch. There is already one corpse here.

It is as if I have been broken apart once, and now am being remade. Not as what I was but as something new. This is not the first time this has happened. When we met, I was shattered and remade, but then it was different. This time it has been a passage through pain. Perhaps this is all life is. A series of breakings and re-formings. Finding new forms in the ruins of the old. But in each new form we retain some of the last, and from you I take sadness, and a memory of who I was when I was with you. Like scars, the ability of smells to reawaken the past, we all carry the past inside and upon us, whatever form we take. The rest: your smell, your voice, I am forgetting, but I take with me the memory of the form I had when I was with you.

In the end I am not writing these words in order to make you feel guilty or responsible for what you have done to me. You did what you needed to do, what was right for you. Rather, I am writing these words to tell you that I understand what it is that you have done, and to say that I understand this process of shattering has engulfed you as well. I am writing this to say that I love you, but that I am perhaps beginning to love another, and that when that happens I will carry you inside me, but it will no longer be the same. And that I hope that you too have found love, or at least a sort of peace with yourself.

Beneath this she signs her name carefully, allowing the strokes of the pen to form its shape precisely. This done she slowly tears the three sheets from the pad and gathers the paper to its center in her hands, crumpling it into a tight ball, as she has so many times before.

MUCH LATER DAVID enters the room, moving quietly in the darkness. She is already asleep, her warmth filling the space. Her breath quiet in the darkness, he finds his way to her, his lips brushing her neck. The rhythm of her breathing breaking.

David?

Shh, it's late.

Is he sleeping?

Mm-hmm.

Your hands are cold.

I'm sorry. You're very warm.

She laughs sleepily, then for a minute, maybe two, there is silence between them. Outside the wind moves through the grass, shapes shifting and scattering in the moonlight.

*T*he past devours everything, snapping at our heels. On the first of November 1755, All Saints' Day, an earthquake struck Lisbon. Its arrival was heralded by an awful roaring not unlike the thunder of an approaching flood, a monstrous sound that burst eardrums and shattered glass in the high windows of the city's churches, and which to the city's terrified inhabitants must have seemed like the trumpets calling out the Day of Judgment. This unnatural thunder followed by an irresistible motion of the earth, which bucked and shook, solid rock liquefying, vast traceries of fissures racing outward, rending and tearing the fabric of the streets. Glass falling like murderous crystal rain. Throughout the ancient city, buildings collapsed in waves, the spired churches and domed palaces tumbling inward, killing the thousands who had fled to them for shelter from the earth's fury.

In the bay, the Sea of Straw receded, forced outward by the frenzied motion of the earth, uncovering the mud and refuse of the harbor floor, while on the banks of the Tagus the ground split asunder, and the Casa da India, the building that had served as the repository for the charts and logs of twelve generations of Portuguese explorers, was swallowed back into the earth.

Finally, as the convulsions began to subside, the waters that had been driven outward returned, sweeping back in to reclaim their proper place, the weight of the water causing the Sea of Straw to break the sea wall and spill into the city, engulfing it. This final act of destruction sweeping thousands of the survivors to their deaths, and drowning thousands more who lay pinned beneath the rubble.

Eventually the waters receded from the streets, leaving in their place the shattered remnants of what was once the great city of Lisbon. The few survivors there were must have stood amid the devastation, looking around themselves in the certain knowledge that this city, which had housed the relics and learning of an empire, was gone, wiped out in a single moment of fury.

In time, of course, Lisbon was rebuilt, more splendid than before, the new city rising on the rubble of the old, its secrets now trodden down by a quarter of a millennia of history, the feet of passersby on the avenues and plazas. The charts and logs of the Portuguese navigators who may or may not have found their way south and east from the Indies to Australia and maybe beyond, lost forever.

The Portuguese Politica do Siglio ensured that all charts and logs returned to Lisbon were housed in the Casa da India. But Mendonça returned first not to Lisbon, but to Goa. And there, the administrative center of Portuguese activity in the east, it is possible these charts and logs were copied by the archivist for safekeeping, to protect their precious contents from the perils of the journey west to Europe.

If so, it is possible that somewhere in the musty chambers of Goa records of Mendonça's expedition and charts of the coasts he followed might have lain hidden, long forgotten; charts that might explain the origins of the Dieppe maps, logs that might record the discovery of the wreck of an earlier expedition cast upon a distant southern shore.

But once again they are denied us; lost, like so many of the records left by the Portuguese, in the hurried and chaotic annexation of Goa by the Indian Government in 1961. Perhaps they were left there, in some lower chamber; perhaps they were returned to Lisbon with the other spoils of colonial conquest. But most likely they were lost. If they ever existed.

*A*fter the night of Kirkby's speech things grew worse. It was as if the Department had closed ranks, excluding us, denying our existence. Even Bill Norman began to avoid us, and although years later he was to tell me he was ashamed of his actions during those months, at the time his was the betrayal I felt most keenly.

Both of us devoted every moment we could spare from our teaching to the search. We would sit in Fraser's office, poring over maps, trying to make sense of the fragments I had retrieved from Goa. His long hands shuffling the papers, smoothing the maps flat, every movement reminding me of her as I imagined those hands on her body, the heroic arch of her sternum, her breasts.

The end when it came was quick, arriving within a fortnight of Kirkby's lecture in the form of a handwritten note summoning us to the Professor's office, the indigo blue of Colmer's fountain pen bright against the paper. Its casual phrasing belying its intent. Fraser brought it to me in the library and stood in front of me, proffering it. I took the paper, read the words. Both of us knowing what this meant.

We walked the linoleum-covered corridor to the Professor's door side by side, not speaking, and it was Fraser who lifted his fist to knock. The Professor's voice came from within, and we entered the book-lined chamber. The room was warmed by a wood fire in one corner, but the Professor himself sat behind his desk. He looked up expectantly as we approached, but when he saw who it was his eyes closed, darkened. Yet his mouth somehow twisted out a smile.

Ah, he said, Fraser, Kurt, come in, sit down.

We crossed the short distance to his desk and took the chairs we were offered. Sitting to attention like children before the headmaster. Once we were seated he spent several seconds arranging the materials on the desk, giving the impression of a busy man. I knew this man, the way he wore his power like a mantle, these tiny games of delay and obstruction used as confirmations, but always so politely, so politely. Finally he pushed his glasses back up his crooked nose (broken years before in a brawl with a Belgian in the Great War and poorly set by an unsympathetic Belgian doctor), leaned back in his chair and steepled his fingers together.

Thank you both for coming, he said, regarding us through his spectacles. When neither of us spoke, he waited before continuing.

I . . . um . . . I heard a story that concerned me very much the other day, he said, his tone regretful, concerned. About an incident at the Historical Society. While Kirkby was speaking.

Again he waited for a reply, but again neither of us was prepared to grant him the pleasure.

I see, he said after another pause. I was rather hoping we would have an opportunity to discuss this in order to reach a conclusion that was satisfactory to all of us. But I see that's not going to be possible. Much as it pains me to have to do this I don't see that your actions leave me any choice. Fraser, I'm afraid there will be no further support for your research; I'm not prepared to allow the Department to continue lending its name to such an ill-conceived and historically suspect venture. Obviously I can't stop you continuing to pursue it in your own time and at your own expense, but you should be aware that if you choose to do so any interference it may cause to your responsibilities here will be looked upon as a dereliction of your duties and treated accordingly.

Throughout this speech Fraser sat in silence, his eyes not moving from Colmer's face. And while his silent pride might not have deflected Colmer from this exercise of power, it was enough to ensure that having finished, Colmer turned his attention to me, Fraser's junior, with relief.

Seligmann, he said, I suggest you apply yourself to finding a position at some other institution.

Appalled, I opened my mouth to protest, but Fraser placed a hand on my arm, restraining me, and then turned his attention back to Colmer, who at last seemed cowed by Fraser's silence, and looked away from us, removing his glasses to massage the bridge of his nose.

I will of course supply you with references of the first order, and assist you in every way I can, but your influence here is increasingly troublesome. Shaking his head he turned back to me.

In the end what it comes down to is my responsibility for

the reputation of this Department. I just can't have my staff pursuing personal research that makes the rest of us look foolish.

I sat, trembling, my stomach churning. I was to be executed but Fraser pardoned? The Professor finished and sat waiting for a reply. Finally Fraser pushed back his chair and rose. Dignified to the end. Without speaking he walked slowly to the door and opened it, waiting for me. I began to stand, afraid my legs would buckle beneath me. At the door Fraser allowed me to pass, then pulled the door closed with a click.

In the corridor outside I kept walking, trying to focus. Dimly I was aware of Fraser behind me. A hand on my shoulder. Fraser's voice.

I'm sorry.

I nodded. For a moment Fraser did not speak, as if he were considering something. Numbly I realized there was more to this than I thought. You knew?

He shook his head. No, not exactly.

Something in the way he said it told me he was lying. A quiver of anger cracked my voice as I demanded he tell me what he meant. For several moments Fraser said nothing. When he finally answered, his voice was quiet, the pride that had sustained both of us in Colmer's office gone, replaced by an edge of shame.

Colmer caught me in the corridor the morning of Kirkby's speech and told me he was concerned about the direction my work was taking. When I asked him to give me a reason he said he was concerned about the Department's reputation. I told him any harm that might have occurred was the result of research being used for political ends by people like Kirkby.

And . . .

Fraser swallowed, looking around guiltily. Then he said that things might go easier for me if I were to let you go. I refused.

I didn't know what to say. Why didn't you tell me?

I don't know. It didn't seem right.

A wave of nausea washed through me. I have to go, I said, and walked away, leaving him there, standing in the middle of the corridor, his hands outstretched. I needed to get away, to think. Fraser had defended me, had refused to abandon me for a reward I knew he sought. But why had he failed to tell me, to warn me? And why was it now me who was to be cast out instead of him?

WHEN CLAIRE ENTERS from the beach David is asleep in the chair by Kurt's bed. His chin resting on the thin rise of his chest. Kurt's breathing slow and shallow. Each breath rasping. A book has fallen from David's hands and lies on the floor, its cover folded under itself. She crosses to him and kneels at his side. Her breath on his cheek. For a second she almost believes she could press her ear to his and hear the whispers of his dreams. An unknown inner world, the hollow world of the mind, the self an illusory sun in the center.

He is dreaming of her.

There is a distance between them they cannot bridge. In their bed their bodies sleep touching, tangled, and warmth passes between them like love. Yet here she sits with her face so close to his that she can feel his breath, smell the scent of his skin, and still he is a mystery to her. He is unknowable. And she knows that she is likewise an unknown country. Sometimes in their bed as they fuck she feels him inside her, moving,

moving, shedding the outer layers of what he is until they are both naked and her body closes around the outpouring of his, her hands cradling the weight of his head, his mouth closed on the heel of her hand. But even then he remains separate. Claire knows that what she is asking for is certainty, and that it is impossible, but her need is not a rational one. There is something temporary, transient about this bond between them. The love of people afraid of themselves.

*A*fter the meeting with the Professor my departure was swift and certain. A meeting of the Department a week later made it official. That morning I sat in my room staring at the papers I had copied in Goa, not seeing them, waiting for the sound of feet outside. Then Fraser was at the door. Entering without knocking, not speaking. He stood behind me, but I didn't turn to face him.

It's done.

When?

At the end of term.

Is that all?

A hesitation. Yes. He was lying, I was sure of it, but I said nothing.

I found work with the Workers' Education Association, teaching history to men with rough hands. I worked three nights of the week, and tutored the children of friends of Fraser's in schoolroom history in the afternoons. Somehow I eked out a living. But still Fraser and I continued our work whenever we got the chance, and for a second time I swallowed my pride, telling myself it wasn't Fraser or Veronica who mattered, but the ship. Always the ship.

Slowly though, winter became spring, then summer. Classes ended, then exams, and suddenly Fraser and I were freed into a space large enough to resume the search. This time there was only to be the two of us, like amateurs, pacing the hills in search of the ship. We arrived on a Wednesday, the car laden with equipment. It had been two years since we had been here, but the hills looked the same, the low scrubby growth of the grass, the white pools and eddies of sand, but it had taken on a new mantle of significance, the words of Quiroga's journal echoing in the space of air, of water, of sand. Echoing down the outstretching years.

That first day we walked together from the shack to the beach and northward, toward the river and the headland. We climbed the rough hill in the evening light, the waves and the wind whispering beneath us. On the bluff we gazed out eastward, over the vast ocean, great mountains of cloud heaving across its rim. The three spired islands reared skyward, their peaks whitened with bird shit as if scattered with snow. The birds coiling and shifting in banks as the evening came, brawling for an aerie in the broken rocks. Lower down, the barking of the seals. Together we stood on the bluff, the wind whistling cold on our cheeks. Both of us knew we had found the right place.

*T*onight the wind is cold, whistling in over the ocean. The dark bellies of clouds scrape the sea, the air chill in the early dark. Kurt sleeps without speaking. Alone in their room David and Claire slide silently into books, losing themselves in other worlds. Claire's shoulders rising and falling with her breath, her forehead puckering between the eyes as she reads. They sit like this for two hours, maybe longer, the wind rattling the tin roof, leaking through the shack's ramshackle walls. Claire moves to draw the blanket she has passed around her shoulders closer, leaning back against the wall beside the bed. The movement stirs David from his book, and he sits, watching her. She turns a page, slowly, her bottom lip pulled in in concentration or concern. David feels a pain inside him as he watches her, an intimacy. He wants her to remain as she is, private, close, and he restrains himself from reaching out and touching her, from placing a hand on her shoulder. He sits watching her for several minutes before she notices and turns to him smiling.

What? she asks, her voice soft, quizzical. The blanket wrapped high around her shoulders.

David shakes his head. Nothing.

A pause for a moment, then she smiles quietly, her eyes returning to her book. David continues to watch, the moment unbroken. But his attentions have disturbed her concentration.

What are you looking at? she demands, laughing.

You.

Again she laughs, then reaches across toward him, one arm supporting the arch of her body, the other holding the blanket at her throat. Why?

I just am. Talk to me.

What about?

Anything. We've been in this room together for two weeks and we still barely know anything about each other.

Two weeks isn't very long.

It can be. Tell me about Paul. What happened?

Paul. The word a statement, a volume of inner knowledge inscrutable to the outsider.

There isn't much to tell.

You don't have to, I just—

No, you're right, I should tell you. It's just not easy; talking about it.

I'm sorry.

Don't be. It's simple really. I loved him, and he said—I suppose he wasn't lying—he loved me. So I went with him to Copenhagen, to the university where he was working. Everyone thought I was mad, leaving here, my job, my friends, just to follow a man. She pauses, smiling ruefully. Except you.

David blushes. Hmm. My advice wasn't the best, was it?

No, but you were right. If we want something we should follow it. What's the old adage? "Better to have loved and lost than never to have loved at all"? It's true. But when it goes wrong it can consume you.

Anyway, after we arrived he began to change. I could feel it. Then one night he didn't come home, and—well you know the old story.

David nods. And you?

I railed and ranted, begged him to stay. But he wouldn't. At least he made it quick, clean. Better that way. And I came home to lick my wounds.

And now?

I'm alive. For the last year that's been enough. Love's a treacherous place, and a dangerous one, it's little wonder people go mad. For a long time I was afraid I would come unraveled, just fall apart, but I guess somewhere I began to heal.

And from here?

She shrugs. There are tears in her eyes.

Finally David reaches out, touches her cheek with the tips of his fingers. I'm sorry.

Claire turns to his hand, his pale skin. So am I, she says, rubbing her face into his palm.

THE SAND IS never still, never quiet. Always shifting, restless, passing forms down its fluid motions. Everything is lost in its wandering. This land unrecognizable as what it was. Two hundred years ago these were long low hills, a tangle of native scrub twisting its long roots deep into the sand, anchoring it, so that it seethed beneath the dark green mat of the scrub, breaking through in crests and washes, spilling in rivulets between the imprisoning roots. Then the Europeans came, with their sheep and cattle and goats, and drove them through here, building their low houses from the sandstone along the edge of the hills, allowing their beasts to strip the grass to the roots, ringbark the low trees, until the scrub faltered and died. Ignorant of the rhythms of the land, they released the sand from its moorings, and driven by the wind, it washed outward, spreading, swallowing up farms and roads and pastures, driving the families that had settled in this harsh land back. Eventually the government bowed to pressure to take action to contain the sand's spread, planting marram grass in strips, the grass spreading quickly, like a cancer, binding the sand in great hummocked ridges. This new landscape covering the old, subsuming it, burying all that had been far beneath itself.

*W*ith love, as with all things, there are stages, points of transition. The first meeting; the point of awakening; the deepening; contact. Sometimes they come easily, sometimes their progress is slow and circular. Ending only where they began, like a return home from war. With the two of us the circles turned inward, a spiral toward a point neither of us could see. Not then, at least. The first point, two days after their wedding. Then for six months our interactions became a constantly shifting web of codes and deceptions. Veronica always one step behind Fraser, his shoulder obscuring her. Neither of us touching. Neither of us needing to speak the danger that was closing in on us. We had become players in a game, which, like all games, was just a proving ground for war.

Then in January 1939 Veronica arrived here. Fraser and I returned from the dunes one afternoon to find her waiting in the shack. She had opened a bottle of beer and was drinking it from a tin mug. The room smelled of cigarette smoke. We entered, and her unexpected presence startled both of us, making us jump. She laughed her deep throaty laugh at our discomfiture. Fraser recovered in time to turn to her and exclaim her name. She half stood as he stepped toward her, and as she did I saw the way her movements were telegraphed as if through deep water, and realized she was drunk. Fraser either failed to notice or didn't want to see, and kissed her cheek.

What are you doing here? he asked, turning back so that he half faced me, thereby including me in the conversation.

Veronica shrugged. I was bored, so I thought I'd come down and see this place you two seem to spend so much time talking about for myself, she said, then laughed again.

The whole time I said nothing, standing back, watching her. I was sure now she was drunk, and wondered whether she had been drunk when she arrived or whether instead she had been sitting here drinking while we were away in the dunes.

Fraser put his hands behind his back, swinging his hips forward as he spoke.

Oh well that's splendid, he said, his smile creasing his face. We could do with a bit of company for a while, couldn't we, Kurt?

He looked at me expectantly, but I just nodded, finally allowing my eyes to stray away from Veronica, who was staring at me intently.

Yes, I said. Splendid.

Veronica smiled, but it was a vicious smile, malign. I had never seen her drunk like this before, and it frightened me. I knew my voice had sounded false after Fraser's cheerful tones, but I didn't care, not even enough to keep talking to save the room from the silence that fell on it. Finally Veronica spoke.

Why don't the two of you sit down, get yourselves a beer? I knew this voice, it was the voice of Veronica when she was with actors, a coarser, rougher Veronica. I wondered if Fraser knew this voice, this person. I was suddenly aware of Veronica as a creature of shifting masks, a person who took on guises as a defense, never showing what lay beneath. Roughly she pulled a chair out from beside her.

Here, she said. Sit down.

I looked at Fraser, and realized he was confused, so I took the proffered chair and sat, hoping this might calm her, help disguise her drunkenness. Once I was seated she turned to Fraser.

Is there more beer out the back somewhere? she asked, smiling disingenuously. Darling?

Fraser nodded, as if startled out of a reverie. Hmm, yes, there is. You'd like some more?

Veronica nodded. Suddenly she was the woman Fraser clearly knew again, clean, elegant, kind, and her return reassured him.

I'll get it then, he said, and turned to leave. Kurt, he said, at the door, you'd like a bottle? I nodded without speaking.

As Fraser left the room, Veronica reached into her bag, produced a silver cigarette case, and removed a cigarette from it. She did not offer me one, but instead lit hers, and deeply inhaled. She smoked the cigarette without a holder, like a working man. Or an actor.

You're drunk, I whispered at her. She shrugged, exhaling as she did, and allowing the blue-gray smoke to coil out her nostrils in long, sensuous knots. And when did you start smoking?

A while back, she said, affecting disinterest. Why?

But your voice . . . I said, and she shook her head, laughing.

My voice? I'm not a singer any more, Kurt, remember? I gave it up. Again she exhaled smoke. So what I do doesn't really matter, does it? Her voice was hard and cold.

As she finished she glared at me, as if a gauntlet was being thrown down, and I looked back, frightened. My heart beat loudly in my ears. And before I could answer Fraser returned with bottles of beer, smiling his stupid smile. Smiling his stupid, naive, gentle smile, like an innocent walking into a minefield.

FOR THE REST of the evening we sat there at the table in the kitchen, drinking beer and watching Veronica smoke cigarette after cigarette. As she finished each one she would reach into the silver cigarette box and produce another, her eyes turning to Fraser as she did, offering him an unspoken challenge that he refused to meet. She drank more and more, but never lost her composure. The dark cloud of her mood spreading outward through the room. Fraser talked compulsively, trying to fill the space between Veronica's and my words, to dispel the pall of her mood, but his attempts were just sucked into the silence. Finally the conversation ran out completely, and for several minutes the three of us sat in the room in silence. Then Veronica ground out a half-smoked cigarette in the plate she had eaten from.

Well, that's enough for me tonight, I'm off to bed, she said to Fraser, pointedly not meeting my eyes.

Fraser pushed his half-drunk glass of beer away from himself, sliding his chair outward. You won't get any argument from me, I'm buggered. He turned to me. You don't mind having the sleep-out, do you?

I shook my head. No, don't be silly. You two just go to bed.

As I spoke Veronica rose from the table, unfolding herself to her full height. She swayed slightly, then fixed me with an unreadable look.

Well, see you in the morning I suppose, she said, then turned, moving toward the bedroom slowly, disguising her drunkenness. Fraser smiled, almost as if embarrassed.

Perhaps we'll start a little later tomorrow? he asked.

I nodded. Sure.

Fraser pushed his hair back from his face, and for a moment I saw that his beautiful blond hair was graying.

Good night then, he said, and turned to follow Veronica.

As they left I pushed my beer away and sank forward, burying my head in my arms. Alone in the kitchen I heard the sounds of them moving quietly around the bedroom, the squeak of the bedsprings, and later, wrapped in my thin blanket, I heard Veronica cry out, the sound echoing through my body, even as I wondered whether it was for Fraser's benefit or mine.

*T*wo more days pass. The wind shifts northward, growing stronger before guttering out, collapsing into gusts and squalls as storm clouds mass to the south. On the second day the air becomes charged with static electricity as thunder rumbles out of sight. A cold wind suddenly breaks free, leading in on a wall of rain, pounding the sand into a shifting liquid that dries each drop even before the next can fall. Every drop exploding upward in a puff of sand as the sand splashes out from the drop. The wind building until the rain falls almost horizontally. In the shack Kurt thrashes and moans, constantly pulling at his sheets, trying to drag his ravaged form upright. Lost inside an inner storm, his words confused and meaningless, everything around him producing dread and fear and confusion. Claire and David sit with him, trying to calm him as the wind beats and rattles on the tin roof, the thin walls. The shack like a fragile shell on the lip of an ocean that has returned to claim the land as its own. At eight o'clock there is an explosion of lightning, shattering the air of the shack, which lasts almost ten seconds, then a rumble of thunder from directly overhead that begins even before the lightning has guttered out. Claire looks at David, who is pressing down on Kurt's struggling chest with both hands, trying to keep him there in the bed. The lights in the room flicker and die, and in the sudden darkness, the thunder shaking the house, Kurt cries out one word, his voice rising above the thunder's tumult. Veronica!

AFTER I LOST her it was as if things had come unraveled. I carried her photograph with me into the jungle, folded across the center. At nights I would take it out and unfold it, but there was no need, her face, the contours of her body came to me unbidden, whenever I closed my eyes. They say sculptors can look at a block of marble and see a shape within it: I had become like a stone, her form written within me, unseen, untouchable, but there, inescapably there.

But that week, alone with her and Fraser in this house, the two of us circled each other, wary, frightened. In the days we worked, measuring, plotting, trying to tie down the shifting pattern of the dunes, the shoal of grass that we knew would mark the leaking nutrients of the wood. In the evenings we talked and drank, Veronica's presence charging the air in this small house so that it crackled, electric. Veronica hung off Fraser, constantly daring me with her eyes and manner. In the night I would lie in the quiet house and hear their breathing as they slept, imagine her cool hand on my body, but then, in the cold light of the morning, this new Veronica who had no use for me would return, her brittle anger like a slap.

The night before she left the three of us walked together on the beach. Fraser, the tallest of us, in the middle. Veronica took the seaward side, and I struggled in the softer sand. We walked toward the water's edge. The moon was full and the water burned with the light of billions of tiny creatures, the waves rising out of the water's mass in softly glowing walls, as the water reared upward in the moonlight and exposed its luminescent belly to the air. At the ocean's edge we stood in a ragged line, not speaking, then we turned and walked back up the sand to sit just above the waterline. The surf boomed in the night air. Fraser turned to us and asked if we wanted to walk on as far as the headland with him. I shook my head, and turned to Veronica. A moment of shifting possibilities, then she shook her head.

No, I'll stay here thanks, she said. Fraser nodded.

I'll be back soon, he said, walking away into the darkness. In the moonlight the air of the beach was misty with the spray from the surf, and as it receded his form wavered and vanished into the night like a ghost.

For a long while the two of us sat there alone on the beach in silence. Our eyes ahead, over the sea, not upon each other. The feeling between us was strange, as if in Fraser's sudden absence the violence and anger were gone.

I was reluctant to speak, afraid I would shatter this temporary stillness between us, but finally I asked. Why did you come?

She didn't answer straightaway, instead sitting forward, wrapping her arms around her legs. Her chin butting her knees in a slow rhythm. Seconds passed, and I began to wonder whether she had heard my question, then she answered.

I don't know.

Was it to see him or me? As I spoke I regretted my ques-

tion, fearful that I had asked too much, and that this temporary truce might collapse, but when she answered her voice was
still low and calm.

Does it matter?

I nodded. Yes. To me at least.

I'm not sure. Even if it were you I wanted to see, nothing
would change, I'd still be married. To him.

I know, but—

No buts. It's my bed, I have to lie in it.

I moved toward her, extending a hand to her shoulder but
then letting it fall. It doesn't have to be like this, I said, almost
pleading. You could leave him.

She shook her head. No, not that.

Why not?

I couldn't, it'd kill him.

What about you?

I'll survive; I have to. As she said this she looked up and
away, and I realized she was weeping.

Do you love him?

She shook her head, then shrugged convulsively. I wanted to
reach out, to touch her, but something held me back.

Maybe, but not . . . not like this, not . . .

Like me?

She shook her head. It's more complicated than that.

I felt my stomach turn, and realized my throat was thick
and full. Afraid to speak unless I too began to weep, I stared
ahead, willing my tears to pass. Finally Veronica spoke again.

Please, she said, can we not talk about this, not now.

I swallowed. If not now, then when?

She lifted her shoulders, then lowered them. Please, Kurt . . .

Hearing the desperation in her voice I relented. It was a long time before either of us spoke again. Veronica drew out a cigarette and flicked the lighter she kept in her bag. The orange light lit her face.

You smoke too much, I said, regretting the tone in my voice instantly. She turned to me, the light from the lighter falling away from her face as the end of the cigarette flared in the new dark.

I know, but I can stop whenever I want.

You drink too much as well.

Jesus! she spat. Who do you think you are?

It doesn't matter who I am, you do. It frightens me.

Does it? Well good, because it sure as hell scares me as well.

Then stop.

Yeah, sure.

Stop while you still can.

Her voice was softer now, weary rather than angry. Fuck off, Kurt.

I laughed and she turned to me, bristling again.

What?

That's the first time I've heard you sound like yourself all week.

Swearing? She chuckled. That'd be right.

I thought she was about to say more, but then Fraser appeared out of the darkness, almost upon us. The next morning she was gone.

VI

The Secret Journey

Beyond the three parts of the world there is a fourth part across the interior ocean, unknown to us on account of the heat of the sun, in whose bounds the Antipodes are fabulously said to live.

ISIDORE,
Etymologies

*T*hroughout history, the idea of the southern world has haunted Europeans. Its nature, its very existence a reflection of their dreams and desires; its absence a blank space into which they cast themselves, imagining a world that was bounded only by their imaginations, their fears.

Five centuries before the birth of Christ, the disciples of Pythagoras imagined the world into five parts; two frigid, two temperate, and between them, dividing them impassably, a torrid equator. This division was a consequence of the Pythagorean belief that at the root of all things lay numbers, eternal, unchanging, their properties and relations defining the cruder world of the senses, and just as music is mathematical so too were the harmonies of numbers expressed in the symmetries of the universe. Five was the number of marriage and unity, the sum of the first odd and even numbers, the first two primes, and this unity was itself contained in the contours of the world. And so, while the Pythagoreans could only guess at the nature of the unknown southern land, its existence was indisputable, made certain by the existence of their own. This imaginary land balancing the weight of the known.

Yet between these two lands lay the equator, a region the ancients after Pythagoras believed so hot as to be impassable. In the fifth century A.D., Macrobius wrote of a *perusta inhabitabilis*, a place so hot as to be uninhabitable by men, dividing the northern and southern *temperata habitabilis*. But to early Christian theologians this idea was a heresy, demanding as it did a land of men not born of Adam and ignorant of the Gospel. For another eight hundred years Christian theology kept European minds turned inward, contemplating the spiritual relations that defined their imaginative realms, the political squabbling and intrigue that divided their material realms, the southern lands fading again, forgotten by Europeans who were made uneasy by its possibility, dubious of its accessibility.

And then in 1295 the Venetian merchant Marco Polo returned from his second journey to the court of Kublai Khan. A businessman rather than an explorer, Polo saw no reason to record his travels, preferring instead to return to his business, until three years later war broke out between his native Venice and Genoa. Imprisoned by the victorious Genoans, Polo began to dictate his story to his fellow prisoner, Rustichello of Pisa, and within the pages of his dictation gave shape to kingdoms that thrived deep within the mythical equatorial region. These kingdoms, Lochac, Pentam, Ciaban, and others, were realms of wealth and grandeur, populated by men who worshiped not the Christian God but idols, whose ways and laws were so fantastical as to be scarcely believable, but who, regardless of their ways, were men, not monsters, and their world was not an inferno but a place of riches and plenty. And south of them lay more, said Polo; south lay Isles of Gold.

Were you to try and trace Polo's journeys on a modern map the task would prove impossible. The lands he described are unlocatable, the kingdoms he spoke of cannot be identified with any certainty, their ways and natures not tallying with the history we have painstakingly assembled. Why this is so we do not know. Perhaps Polo's memories were confused or embroidered. Perhaps the stories he told Rustichello were only half truths, a mongrel assembly of stories and conjectures based on information Polo gathered at the borders of his family's trading empire, which extended as far east as modern Turkey, and Polo himself never ventured into the lands he described. Or perhaps they were no more than the lyrical dreams of a restless mind, fueled by avarice and desire. Whatever the truth it is unlikely we will ever know the answers to these questions for sure. What is certain is that Polo turned his mind outward and saw wealth and opportunity, and regardless of whether the tales he told were his own, corrupted assemblages of the reports of others, or mere fantasy, he had taken this vision and painted a shimmering line around the unknown arc of the planet, his stories beginning to dissipate the fabled heat of the equator.

But for the sailors, kings, and merchants of Europe, the world they inhabited was still a narrow one, a slender ribbon of half-truth and conjecture snaking from Greenland to Norway to the courts of the Khan in the mythical East. To the north their world was bounded by the frozen wastes of the Arctic. To the south lay the vastness of the Sahara, the kingdom of the mythical Prester John and the perils of Cape Bojador. And westward lay the shifting enormity of the Atlantic. It was to be almost two centuries until Columbus would sail west in search of a passage to China and stumble upon the borders of the New World, and the ocean still formed an impassable barrier to the European mind. What lay beyond the natural barriers to the south and the west was a mystery. Perhaps there were lands of unimaginable strangeness populated by men who wore their faces on their chests, or backward, or carried them beneath their arms, lands prowled by creatures hideous of shape and countenance that feasted upon the flesh of humans. Perhaps there were kingdoms populated by men and women who worshiped idols and demons and were ignorant of the word of the Christian God. Or perhaps there was nothing at all, the ocean beyond the lonely Azores stretching out to infinity, the lands of the Sahara growing drier and lonelier until all life ended. Or worse, perhaps the end of the known world was more than a border of knowledge, and beyond the ocean lay nothing and nowhere. Sailors imagined a point not far beyond the treacherous waters of Bojador where the ocean fell away into nothingness, giving this terrible nonplace a name that has the ring of finality and despair deserved of such a place: Abyssus Abyssum. The end of all things. The Abyss. The educated imagined a more figurative boundary, assured by the knowledge that the world was round; theologians imagining a limit to the spread of the Gospel (*a quae Deos deu por termo do habitação dos homens,* wrote de Barros; "that which God gave for the time of man on earth"); others imagined the Sahara to be the northernmost limit of the uninhabitable equatorial region predicted by Pythagoras, Macrobius and Isidore. What lay beyond was a matter of debate. Or faith.

But the stories of Marco Polo and the growing trade with India and Asia, coupled with the knowledge guarded by the Arabic world that had begun to filter back into Europe after centuries of animosity, increasingly demanded these limits be tested. Land routes imposed restrictions the Europeans could not afford, the winding lines of trade preyed upon by brigands, capricious kings and greedy middlemen, their vicissitudes meaning pepper frequently cost more than its weight in gold, silk more again. What was needed was an ocean route to the East.

A journey of such magnitude had never before been attempted, but in 1419 the young Prince Henry, fourth son of King João, took his court to Sagres, the westernmost point on the European coast. Here, on this mighty headland, the young Henry read and studied, succored by the knowledge of geometry and navigation that was slowly returning to Europe from the Arab world, redrawing the maps in physical, not spiritual terms. The Middle Ages were waning; Jerusalem was no longer the center of the world; and as the maps began to be redrawn Henry began to see how the dangers of Cape Bojador might be passed and such a route be found. With the arrogance of those who wield power, he devised a plan to pass Bojador, not by navigating its dangers but by avoiding them. Instead of sailing along the coast, plotting courses by landmarks and memory, Henry ordered his captains to sail westward, into the ocean, where their only hope of return would be faith in their charts and lodestones, and then south, so that their routes

described a semicircle, returning to the coast of Africa beyond
Bojador. And if they did not return, he would order more ships
out, with directions to take their arc further, and if they failed,
further again, until the coast was regained safely, and eventually, a route to the lands of the East and their riches discovered.

Henry's captains were successful, and slowly, year by year,
the Portuguese crept south, passing the equator in 1473, then
south to the Congo, and south again, to Cape Cross, their land-
ings gentle concussions in the muffled thunder of Africa's
history. In 1487 Bartolomeu Diaz reached the southern
boundaries of this known world and continued onward. The
winds blew well for him, and he passed out of sight of land,
coasting ever southward, until caution drew him to turn east,
then northward, and land reappeared off the bow. Transcribed
on a map, this arc had taken his tiny vessel outward from one
side of the Cape of Good Hope and around into the Indian
Ocean, without the knowledge of Diaz. He named the place he
had landed Mossel Bay and, under threat of mutiny, returned
the way he had come, but his voyage had shown the way for
the next wave of Portuguese conquests, which were to be eastward from the Cape, to India, Java, and beyond. But more
importantly he had cast the Portuguese vision of the world
onto the blank space he had passed into, however briefly, transforming the lands to the south into reflections of the lust for
wealth, conquest and trade that was to drive this next vanguard of discovery.

The first time happened almost by accident. We were alone in their sitting room, talking. She laid a hand on my arm to emphasize a point. Suddenly I leaned forward, placed my mouth on hers. One kiss, then she tore herself away. Her lipstick smeared. Neither of us could remember what we had been talking about. You taste of whisky, she said.

The next time was more calculated. Summer 1938–39. That long hot summer when the world seemed poised on the brink. Echoes in the hot nights of English accents crackling on the radio, warning, warning. Caution becoming concern. A dinner at Fraser and Veronica's. All night opposite each other, the air pregnant. Hardly listening to the chatter. Later, the others inside, the sound of a record spilling from the open doors. I went outside to smoke a cigarette. Knowing she would follow. The harbor below, the green damp of the vegetation. Lights of boats on the water. She appeared next to me, almost as tall as I was, a deep green dress wrapped around her.

You know what we're doing, don't you? she said.

I nodded. Does he?

No. It would break his heart.

I said nothing.

Do you hate me? she asked.

I shrugged. Perhaps. Does it matter?

Her face stared out over the water, betraying nothing. Maybe. But there's no going back after this.

I know.

A ship blew its horn in the distance. Her lips on mine, her body against my skin. Something frightening, primitive about our hunger. Fraser's laugh echoing across the balcony. A week later I woke and cried out her name in the darkness. I had dreamed of her lost and burning. And of myself, searching in vain.

AFTER THAT IT happened often. A network of lies and half-truths to conceal us. Dressing and undressing in hotel rooms, in my bedroom, in their home. Hungry for each other; desperate couplings in hallways and empty rooms, in spare rooms at parties. Making love in an arbor in the Botanic Gardens in a sudden downpour, our clothes sodden, plastered to our skins, our mouths burning, her breasts and clavicle open to the water and the sky, her nipples hard under my lips, our skin alive like the rain, the smell of the flowers and the bark and the rain and the mulch filling our heads.

The sweat on our bodies in the heat of the Sydney summer.

LATE IN THE afternoon David leaves Kurt's side, walks the twenty feet to the front door and lets himself out into the light. The sun shrouded by clouds, the light soft and diffuse. Outside he lets his breath out in a long sigh. He stands uncertainly, unable to sit, too nervous to move away, his body coiling tight, twisting in on itself. He feels the need to move fast, run, release the contortions within him in violent movement. But the violence inside him eats its own tail, turning him inward, making such a release impossible, so he just hovers here, nervous, agitated, a fuse burning inside of him, until finally he sinks to the ground on the edge of the veranda and sits, his arms cradling his body.

He is still there half an hour later when Claire returns, walking over the dunes toward him. She smiles when she sees him and waves, and he raises a feeble hand in reply. Concerned, she hastens her step to his side.

David?

Hi, he says, looking up at her, his arms still locked tight around himself. From her vantage point above him he looks like a man on the point of breaking, filled with a pain he cannot contain or rationalize.

What is it? she asks, kneeling by his side. Is something wrong?

When he doesn't answer, she has a sudden sense of premonition.

Is it Kurt, is he . . . ?

David shakes his head. No, he's fine . . . or at least he's no worse, it's just . . .

Her hand on his shoulder. Just what?

David pulls away, his confusion palpable. He's dying, he says, the words coming in a rush now. And I'm still no closer to finding it. And if he dies without telling me, then . . . then I'm not likely to ever find it. We'll never get the money to come looking again. The museums think we're chasing phantoms anyway, and without the ship itself we've no hard evidence. Just hearsay and relics that we can't prove to be what I'm sure they are. As he finishes his voice trails off.

But you've known this for years.

I'm so close now, though, I can feel it, but he just talks round and round and . . . and I'm scared he'll just slip away any time now and I'll never know. He turns to her, his eyes pleading. And if he goes then the ship might as well be gone forever.

Claire reaches for him again, feeling his mood subsiding, strokes his hair.

No, you'll just be back where you were before this all began.

David allows himself to be drawn to her. I know. That's what frightens me.

*O*ur bodies like a cipher, a code, a litany of tiny injuries trailing clues across our skin. Her nails cutting into my skin, her white teeth breaking the skin on my shoulder. A yellowing bruise circling the incision of the bite. Sometimes our loving was like a punishment, as if each of us were trying to destroy the other, to eradicate all traces of them from the earth. Blood in my mouth, the back of my hand against her arching cheek. As if this love could be burned to the ground, erased, expunged, destroyed. As if we could be released. Both of us knew it could not last. How she hid the marks from Fraser I don't know. Maybe she would cloak herself in shadow, or hold his gaze and never let his eyes stray below her neck. The time I blackened her eye she told him she had been hit by a ball at tennis. He must have known she was lying. All that summer this thing inside us spread like a disease.

KURT'S VOICE IS low, the words indistinct. Claire is beside David tonight, watching, listening. A distance between them. She is afraid for David, the game she is watching frightening her. His body growing thinner, more angular. Dark bruises pooling beneath his eyes. His need for the ship palpable. In their bed he hardly sleeps, his body a tangle of sharpness, coiled emotion. Their lovemaking has an urgency that is new, a need in the way that he cradles her head as she rides him, as his eyes roll back as they come. The frailty of his neck and clavicle, his throat exposed like a penitent. Sometimes she wants to shake him, to take his hand and drag him away from this place. The shifting sand and water like a sinkhole, a graveyard where lives vanish in a flicker of the changing light, matter rendered insubstantial as shadows by the past. The lines of gravity passing through the hidden ship, drawing them inward on a slowly turning tide. David looks at Kurt and sees a way forward. Claire looks at him and sees a drowning man who will take the hand David offers and pull him down with him.

THEN IN THE winter of 1939 the war began, and everything changed. Not immediately, and at first not discernibly, but things were different, and the more time went by, the more the change became apparent. An expectancy in the air, an atmosphere of heightened excitement, like the mood before a race or a fight, an exultant giddiness that could change quick as lightning from sudden love to an ugly, vicious violence, brutal and cruel. Young men were the most affected, and in the trams and on the trains, in the streets and in the pubs they talked of little else. Who was joining up, when they were going. Who they were leaving behind. Uniforms began to appear in the streets, groups of soldiers roamed the Cross, Bondi, Manly, their uniforms releasing them from the everyday world that had once contained them so they could hoot and holler and drink and shout. For the first few months it was almost like a game, if you could ignore the looks in the eyes of the older men, the women with the shadows in their faces who remembered the last time this game was played; if you never saw or spoke to the men and the women in their shabby dark suits who began to filter into the city, bringing with them tales of rape and murder and worse, telling their stories in their halting, heavily accented English. But then the voices on the radio, the stories in the newspapers, grew darker as France collapsed and what little remained of the Allied forces fled across the Channel. The first Australian troops began to fall, and slowly, the chill reality spread outward. War.

Fraser and I joined up in 1940, he as a lieutenant, I as a second lieutenant. We were trained for six weeks at Victoria Barracks, then left waiting, on an indefinite leave, waiting for the call or telegram to say we were going. Veronica raged at us, telling us there was no need, that there were others who could go but she needed us here, with her. Alive. But Fraser said he had to, he couldn't live with himself if he didn't feel he was doing his bit. I felt the same, the need to help. But I was afraid.

*T*en years after Diaz rounded the Cape of Good Hope, Vasco da Gama set forth from Lisbon to seek out trade and conquest. In 1497 his expedition rounded the Cape and anchored at Mossel Bay, as Diaz had. Then, once again, the ships sailed out of the known world and into the realm of supposition and rumor. His ships made north and east, up the coast of Africa to Mozambique and Malindi, where da Gama obtained the services of the celebrated Muslim navigator, Ahmed ibn Majid. The Arabian nations having already established intricate trading relationships throughout the Indian Ocean, Majid was able to provide da Gama with their knowledge, and guide his ships eastward to India and Calicut, where da Gama obtained a cargo of spices and then turned homeward, returning to Lisbon two years after he departed.

The spices obtained by da Gama's expedition were enough to whet the considerable appetites of the Portuguese. Pepper and cinnamon were as valuable as gold in the fifteenth century, and da Gama's reports of the wealth of the eastern coast of Africa and India were to prove irresistible. Six months after his return a second expedition was sent, better equipped and better armed than the first, and after some resistance, its commander, Pedro Alvares Cabral, established a Portuguese trading post in Calicut. In 1502 da Gama returned, this time at the head of a fleet intended to humble all opposition to Portuguese trading hegemony in the Indian Ocean. Five years later, determined to oust the Arabs, the Portuguese took Ormuz, establishing a military and naval base there, then Socotra and Goa.

And all the while the Portuguese were continuing eastward. In 1506 they sighted Sri Lanka, its mountains rearing out of the ocean, shrouded in a mantle of mist, its shores carpeted with lush vegetation. They called this land Ceylon, but it had already had many names, including Serendib, meaning "good fortune," the name given by Muslim traders in the eleventh and twelfth centuries, the antecedent of our "serendipity." From Sri Lanka they struck east again, reaching Malacca on the Malay Peninsula in 1511, then the Moluccas and finally, China. Soon a string of Portuguese bases ringed the Indian Ocean and snaked through the Philippines and Indonesia. In 1516, drawn by the fragrant sandalwood, they came to Timor, a mere two hundred and eighty-five miles from the northwest coast of Australia.

With Timor secure, the Portuguese had created an empire the likes of which the world had never seen before, an arc of fire and steel that stretched from the Cape of Good Hope to less than three hundred miles from the Australian coast.

HOW DOES THIS end? she asked me one afternoon.

I woke from a half doze. What do you mean?

This, us.

I turned on the bed to face her. She was sitting upright, the window open behind her. We were in their bedroom, where we had been all afternoon. She looked down at me, the sheets tangled across one leg, pooling at her side, her stomach and breasts exposed to the warm sun from outside, exposed to me in the way only lovers can be. Late autumn, 1939. Fraser was at the University. Unsure what to say, I shrugged.

How do you want it to end?

I don't know.

Leave him.

No.

Never?

You know that.

Then why are you here?

I don't know that either. Because I need to be. But I know this is wrong, for both of us.

I took her wrists in my hands, pressing them together. It's not, I said, pulling her toward me. You know it's not.

She pulled away but I refused to release my grip. Kurt, don't . . . she said, but I pulled her back, my mouth on hers, hungry for her.

Stop, you're hurting me! she said, more loudly this time, but I couldn't. I released one of her hands and grabbed at her breast, but she slapped at me with her free hand, her ring biting into my cheek. Startled, I pulled away. She fell away from me as I released her, grabbing at the sheet and pulling it up to cover herself. I felt gingerly at my cheek, my hand coming away sticky with blood.

Get out, she said, her voice thick with hatred. Get out now!

I stood without speaking and gathered my clothes from the floor, dressing in silence, aware the whole time of her eyes on me. Once I was dressed I looked at her, and she glared back, refusing to meet my eye. When she said nothing I turned and left, closing the door behind me. As I walked away I thought I heard her weeping, but I couldn't be sure.

$\mathcal{I}$n the middle of the fifteenth century, seeking to protect the lands they were discovering in their relentless progress south, the Portuguese court petitioned the Vatican for a declaration that they alone were charged with the role of converting and subjugating their discoveries. While the effect of such a declaration would be political, assuring Portuguese primacy in Africa and the Indies, its wording placed it squarely within the spiritual dominion exercised by Rome, and accordingly, despite the protests of the Spanish king, the Vatican issued a series of papal bulls: *Dum Diversis 1452*; *Romanus Pontifex 1455*; and finally, the notorious *Inter Caetera 1456*. Taken together these gave the Portuguese a license over all lands south of the Canary Islands from Cape Bojador to the Indies.

Then in 1492 Christopher Columbus sailed west in search of a passage to China. Columbus, Genoese by birth, had lived most of his life in Portugal. Columbus' brother was a mapmaker in Lisbon, his business buoyed by the voyages of Portuguese captains, while his wife was the daughter of a Portuguese captain. But Columbus, his vision of a westward route to Cathay spurned by King João of Portugal as too expensive, turned to the Spanish for support, and it was under their flag that he sailed west.

When Columbus returned, only seven months later, bringing with him stories of a fertile and friendly land to the west, Portugal suddenly found herself with a rival. Unable to match Spain's military might she instead turned to the *Inter Caetera*, but Spain responded by declaring that since the lands Columbus had discovered lay to the north of the Canaries the Pope's ruling did not apply. Like Portugal forty years earlier, Spain now turned to the Pope for support, arguing that she should be granted exclusive rights to bring spiritual salvation to the inhabitants of these new lands to the west.

The Pope of the time was Alexander VI, a Borgia and a friend of the Spanish court. Not surprisingly the Spanish request was granted, and at Columbus' suggestion a line was drawn approximately one hundred leagues from the westward tip of the Azores, dividing the Atlantic in half. Whether or not Portugal already knew of Brazil (and it is likely that the outward journeys of her captains had already led her to the shores of South America several years before Columbus' journey), she undoubtedly had considerable fishing interests to the northwest of the Azores, and as a result the Portuguese court protested against the terms of the papal decision. And so, in 1494, after much posturing by both sides, a new treaty, the Treaty of Tordesillas, was brokered between Spain and Portugal, which agreed:

... a boundary or straight line be determined and drawn north and south on the Atlantic sea, from the Arctic Pole to the Antarctic Pole. This boundary or line shall be drawn straight, as aforesaid, at a distance of three hundred and seventy leagues west of the Cape Verde Islands, being calculated by degrees or by any other manner as may be considered the best and readiest, provided the distance shall be no greater than aforesaid.

In this way the world was divided. And although the line the Treaty of Tordesillas drew was fictional, an arbitrary division on a map that was, although increasingly detailed, still predominantly blank, its existence determined much of the course of what was to come. Because of it Spain drove west, while Portugal continued east. For a time this was enough to prevent their collision, but on the opposite side of the globe the two empires' hemispheres were drawing closer, closing a circle that had begun with the first Portuguese journey south, and threatening the uneasy peace between the two countries. Once again a decision was needed about the limits of each nation's domain. Informally it was determined that the line set by the Treaty of Tordesillas continued onward, slicing the globe in half, and although they did not realize it at the time, passing through the Australian continent somewhere near the West Australian border.

But the terms of the original treaty were never as clear as they sounded. Spain and Portugal had bickered for two and a half decades about whether the line was to be drawn three hundred and seventy leagues to the west of the easternmost or westernmost of the Cape Verde Islands. A few hundred miles of Brazilian jungle might have been a source of mild tension, but on the other side of the world the stakes were higher, and if a new line was to be drawn both sides needed to know as much about the lands that they were arguing over as possible. So as the second decade of the sixteenth century drew to a close Portugal began a series of expeditions east from Timor and Malacca. These expeditions were charged with the vital task of penetrating the shadowy realms to the south and east, the political value of the knowledge they would bring justifying the transgression into what was nominally Spanish territory, while simultaneously demanding secrecy.

*B*ut still Fraser and I were bound together, not just by Veronica, but by the ship. In the evenings we would sit with our charts, our surveys, and map out likely locations. Imagining all the possibilities, investing them with such meaning that if a ship could be made out of nothingness then we would have done it. Sometimes Veronica would be there, other times not. When she was she would hover near Fraser, placing a casual hand on him, on his shoulder, his arm, his leg, almost as if she were daring me, each touch a muffled thud deep within me. She would bring us tea in the study, smiling like a wife, and Fraser would nod at her, distractedly, not able to see the web that danced between the two of us; his wife and his best friend.

I began to feel that what we were doing was like a game to her, an ever escalating game of truth or dare. Our meetings became riskier, the line between secrecy and discovery shrinking. Her need, her desire seemed to increase with the risk of discovery, and I, like a fool, allowed myself to be drawn in, to be seduced into complicity. One night late in the autumn she entered Fraser's study without knocking.

Telephone, she said, smiling at Fraser. He looked up.

Who is it?

She shrugged. I'm not sure, they didn't say.

Fraser turned to me, removing his glasses from his nose to lay them on the chart before us. I'm sorry, Kurt, I'll have to see what this is. I nodded. It's fine.

As Fraser stood to leave Veronica hovered by the door, making no move to follow him. We had spent the afternoon in my bedroom, entangled in front of the gas fire. I was unsure what to say, her moods when Fraser was around were so unpredictable. But then she crossed the floor to where I sat and grabbed my hand, pushing it roughly into her skirt, forcing my fingers between her legs, roughly cramming them into herself. Startled, I let her do it, realizing she was naked beneath her petticoat.

Feel that? she demanded. That's yours.

My semen warm from within her coating my hand. As she spoke she dragged me upright with her other hand, pulling me toward her, her lips hot on mine, her hand pulling at my hair as she fumbled with my belt and fly, bracing herself against the wall behind her, wrapping her legs around me. Fraser's voice coming low from the telephone two rooms away. I tried to listen for its cessation, the click I knew must come as he hung up, his footsteps returning, but I couldn't, his voice fading into the grunting rhythm of our congress, finishing in a brutal red shudder from deep within, the sharp intake of her breath, her muscles convulsing tight as I came deep within her for the second time that day.

Then as quickly as it had begun it was over, each of us twisting apart, gasping at the air. I was still fumbling with my trousers when I heard Fraser outside the door, certain I would betray myself, but Veronica turned to him as he entered and smiled.

Who was it? she asked, her eyes clear and direct. Fraser pushed his hair back.

It was Hoskins, he said, and at the name of our commanding officer I looked up.

What is it?

Orders, at last. We're being sent overseas.

Where? When?

Singapore, in a week.

As he spoke Veronica stepped forward toward the two of us. Both of you?

Fraser nodded. Both of us.

Watching the two of them now I felt something slide out of place, the beginning of a movement away from order and into chaos, disaster, and suddenly, suddenly I realized the enormity of the risk we had just taken, and was deeply, terribly afraid. And ashamed. Of myself, of Veronica, of what we had just done, and of what we were doing to him. To Fraser. Fraser saw me cup my head in my hands.

Anything the matter?

I looked up, shook my head. Just tired, I said.

*F*our A.M. and David wakes to the sound of Kurt coughing, the sound echoing through the quiet of the sleeping house. Almost immediately he is at his side, the electric light blazing, stroking his brow, the old man's skin burning beneath his hand. Kurt thrashes and pulls away from David, moaning and grasping at his sheets. Claire! he calls, crying her name out, his voice breaking raw panic, but she is there beside him even as he cries out, pulling a singlet on.

He's burning up, we have to do something.

Let me look, she says taking his arm and pulling him aside. As he steps aside she puts a hand on Kurt's brow then turns to David. And you need to calm down. He needs antibiotics. She pauses, looking at David, who is hovering behind her. Jesus, she says softly to herself.

Together they work side by side, calming Kurt, slowing his frenzied movements with painkillers. Finally, after half an hour or even longer, his fit subsides, his breathing slows. As it does they step back, Claire wiping her brow. Without speaking she looks at David, then looks away. The reproach in her look is unmistakable.

What? he asks, knowing the answer already.

This. It needs to end, she says, walking away from him, back to the sleep-out.

Later, Claire and David lie beside each other in silence. Their bodies back to back, distant in the narrow bed. Not long before dawn they sleep, but wake quickly in the soft gray light. Neither speaks, their eyes sore from lack of sleep, nerves jangling. A conversation that must be had hanging between them. Finally David turns to Claire and places one hand on her belly, pulling her hair away from her face with the other.

What's wrong?

This. Him. You.

What do you mean?

She is silent for a moment, then her reply comes, her voice weary, but her words charging it as she continues, her tone rising.

Don't you think this is weird? You, that evil old bastard out there, and me, all here in this one house. He killed him. We both know that. That body up in the fridge in Sydney is Fraser, his best friend, and he killed him and buried the body, and what's worse, he got away with it. And you, you just sit there listening to him, watching him die and waiting for him to tell you where the bloody ship is. She pulls at his hand, pushing him away. And don't touch me, there's something . . . I don't know . . . dishonest about you, and the way you touch me. Just don't!

Claire leaps to her feet, and backs away in the darkness.

David, confused by the ferocity of her attack, sits up, reaching out to her.

Wait, Claire, he says, and she stops, swaying from side to side in the dark. I don't understand what's wrong. Please.

Claire does not move, her anger holding her there, then suddenly it breaks and tears flood forth. Fuck, she says. Fuck, fuck, fuck.

*A*t the end of the second decade of the sixteenth century, the Portuguese in Timor began to hear stories from the native fishermen of a great land to the southeast of Timor, a land of such vastness men could walk a year and not see the ocean. This land, the fishermen said, was inhabited by a dark-skinned people who lived by hunting and fishing, and with whom the fishermen sometimes traded. The stories were vague, but they were enough to convince the Portuguese that these lands were those that Marco Polo had described as the Isles of Gold, and by 1519 the Portuguese commanders in the East began to contemplate a secret mission southward to investigate the claims of the fishermen.

The obvious candidate to command such a mission was a young captain, Jorges de Cueva. Lisbon-born, de Cueva had served in the attack on Malacca ten years earlier, and had been commended by Albuquerque for his services there. An enigmatic record exists of a young captain who petitioned Diogo Lopes, Portuguese Governor in Goa, for the resources to mount an expedition to a land he believed lay south of Timor, but this record is silent as to the identity of the captain, although it seems not unlikely it was de Cueva. But whether it was or not, de Cueva had certainly impressed many, including Albuquerque himself, with his determination that there were lands to be found to the south.

And so, in 1519 de Cueva was assigned three caravels and ordered to sail in search of this mysterious southern land. Whether the expedition had the formal sanction of the Portuguese court is unknown, but it is unlikely such an expedition would have been mounted without at least tacit approval. Perhaps the paucity of information about it, the lack of any official records beyond a note regarding its disappearance in a journal kept by de Barros (and not included in his official history of Portuguese expansion, *Da Asia*), is testament to its secrecy. Or perhaps it is merely that the records are lost to us and any inference about its secrecy is mistaken.

Whether there was official approval or not, de Cueva was commanded to sail not just south but east, into Spanish waters. His mission violated the tacit agreement between the Spanish and Portuguese empires that the line drawn by the Treaty of Tordesillas extended into this hemisphere as well, and had they known of its existence, would have been as provocative to the Spanish as Magellan's incursion was to the Portuguese two years later.

From Goa de Cueva traveled southeast to Timor, where he took on supplies, then south and east again toward the unknown land. These few details we know from letters and journals, although they contain no more than dates and figures, no hint of the mission de Cueva and his men were upon. From Timor there is no record of them, save a brief reference to their disappearance in the annals of de Barros and a letter written in secret to the father of one of de Cueva's officers by Mendonça's navigator, telling of a wreck on a distant shore. And if Mendonça found the wreck of one of their ships did he find survivors, charts, secrets, that he bore back to his masters? Or was there nothing but the blackened hulk and charred bones found nearly three hundred years later by Bell and recorded by Townshend; de Cueva, his men, their records, consumed by a storm or a fire or murdered by the land's inhabitants? And what of the other two ships? Were they wrecked as well, and if so, where? With so little knowledge questions multiply, unanswered, unanswerable, doubt threatening to consume us just as it does the stories of these secret expeditions themselves.

VII

The Burning City

There are contemporary maps which might tell us much if we could read their secrets. These maps are a dangerous type of evidence; too much study of them saps a man's critical faculty. Henry Harisse knew as much as any man of the Renaissance maps, and one may see from his works that as his learning increased his judgement deteriorated.

J. A. WILLIAMSON,
The Voyages of John and Sebastian Cabot

$\mathcal{T}$ime is not a stream flowing equably, constantly, from the beginning of all things to the end of all things as Newton believed. Instead time is an intricate web of is and was and will be, all coexisting in a continuum of time and space, each fraction of a moment a point in the continuum. All times exist at once, and the future, just like the past, is already there.

But such an understanding of the world is denied to us. Our physical bodies, our minds, are created in such a way that we can only see time as a progression from one moment to the next, where the future is unknown and the past only remembered. We feel time's pressure, but not time itself, our access to the universe limited to a dim and faded understanding of its possibilities, so we live feeling the past slip away as we fall into an unknown and constantly fluctuating future. And within this illusion there is nestled another, even more terrifying. Although we believe we remember the past, it is no more accessible to us than the future, what it holds lost to us forever, as our minds and bodies blind us and condemn us to no more than a half-remembered dream of what was. The past is as inaccessible as the future, and as untrustworthy.

BY MORNING KURT is stable, his ragged breathing calmer, but it is clear that the previous night has pushed his body far closer to death. When he wakes David is sitting behind him, his elbows on his knees, his eyes and head filled with the aching alertness of exhaustion. As David says Kurt's name there is a flicker of recognition in the old man's eyes, and David, who has been half sure that his fit would have robbed him of the last of his faculties, leans forward further, until his face almost touches the old man's.

Kurt, he says, I need to know where the ship is, now, before you're not able to tell me any more. Avoiding the words still, even now, when it is the only way forward.

Kurt's voice low, little more than a whisper. Soon, soon, he says, and David looks at the ground, shaking his head. But you need to understand all of it before you hear the final part, the ship itself.

Please, Kurt, no more games, just tell me.

A shake of the head.

No, you need to know the rest, he says, extending one hand weakly to touch David's. There's not much more to tell.

Claire standing behind the two of them, her arms folded.

IT WAS EARLY 1941 when we arrived in Singapore. From the electrified atmosphere of an Australia that knew it was at war we entered a place of colonial languor. Officers spent the long afternoons talking with their feet on the tables, while the men spent them sleeping or playing cards. The papers and the voices on the radio were British, and our news was all of Europe and North Africa, and so, slowly, steadily, we were lulled into a sense of security, dozing behind the mighty guns of the harbor that guarded our impregnable fortress city. No one wanted to believe we were at risk from the Japanese, although the knowledge of their presence was always there, in the background, lurking. We heard rumors of disagreements between Bennett and the British, of his insistence that the troops be made ready for an attack from the Peninsula, but little was done. More troops arrived and were quickly absorbed into the general torpor.

Fraser and I were assigned to a minor command, handling various administrative matters. Each day was like a normal working day, beginning at nine, an hour off for lunch, home at five. Except that there was little for us to do, and we grew lazy, unfocused, took to drinking in the afternoons with the other officers. I learned to handle strong liquor, and within months could drink two-thirds of a bottle of gin without blinking. In the evenings we ate and drank with other expatriates, an endless round of parties and clubs and dinners. My spare frame began to fill out, my middle thickening to a point where I began to be concerned about my weight.

Fraser and I were billeted out to different places; he to the home of a wealthy but elderly woman, whom he rarely saw, she being more concerned with bridge than her guest; me to a private hotel, but we worked in the same building, our offices three doors apart, and most days we spent our afternoons together in one or the other of our offices, drinking, talking, waiting. Always waiting. In the beginning we talked often of the ship and our work together, but as the months went by we talked of it less and less as we slipped deeper and deeper into the torpor of Singapore society. But this torpor was an increasingly uneasy one, as the reports from Europe and North Africa grew worse and worse. The men, with little to do, anxious to be doing their bit, grew restless, sullen, and there began to be fights, punch-ups in bars and in the barracks, stories of enlisted men harassing Singaporean women, in particular the Eurasian women.

In the evenings, alone in my room I would write letters to Veronica, but the correspondence was irregular, tempestuous. Weeks would pass without a word, then one of us would write twice, three times in a day, trying to articulate the violence of our feeling, our desire. And always, throughout it all, I ached for her, starting out of uneasy sleep to the shrieks of bats, hidden movements in the dark, suddenly certain that she was there, beside me. The smell of her skin on my hand like a passing dream.

Then suddenly, in October, I received a telegram telling me she was on her way. No explanation, just six words: *Coming Friday, talk then. Love Veronica.*

The next morning Fraser came into the room where I worked. I looked up, aware that when he told me the news I would have to appear surprised, which I duly managed. But there was something odd about the way he related it. Rather than being pleased, as I would have expected, he was cautious, almost reserved. Not for the first time I wondered if he suspected, but he gave no clues to the reasons for this lack of enthusiasm.

*V*eronica arrived in a rainstorm, water pouring in a glassy sheet from the dome of the steward's umbrella as she made her way down the gangplank. I stood beside Fraser and watched her move toward us, watched him take two steps forward, his umbrella falling away as he drew her close, the rain soaking his shoulders and the back of his uniform. The way his mouth only brushed hers. Then Veronica turned to me, her lips dark. I remember feeling as if I was going to be sick, the lurch in my stomach as her dark eyes met mine. Her smoky voice counterpointed by the thunder of the rain. I smiled, managed to stutter out a greeting. She took my hand and kissed my cheek and I allowed my umbrella to fall aside, the rain on my face masking my sudden tears.

FOR THE FIRST two days we were never alone, not even for an instant. Both of us were tensed, like cats ready to spring, waiting for the moment, neither of us sure what we would do when it arrived. The third evening the three of us attended a dinner at the home of the uncle and aunt she had used to arrange the visit. Standing in the drawing room with Fraser and several others whose names I barely remembered that evening, let alone now. The house immense, set among gardens that could have been brought from England, Indian servants in white suits and turbans pouring champagne. The conversation swirling around me, only half heard, as if the others were talking through deep water, Veronica circling in front of me like a planet, her eyes darting nervously to me and away again; my eyes following her in a giddy circle. A butler appeared and the aunt ushered the eight of us in, smiling and talking, her words indistinct. Veronica waiting behind, allowing the others to pass through the palm-fringed doorway, then stepping forward, pulling me aside and falling into me, her tongue deep in my mouth, her fingers in my back. Just one kiss, but enough to feel myself dissolve into her, feel her dissolve into me, the champagne sweet on her breath. The smell of jasmine from the garden. All night watching each other over the table. Blood in my mouth from her kiss.

FOUR MORE DAYS passed like a famine. Then my doorbell rang in the early evening. I called to the person outside to enter, expecting it to be the maid, and continued dressing. The sound of the door opening, followed by a silence, then cool fingers on my cheeks, my eyelids, her lips warm on my neck behind me, her breath making my scalp contract reflexively, my groin twist, my breath catch. I turned, pulling her to me, her face and dress soaked with the rain, her skin cold, and we clawed at each other, bodies forming crazy angles as we burrowed flesh into flesh. No hurting in this now, only love. And need.

Later, we lay huddled together, my arm and chest cradling her, our hearts subsiding. Veronica's face against my chest, her lips lingering on my skin.

What about Fraser?

I'll tell him I got caught by the rain and had to stop in the hotel with you for a while.

Will he believe you?

Do you care? she asked, looking up at me, her eyes full of laughter. I was suddenly aware that she was genuinely unconcerned.

I grinned and shook my head, her happiness infecting me. No, now that you mention it, I'm not sure that I do.

Then we were quiet again, and as I played with the dark weight of her hair, the strands separating in my hands, I realized that something had changed.

HERE, NOW, IT was harder than it had been in Sydney, fewer places to go, more restrictions, but still, after that first week, we could find time to be together. But something was different. Where before our unions had been savage, more like animals in heat than rational beings, now they were suffused with such tenderness it frightened me. The round curve of her stomach after a long lunch, pressing my ear and nose and mouth and eyes to the curve of smooth skin, the intricate workings of her womb and belly beneath my cheek. Her hand splayed open across the skin beneath my sternum, where a knife could enter my heart without resistance. There was something new between us, a sureness, the trust of older lovers reunited. But between us there was also Fraser. And the ship.

$\mathcal{T}$hat night there is still a tension between them. Their bodies in the bed a tangle of elbows and angles, the narrow mattress twisting between them, lumpy. As David slips into sleep Claire turns to him and says, I'm leaving. As simple as that. David rolls toward her, lifting himself on one arm.

I thought you would. When?

She reaches out, brushing his forehead with one hand, pushing his hair away from his face. Her tenderness telling him how hard this is for her.

The day after tomorrow. My leave is finished, I have to.

David nods. When this is over, when he . . . is dead, and I come back, what then?

I don't know.

He feels tears in his eyes, stinging. I understand.

She looks at him, her eyes looking deep into his. He sees she is crying.

Do you?

He nods, and she pulls him down toward her, their lips mingling with tears.

How did this all become such a mess? she asks, and David shakes his head, their faces moving wetly across each other.

I don't know, he says, and suddenly both of them are laughing, choking on their tears.

THE NEXT MORNING Kurt is awake when David enters from the glare of the morning. When David approaches him, though, he barely turns, his body now so weak moving his head is more than he can manage. His one good eye peers sideways at David.

You must listen, he tells David, his voice little more than a whisper, I haven't got much longer, and you need to understand why I did what I did.

David shakes his head. Did what? Killed Fraser?

A sudden flash in his faded eye. That too.

IN EARLY DECEMBER 1941 Fraser was sent up country on a forward command detail. The night before he left he came to my hotel. I answered the door to find him standing there alone. Surprised, I asked him in. He sat in one of the chairs by the veranda. For a long while he didn't speak, just sat sipping the drink I had given him, looking through the open doors into the deep tropical darkness. Finally he put the drink down on the arm of the chair, looked around at me.

There's something brewing, he said, looking past my shoulder. Something big.

What do you mean?

He shook his head. I don't know, but something's up. Something's going to happen, the brass know about it but they're keeping mum.

The Japanese?

He shrugged. Maybe. It was the first thing that came to my mind as well, he said, his face grim. I'd hoped you might have other ideas.

As he spoke he picked up the glass and threw back its remaining contents in one gulp.

You think it's why you're going up country? I asked.

Again he shrugged, this time peering down into the dregs of his glass.

Again I don't know.

I leaned forward, my eyes following the patterns on the carpet. If it's the Japanese, why now?

What better time? Most of our troops are in Europe and North Africa, where things are going badly, so we're not likely to put up much of a fight here. His eyes not lifting from his glass as he spoke.

I don't know about that, I said, allowing my voice to rise, Fraser's remark having wounded a pride I was surprised to feel.

Fraser fixed me with a look of such sorrow I was immediately silenced.

Don't you? Just look at us. No training, no discipline, no experience. The British troops are even worse if anything. And their officers may be good men, but I wouldn't trust them to run a parish picnic, let alone a war. Face facts; if the Japanese do attack they'll steamroller us flat in weeks.

As he finished I just nodded, sobered by his tone. For several minutes we sat without speaking.

When he continued his voice was different, as if this were a speech he had thought out before coming. Kurt, he said, we've known each other for years. I trust you, and I just wanted you to promise me that if something were to happen while I was away, that you would make sure Veronica was safe.

My face flushed, my stomach turning with revulsion at my deception. Suddenly I wondered how I could hurt this man.

Would you? he said, looking at me.

I nodded. Of course, I said. Of course I would.

Once I had spoken he was quiet, and I sat choking on self-disgust. Finally he put his glass aside again.

I have to go, he said, handing me the glass. I put it down and he extended his hand, which I shook.

Good luck, I said, and he nodded.

I could be wrong about all this, he said.

But he wasn't.

THREE DAYS LATER I was woken by a pounding on my door. Veronica pushed away from me, her hair shrouding her face. Grasping about for a robe, I stumbled toward the door, halfway there colliding with a chair in the darkness. As I swore I heard Veronica groan, sliding back down into the sheets, but then I swung open the door, blinking in the bright light of the hall, rubbing my leg and scowling in pain. A young soldier stood there, nervous, his face pale.

It's the Japs, sir, he said. They've bombed Pearl Harbor.

AS DAWN BROKE, I was in at the headquarters, the corridors filled with men and women tumbled out of bed, running and pushing. No one seemed to know anything. There was garbled talk of Japanese troops having landed at Kota Bharu to the north, but it was not until midday that we began to get a picture of how bad things really were. The American navy was gone, sunk to the bottom of the ocean. Then we learned Kota Bharu had gone, fallen. The Japanese were on their way south to Singapore. And Fraser was somewhere up there, among the flames, maybe dead already, his wife asleep in my bed.

ALL MONTH THINGS grew worse. Twice I spoke to Fraser, his voice crackling down the phone line. Both times he asked me to make sure Veronica left as soon as she could. Both times I stuttered before I answered.

But Veronica refused to leave. Every day the ships at the harbor filled with civilians fleeing, dragging bags and cases with them, everything they could carry piled high on their backs. Their servants all gone, abandoning them. In the nights the anti-aircraft guns boomed as Japanese planes whined through the shifting maze of searchlight beams, the streets filled with looting gangs, dogs running wild, refugees spilling in from the north. The sirens wailed constantly, smoke staining the air, everything moving, dislocating beneath us. Every night Veronica waited in my room for me to return, and we would lie together, talking, trying to make sense of what was going on around us. And all around us, things were spinning out of control.

BY FEBRUARY EVERYONE could see that things were hopeless. Guam and Rabaul had fallen, and around us our troops were on the run, fleeing in disarray before the Japanese. We all knew we were next, although the British could barely believe what was happening. You could see the fear and confusion in everyone's eyes, troops pouring back into the city in transports, the wounded and the dying choking the streets. The wind from the inland bringing with it the smell of smoke. The banks ordered the burning of currency, and piece by piece, note by note, their reserves were fed into the furnaces to stop it falling into the hands of the Japanese; farmers slaughtered their animals, burned their fields; Europeans abandoned everything they couldn't carry. Everywhere the talk was of escape and defeat.

And then finally there was a place for Veronica on a ship. The night before she was to leave we lay in my room, listening to the sound of gunfire in the distance. She didn't speak, allowing me to cradle her to my chest. Both of us wondering where Fraser was. Some time after two she rose, crossing the floor in the dark, her skin glowing in the deep blue air, luminescent. I stood and followed her, and the two of us stepped out onto the balcony. Fire lit the sky to the north, searchlights to the south. In the distance there was the muffled thunder of a bomb, then another. Without speaking I drew her toward me, the curve of her back and buttocks against my chest, stomach, groin. My left hand cupping her left breast. She turned her face to me, the light from the sky painting her pale skin a deep orange, and her lips brushed my shoulder. Then she turned away, drew breath, and began to sing, the sound so pure, so rich, soaring, *Un bel di, vedremo,* declaring her love and faith that her husband shall return, and as I held her, felt the mighty draw of breath into her chest, the sound filling her body so that it hummed, resonated with the song, I too began to weep, the sound of Puccini spilling out across the streets, heads turning to this balcony, where a naked woman sang as the city began to burn, the majesty of the music refracted through the crucible of her body.

.   .   .

JUST BEFORE DAWN the phone rang, and I stumbled for it, pulling the receiver to my ear. A torrent of static, then Fraser's voice, distant, broken up by spitting waves of broken sound.

Kurt! Kurt! Is that you?

I nodded, reaching out for Veronica with my free hand so she drew herself in, pressing her ear to the other side of the receiver.

It's me, I'm here, where are you?

A pause, then, I'm in Kulai, but they're almost here.

Are you all right?

I'm fine. Is Veronica . . . ?

She's in the other room, she's fine. There's a place for her on a ship this morning. For us too. As I spoke I realized there was something I had to do.

I'm coming to get you, I said.

No, it's not safe. Everything's going to hell.

I'll meet you outside the bank. Wait there, I said, and hung up.

As I put down the receiver Veronica looked at me.

You can't, it's too dangerous.

I shook my head. I have to, I owe him this much at least. As I spoke she swung from the bed.

Then I'm coming too.

No, absolutely not. I'll meet you at the dock.

Please, Kurt . . .

I have to, I said again, and went to kiss her, but she twisted away.

I don't want to lose you, she said. Not now, not now that we've . . .

I held her arms, staring at her. What?

She looked away. I love you, she said, I want to be with you.

I didn't reply, instead looking away and saying, I'll help you get your things, as I let her arms fall.

In the street outside it was almost light and already chaos reigned. Soldiers and jeeps and trucks and rickshaws, all scrambling for the docks. I saw a jeep with two soldiers in it and hailed them to stop.

Get her to the docks, I said, as we threw her bags in the back. The soldier behind the wheel turned to me.

No worries, mate, it's where we're headed ourselves, he said. I nodded, and turned to Veronica, who stood beside me.

What you said back there? I said. Did you mean it?

She nodded. Of course. Just you be careful. She was about to say more when the soldier behind the wheel hit the horn. We looked around and he grinned.

You'll see each other soon enough, he said. But we've got a ship to catch.

Veronica turned back to me and drew me close to kiss me, and as she did I felt her breathe into my mouth, felt the taste of her. I love you, she said again, and I nodded.

I love you too. Now go!

As I spoke she stepped up into the jeep, the soldier in the passenger seat helping her up with one hand. She turned and waved, and I waved back, then set off to find a car for the trip north.

WITHIN HALF AN hour I was driving a jeep northward, toward Kulai. Driving was difficult, the streets jammed with troops and civilians all fleeing southward. Overhead the Japanese aircraft swung low, their guns chattering. The ground shook with the release of bombs, the pounding artillery. By the time the sun was properly up I had crossed the causeway. Beneath it the Strait was awash with burning wreckage, fires raging along its shores. By mid-morning I was in Kulai itself. On every side things were coming apart at the seams. The roads choked with refugees, ambulances pushing and jamming through the confusion down the Peninsula and back to the front, jeeps and soldiers and trucks, everyone running, screaming, a chaos of engines and voices and blaring horns. In the distance the ever-present sound of shelling, dull thumps booming out at irregular intervals. On the outskirts of the town a soldier shouted directions, and I managed to find my way across town, to the main street and what remained of the bank, its once impressive structure destroyed by a shell or a bomb from an aircraft. And there, out the front, was Fraser, his uniform torn and filthy, his eyes staring, but intact. I swung the jeep around and as I did he saw me and began to run.

You made it! he cried, the sound of a passing truck almost drowning him out as he clambered in. As I looked at him I saw the hollow cheeks and staring eyes of an exhausted man.

I nodded. Are you all right?

I'm fine. I don't know whether to thank you or punch you for being the biggest damn fool alive, he said, and I laughed.

Why don't you work that out later, I said. We need to keep moving.

Is Veronica . . . ? he asked, and I turned to look at him as I headed back the way I had come. When I answered my voice was quiet.

She's fine. She should be safely on the ship by now.

Fraser looked away, into the chaos.

Thank God.

TOGETHER WE DROVE back, fast, using everything the jeep had to force our way through the terrified crowd that filled the roads. Chickens squawking, dogs barking, the roar of the planes overhead. Just outside the city a Zero flew low toward us, strafing the crowded road, a line of dancing tracers slicing a line through the chaos. Without thinking I pulled desperately at the wheel, dragging the jeep to the side of the road, the bullets so close we could taste the stink of burning metal singing through the air. Beside the heaving form of the jeep a woman fell screaming, a sea of red blood pumping from a ragged hole in her middle. I watched in horror as she pushed and fought with the blood, almost as if she thought her wound could be wiped away. I looked around wildly, expecting some kind of help that was never going to arrive. All around her the crowd stood unspeaking. Her screams awful to hear. Finally instinct took over and I let go of the wheel, moved toward her, but before I could reach her I felt Fraser's hand on my shoulder, pulling me back. I turned to him, heard him screaming my name. Some other sound drowning him out. I followed the line of his arm upward, saw the Zero, no longer alone, beginning another sweep, then his hands dragging me back into the jeep, his hand pulling the wheel in my grip, so the jeep slid out sideways, further up onto the verge, the bullets from the planes exploding in the dirt on either side of us and then we were away, the look on that woman's face, the disbelief filling my mind.

Inside the city shells were falling, their impact making the jeep's steering kick and buck. Fraser drew his revolver, using it to threaten the sea of hands and faces that clamored to join us in the jeep. The heat of the burning buildings searing our faces and hands, my palms blistering against the metal of the steering wheel. As we drew closer to the docks the roads became impassable, and the two of us abandoned the jeep, fighting our way through the crowd for the last half a mile, running, grabbing strangers and demanding to know where the ship was, whether they'd seen her. The uncomprehending faces of the panic-stricken. For both of us her name like a prayer, repeated over and over. Climbing past the shouting guard onto the ship itself, pushing past a screaming woman with a baby that will not be stilled, the smell of gunpowder and salt and oil. Then those awful minutes, hours, years, searching the decks, the cabins, the corridors, until we finally understood that she had never arrived, that she was back there in the burning city and that all this noise, all this searching, was in vain, until we realized with a sudden and terrible certainty that she was gone.

As Kurt finishes speaking, falls back into the tangle of his mind, Claire adjusts the drip in his arm. Outside the wind blows against the tin roof.

Not long now, she says, and David raises his eyes, sees a concern for the old man on her face that he has not seen before. She, for her part, sees the rings circling his eyes, the fear in her lover's eyes. Realizes she has called him "her lover" to herself.

VIII

Wrack

Life's but a walking shadow, a poor player,
That struts and frets his hour upon the stage,
And then is heard no more; it is a tale
Told by an idiot, full of sound and fury,
Signifying nothing.

Macbeth, V, xvi

ut Java la Grande was to vanish too.

After 1550, as the sixteenth century waned, this mysterious continent with its shadowy inhabitants and marvelous fauna began to fade, the clear outlines of the maps vanishing back into the glare of the sun, reverting to a chimerical place of no clear dimensions or shape, leaving nothing but questions and uncertainty in its wake. So many of the maps of the Dieppois are now lost to us, consumed by the fire and war that have riven this century, burned in Dresden, destroyed in Vienna, that it is hard to trace the decline of this fabulous realm, but those that remain mark out a steady loss of definition and form. For twenty years the maps of Nicolas Desliens mark out the coast, but leave the interior, so lovingly rendered by Desceliers, Jean Rotz and Le Tetsu, blank, as if this land was being progressively forgotten, its detail vanishing from the imagination first, then finally the outlines.

Why this should be the case we do not know. Perhaps attention turned elsewhere; perhaps the charts from which the maps were made were lost or stolen or fell into disrepute. Or perhaps this place was never anything more than a figment of the Dieppois imagination, and was eventually erased, cartographical fantasy best forgotten. Whatever the case, the last of the Dieppe maps to show Java la Grande is the "Livre de la Marine du Pilot . . ." Marked 1587, this chart shows the upper portion of the continent, the familiar outline, so seductively similar to Cape York and Arnhem Land, the coastline lovingly detailed. But it is unfinished, and, perhaps prosaically, the name of its author has been smeared and is now illegible.

So, by the end of the sixteenth century, Java la Grande was gone from the imaginations of Europeans, the continent that the vanished land occupied left to await a new wave of sightings by the Dutch, and then later the English in the eighteenth century.

$\mathscr{B}$y evening it is clear Kurt will not make it through the night. His breath coming raggedly, in weak gasps. His one good eye staring blindly. David is hunched over him, spurring him on. Outside the weather has turned cold, a thin rain falling in veils, the wind hurrying off the deep gray ocean, and Claire works to warm the room, burning wood to ward off the damp that rises through the floors, spills in the windows. The air rich with the smell of salt and seaweed. Kurt's sentences falling down, breaking apart, as his mind collapses from within, but out of the fractured, twisting skeins of his mind, some sense still struggles to the surface.

FROM SINGAPORE OUR ship made south and east to Darwin. There was so little information, so much confusion that I could have let myself believe that Veronica was still alive somewhere, on a ship, or perhaps already safe in Broome or Townsville. Or perhaps a prisoner of the Japanese, but still alive and intact. Fraser refused to accept that she was gone, but I knew, somehow, that she was lost to us, forever and irrevocably, and I

could not escape this knowledge. Through the trip I stood by
Fraser, filled with the leaden certainty that not only was she
gone, but that this man, whom both of us had betrayed, was
prepared to believe in her when I was not.

But in the end my faithlessness was prescient. She was gone,
vanished into the confusion and chaos of that burning city,
swallowed up like so many others without a trace or a ripple.

Two days out from Singapore we received confirmation
the city had fallen, only hours after our departure, and each
day thereafter the news grew worse. The ship, crowded with
refugees and servicemen, took on an air of despair, people
barely speaking to each other, their days spent staring silently
out over the immensity of the ocean.

It was the end of the month before we reached Sydney, walking blinking into the hot sun. We had been gone for a year,
and things had changed. The air of excitement was gone,
replaced with a mood of foreboding and loss. The two of us
walked side by side down the wharf, still dressed in the uniforms we had been wearing that last day in Kulai, our eyes forward. An officer, his face impossibly young, stepped forward
from the crowd, speaking our names as a question. The two of
us turned, with looks that belied what lay inside us, allowing
ourselves to talk amicably with this young man as we walked
from the wharf to the waiting car.

WITHIN A WEEK we were reassigned. Fraser to remain here in
Sydney, me to the highlands of New Guinea, where our commanders fed troops into the narrow trails, feverishly trying to
hold back the relentless advance of the Japanese. I remember
receiving my orders by phone, nodding, then replacing the

receiver. Too numb to reply. In the nights I would wake
screaming, hearing the rattle of gunfire, the drone of the
Zeroes. My heart loud in the quiet room. But even awake I
could still smell the smoke, the stink of burning.

And Fraser, coming apart at the seams, unraveling into his
grief. Waking me at 2:00 A.M. with a phone call, asking for a
detail of the last time I saw her that he thought might somehow be relevant. Alone in my dark hallway I listened to him
talk on and on, his words slurred with drink, finally ringing off
abruptly to leave me there alone, my head butting against the
wall, first gently, then with a violence that broke the skin, the
pain sharp and high in the whining numbness that was envelop-
ing me. Too tangled within my own grief to help anyone.

Her loss creating in me not so much a pain as a cessation of
belief and meaning. Words moving without fixture, time passing without seeming to touch me. My grief isolating me from
everything around me.

But what about the ship?

The ship? That came later . . . much later. First there was
the night . . . the night when Fraser, when I . . . his voice rising with sudden agitation . . . Please, you have to understand,
it wasn't my fault.

David and Claire exchange glances.

What wasn't your fault? David asks, solicitous, hearing the
note of treachery in his voice.

He was drunk, you see, he had a gun.

Fraser?

He turned up late, woke me up. Hammering on the door
like a madman, a steady rain of blows, not pausing until I
came, a pair of pajama pants around my waist.

When? Claire asks. When did this happen?

Just after we arrived back from Singapore, Kurt whispers, and Claire glances significantly at David.

It was raining outside, and half asleep I demanded to know who was there. He shouted his name, and like a fool I opened the door. Fraser exploded inward, knocking me back, his service revolver in my face. Outside the rain was coming down in a torrent, and he was soaked to the skin, his hair plastered flat on his face, his eyes staring. The sight of the gun making me shake as he advanced on me, a vase suiciding sideways off the telephone table as I backed into it.

Fraser, I stammered, please . . . But instead of stopping he sprang forward, pushing me back, the gun stretched before him, his body crashing into the door frame, the wall, as he slipped from side to side.

How could you? he demanded. You of all people?

My guilt strangling me I just shook my head, watching the gun move in front of me like a snake, mesmerizing. Two drops of water hanging from the barrel, the darkness within the muzzle so close I could see it consume the arcing grooves of its interior. Finally I managed to stammer out, I'm sorry, I never meant—

You were supposed to be my friend.

Here, finally there was no answer, my crime undeniable.

I trusted you, I trusted you to care for her, to protect her—

I tried, I shouted, God knows I tried, but—

But what?

I just shook my head. How did you . . . ?

In her things. A letter. At first I didn't . . . couldn't believe it, but then it all began to make sense. As he finished he looked upward, blinking back tears, but I hardly noticed, all my attention focused on the gun in front of my face.

Did she love you?

The presence of the gun telling me to lie. I hesitated, but that was enough. Fraser looked at me and I could see that he knew. My teeth chattering with fear I began to speak, words tumbling out in a desperate attempt to explain, to justify, to placate, but Fraser just shook the gun in front of my face, silencing me.

How long, he asked. How long were you together?

I shook my head. Please Fraser—

Just fucking tell me! he bellowed. How long were you together?

I swallowed before answering, my voice cracking midway. Since the end of 1938, about six months after you were married.

Were you together in Singapore?

I nodded, convulsively. As I did Fraser folded over, a howl rending his body, the arm with the gun in it swaying in front of me still, shaking as each sob shook him.

Please, Fraser, I said. Don't . . . But he wasn't listening. A moment passed like hours ticking by, and I suddenly knew without a doubt that Fraser was capable of doing what he threatened, like a creature so wounded it no longer cares who it hurts, just as long as some measure of vengeance is exacted. I stepped forward, my hand raised to deflect the gun to one side, knocking it from Fraser's grasp so it flew, end over end, upward and over, striking the wall to my right and bouncing downward. Fraser stood, lurching back, and I dived for the gun. My fingers closing around it as Fraser's knee hit me in the

gut, knocking the wind from me, sending me sprawling backward, down the hall. Next thing his boot striking me, hard,
his weight across my body as I tried to crawl back, away from
him. Blows raining down on me as I tried to back away, blood
in my mouth, in my eye. Then lifting the gun, and without
thinking pulling the trigger, the gun exploding with a roar as
the first bullet struck him in the wrist, flinging his arm back
and opening his body to the second, third, and fourth, which
struck his chest from left to right. Then, suddenly, a silence
as he stepped back, slumping to the ground, his good hand
clutching at the hole in the center of his chest, the fingers
scrabbling desperately, clawing at the rapidly spreading stain.
My breath coming fast and loud, then his surprised face looking up at me. I could smell the alcohol on him as he opened his
mouth, blood spilling forth, running down his chin as he
slumped back, against the wall and onto the floor, the good
hand still clutching his chest, the other falling out from
beneath him. Two more gasps, six quick panting breaths, and
then his eyes dulling.

OUTSIDE IT IS dark, and the rain has become heavy. Kurt's
breathing less regular, shallower, but still the words come.

I DON'T KNOW how long I sat there in that hall, watching the
blood spreading outward. All I remember is being woken from
a stupor by a convulsive motion in my stomach, running out
into the garden and falling to my knees in the rain as my stomach emptied itself, again and again, until my mouth and throat
and nose were choked with the sharp taste of bile.

Finally though I stood and went back inside, knowing I had

to do something about the body. I didn't know whether the neighbors had heard, what they had thought if they did, but no one had come. The sound of the storm masking the sound of the gun. The blood had spread until it covered half the hall, and I knew the first thing I had to do was get the body outside, stop the blood. Unable to think of anything else to do I found an army blanket, and managed to roll the body into it, the warm blood covering my hands. Each time his face turned back to me, his head lolling lifelessly, I looked away, the bile stinging in my throat. Once I was done I dragged that terrible parcel out to his car. With my hands trembling uncontrollably and my knees shaking beneath me I slid it into the backseat, covering it with another blanket. Finished I slammed the door, slumping against the car, trying to find a footing as vertigo consumed me. I knew that I needed a plan, but my mind felt paralyzed, the moment when the gun jumped and roared in my hand, Fraser's spinning body, filling my head, over and over. Finally I knew what I had to do. I made my way round to the driver's door, which hung open where Fraser had left it, the rain pooling on the floor. I groped in the dark for the keys, finding them in the ignition where Fraser had left them in his haste, turned them. The engine roaring into life, the gearbox screaming as I skidded away from the curb, suddenly desperate to get away.

MY FIRST STOP was Fraser's, where I knew he had reserves of petrol hidden in a shed. I remember finding my way into the shed in darkness, afraid to use the lights, finding the cans by the light of a match. Loading them into the boot, one after another. Taking a shovel as well.

I arrived down here mid-morning, the clouds clearing away,

the damp air making me sweat. A cut in my forehead throbbing. There was a sign on the edge of the dunes I had not seen before, declaring the area was prohibited, that beneath its surface there were land mines, but I ignored it and unloaded Fraser's body, dragging it behind me as I moved deeper into the dunes to begin the grim work of digging a grave.

Later, as darkness began to fall I completed the job, rolling the swaddled body in. I remember standing above him, pulling at the blanket to reveal his stiffening body, the glazed eyes staring upward, as I groped in his jacket for his wallet, then clambering out, watching the tumbling clouds of sand that rained from my shovel swallow him. Finally done I retraced my steps, following the trail I had left on the way in, the trail Fraser's body had made as I dragged it through the sand, a ribbon of safety. By torchlight I cleaned the car, then began the long trip back to the city.

I left Fraser's car by the Gap, climbing out and walking away from it, having wiped the steering wheel with my shirt. It was dawn when I left it there, and before I left for good I walked to the edge, stood looking out over the restless sea before taking his wallet from my pocket and casting it out into that blue space. The birds wheeling in the rising sun.

I don't know how long I stood there, but finally I turned and began the long walk home. Consumed by exhaustion in the quiet dawn streets I walked slowly, and as I walked I felt a revulsion for what I had done; to Fraser, to Veronica, to myself, a revulsion that would not wash off under the heat of the shower, where I scrubbed and scrubbed until my skin was raw and bleeding, a revulsion that followed a trail from the center that had drawn us all together. The ship.

Later they were to come to me again and again, asking me questions, trying to find a contradiction in my story, but I gave them nothing. Knowing that given nothing else to hold on to the police would find the car and believe he had taken his own life.

AFTER KURT FINISHES there is a long silence, the sound of the rain filling the room. The isolation of the shack almost tangible. A piece of tin on the roof lifts and drops with a clatter. His breathing low, the breaths further apart than before, each one terminating in a long wheezing sigh. Finally he speaks again.

THEY SENT ME to New Guinea after that. Two weeks in Port Moresby, then up into the high country. Three weeks marching up the trails, watching the wounded and dying feeding out along the track, back the way we had come. Men dying every day, freezing with fever, their bodies unable to hold food. Snipers everywhere. The ground beneath my feet slippery with blood and rain. After a week I had the fever too, and at night the darkness loomed huge around me, its expanse punctuated with crashes, splintering cries, marsupial shrieks and fear. The bush shivering like a living thing, drawing into itself like the breath of some ancient serpent, its confusion of shadowy forms preening themselves into a ragged, shrieking semblance of life. Bats the size of cats blundered through the foliage, fires erupted from out of nowhere, burning white hot in the clammy dark, cascading sparks into the air and scattering them across the sky like fireflies. Sporadic gunfire in the darkness, counterpointed by the deep rumble of artillery. Intermittently planes droned overhead, low and ominous, their engines throbbing through the thick night air, evil, threatening. A month dreaming of Veronica, of Fraser, a month of waking screaming in the darkness, my limbs flailing as my men tried to control me, their muddy hands covering my mouth to keep us hidden from the snipers.

I think all that time I wanted to die, I was looking for death, but when it came it was a surprise. The shell detonating like a silent wind, lifting me off the ground. Or a heartbeat. As if I were as light as a feather. No pain, just a roaring noise, like a dam breaking, then, as suddenly as it started, there was nothing, just silence. Then the darkness, not the warm dark of sleep, but a burning, thundering darkness.

They say that victims of trauma seldom remember it, their memory fails to commit the details of the event that caused the trauma to memory, to protect the organism, to keep their mind from harm. But I remember. I remember all of it, every conscious moment.

The nurses said I was screaming when I came in, but that my mind was elsewhere. They told me I screamed for hours without waking, until my voice was hoarse and broken. When I finally awoke, I was still screaming, but my tone must have changed, because I remember the nurses appearing above me, their hands on my face, my chest. Then I realized their mouths were moving, but there was no sound. No sound but the sound of my own voice.

When I stopped screaming I realized why I had been screaming for all those hours. I was deaf. Not deaf from loss of hearing, but deaf because the blast had lingered, roaring incessantly in my ears. My screaming was the only way to drown it out.

It was months before my hearing returned, months. And the whole time I lived with the thunder of the shell locked away inside of me, unable to speak, unable to communicate. When I finally began to hear again there were doctors who wanted to speak to me, but I didn't want help. Just silence. Perhaps they should have tried harder to reach me, seen the sickness that was eating at the ragged self that remained, but it was a busy time for the doctors, they had other people to see, ones who did want to speak with them, and eventually they just did as I asked and left me in peace.

It was two years before I was out of the hospital, and by then the war was nearly over. I shuffled through the streets, feeling the eyes of the people I passed on me, the revulsion that shook them before they had time to hide it. I stayed one night in my old house, but found it too crowded with ghosts, the report of the gun still echoing in the dark cavities of the walls. The next morning I left and took a room in a boardinghouse. Before long I stopped going out, staying in with the radio instead, listening, listening. The morphine releasing me from the pain, then slowly, from the need it had created for itself. Outside the world moved on, the war ending, the white heat of atomic fire engulfing Hiroshima then Nagasaki. The night of the peace I sat in my room, floating in the fluid ocean of the morphine, feeling my mind open, time disconnect from space, and as I listened to the dance music on the radio, the beeps of cars in the streets, I knew what it was I had to do.

The next morning I drew out the charts, and began to try to make the connections we had always missed. The morphine bringing the pieces into conjunction. Within a month I saw the clues we had missed before. And a week after that I came back here. My pension enough to pay for this place, the owner happy to be rid of it, eager to leave the town for the city. And then I began the process of crossing and recrossing the sand, looking for the pooling of scrub, stains in the sand. It took me a year, but eventually I found the place. That night I treated myself to a dozen bottles of beer and morphine, waking the next morning on my back in the hall, my own vomit caked down my front. I drove to town and bought the materials I needed, ignoring the children who stared at me, the way the lad in the store started away reflexively, and drove back here. And finally, I began to dig.

WHERE? ASKS DAVID. You have to tell me where.

Kurt's breath escaping in a low hiss. In the cupboard, there's a chart. A wheezing spasm, more a contraction of his shallow lungs than a cough, But it won't help you, you won't find it.

Hearing the edge of hysteria in David's voice Claire reaches out to touch him, seeking to reassure with the gentle pressure of her skin.

I don't understand, David says, Claire's hand on his shoulder now, holding him back. Didn't you say you found it?

Kurt begins to laugh. I found it, but no chart's going to help you find it, he says, his laugh monstrous, pathetic.

Why not? David asks, his voice rising, barely able to control himself from reaching out and grabbing the dying man, from shaking him until he divulges his secrets. Why won't I? he almost shouts. Stop laughing, just tell me why I won't . . . His voice trailing away as he suddenly begins to comprehend the joke.

No, he stammers, you couldn't have . . .

Still Kurt is laughing. Oh yes I could. Don't you see, I had to, I had to be free of the past.

Claire looks at David, confused. What's he talking about?

David swallows, his face pale. He did something; to the ship. Still Kurt is laughing.

No something about it, I burned it, I burned it to the ground.

Claire looks in horror from David to the wheezing body of the old man and back again. No, he couldn't have, it wouldn't have burned, would it?

David nods, his arms wrapping behind his head so that he cannot see the older man. Why? he keeps asking, Why? but all Kurt can do is laugh. Tears on his sunken cheeks, his voice barely more than a whisper.

Because the past is nothing, and we are nothing, and you, you're still foolish enough to believe. You come here with your pious belief in the past, your desire to understand, but you're too stupid to realize that none of it is true, none of it. Faith is a lie. Love is a lie. Only death is certain, and you, you're too blind to see that.

Then David is on his feet, his chair clattering to the floor behind him. He sways unsteadily, and for a moment Claire thinks he will attack the older man, drag his shriveled form up from the bed and shake it until it breaks, but he doesn't, instead lurching away, across the floor to the hall, where he turns and looks back. She stands, calling his name, but he doesn't look at her, just staggers away, down the hall to the door, and out, into the darkness, leaving her alone with the dying man.

urt dies some time just after 2:00 A.M., slipping gently out of sleep, his breathing slowing, growing shallower, until finally it stops. Just before he dies David returns, entering the room quietly from the hall. Claire turns to him, her eyes telling him that there is no more time for questions. David doesn't speak, crossing quietly to where she sits and touching her shoulder. His skin cold from the rain outside. She places a hand over his, squeezes it.

NEITHER OF THEM sleeps, instead sitting in the small room with the body, neither of them wanting to speak. At seven they ring the doctor from the town, arrange for an ambulance, and Kurt's stiffening body is borne away by ambulance workers. The doctor stays for several minutes after the ambulance departs, then he too goes, leaving David and Claire alone. The two of them standing close, not touching. For a long time they stand outside the shack, watching the path the ambulance and the doctor took, then finally they go inside, begin the slow task of cleaning up to leave.

In the end, nothing is true, save that which we feel. Nothing we remember, nothing we believe, all are just stories and echoes. The past is a shifting sea where nothing is certain, and where the things we seek cannot be found, a place where we seek lands that rise from the mist into the glare of the sun and then vanish again, as quickly as they arrived. A shifting sea with nothing at its center, except illusions, and loss.